THE MAN WITH A MASK

A Novel
"The Spencer's Mill Series"

CHERIE HARBRIDGE WILLIAMS

All scriptures referenced in this book are
from the King James Version.

First paperback edition September 2023

ISBN-13: 979-8-9874296-4-8

www.CherieHarbridgeWilliams.com

Acknowledgments

I am deeply thankful that God, in His mercy,
took me from where I was and brought me to where I am,
allowing me to write.

Thanks to my husband, Conway Williams, for his
extravagant support and patience.

With great appreciation to the rest of my support team:
Sara Bryant, Gail Anderson, Jeanne Boyce, Nancy Mills,
Janice Shoe and Jerry Nebergall.

Thanks also to Shaun Baines, editor.

Table of Contents

Important Characters

PROLOGUE

Toledo, Ohio
1889

Julia's face was hot-red, and the veins of her neck bulged. Every muscle in her body was poised to fight, and no description of anger could be too vivid. She was furious...spitting mad...outraged. She had just been committed to a sanitarium against her will by a vengeful husband. She was perfectly sane but had been warehoused in that horrible place to keep her mouth shut.

Shortly after she entered the institution, large, white-coated orderlies forced bitter pills of mysterious ingredients down her throat while she gagged and choked. They kept her drugged, unable to fight or speak clearly...not that anyone would have paid any attention.

How could she ever get out? Did anyone know where she was? Whenever the drugs wore off, she would beat on the window and scream, hoping someone out there would hear her. Sadly, the orderlies always heard her first. They would rush in with more pills, and she would fall back into bed in a deep, unconscious sleep. Days passed without seeing another human being, except the nurse who brought her food and the orderlies

1

who administered the pills.

She hated being confined in a ten-foot square room. She had memorized every smudge on the walls and every spot on the ceiling. The odors of disinfectant and urine were ever-present. A breath of fresh air and a clear thought seemed like distant memories.

After months in captivity, it was surprising that she was still aware her foggy thinking was due to drugs. It was clear the orderlies wanted her to believe she was mentally incapacitated. In her lucid moments, she decided to be more cooperative, hoping to get the orderlies to relax. Maybe she could wangle some small amount of freedom.

Over time, Julia forced herself to be more cooperative with them, even pretending she was glad to see them. In a few weeks, they began handing her the pills instead of forcing them down her throat. That small victory was, to her, monumental. She swallowed a few but dropped most of them into a glass of water, allowing them to dissolve. Then, she poured the contaminated liquid into the washroom sink.

She had been cruelly cheated out of the life she should have had. Only six months before she was put in the sanitarium, she had married a dashing man who adored her. Life had been full of promise. How could anyone know how severe a turn her future would take?

The months dragged on. Seasons came and went. Julia had been there for five long, hopeless years before it occurred to her to pray for divine help in getting out. She didn't have much faith, but she prayed every day, hanging on to the little faith she had.

Then a miracle happened: she was allowed into the common area for two hours a day, where women played table games or chatted in the afternoon over a cup of tea. They were always guarded by orderlies, but soon, she made friends with some other women, particularly a blonde girl who had probably been pretty when she was admitted. Now, she bore the look of one who was devoid of emotion. The girl's name was Annabelle.

Julia entered the large, sunny room where Annabelle was seated in a rocking chair. Hot tea was available on a tea cart for residents and visitors, so Julia poured two cups and offered one to her friend. Taking the chair beside the girl, she opened a conversation that took longer than usual because of Annabelle's difficulty pronouncing words. They went through the usual small talk.

An orderly moved closer to them, so the women dropped their voices.

Annabelle searched the face of her new friend. "You...seem...upset. Are...you well?"

"I'm angry. I've been stuck in this place where I don't belong. Did I tell you why I'm here? I witnessed my husband commit a crime; then he put me in here to shut me up."

Annabelle's eyebrows arched. "That's...horrible."

Julia let the effect of that information sink in, then said, "Why are you here? You don't seem like you belong, either."

Annabelle took a deep breath and wagged her head slowly. "My...speech...problem," she said.

"What? Is that why you were put here?"

Annabelle nodded and dropped her head. "Pa...running...for mayor. I'm... an embarrass...ment."

Julia stared at her hard. "Your situation is as unfair as mine."

The orderly strolled by again as Annabelle brushed a long strand of pale hair from her cheek.

"At least...sister comes...each week," she said, still struggling. Julia listened patiently.

"That's a blessing for you. I don't have anyone to visit me. My parents don't even know where I am. I would give anything to tell them I'm here."

Annabelle grasped her hand and whispered, "Find...a way...to write...letter. My sister...mail it."

A ray of hope flooded Julia's heart. Her mind kicked into high gear, thinking of a way to get paper and a pencil. She decided to risk asking the receptionist.

After thanking Annabelle, Julia walked casually toward the

reception desk. She was aware of being shadowed by an orderly, but it couldn't be helped. She approached the desk and asked, "Could you give me a piece of paper and a pencil? There are some flowers outside my window I'd like to draw."

"I'm sorry, Mrs. March. That's against regulations."

Julia's heart pounded. This was too important to give up easily. A short stack of stationery lay on the desk, and pencils stood akimbo in a cup like drunken soldiers. It would be so easy to pluck one out if no one were looking. The receptionist noticed her staring at them and pulled them away. What to do? Julia turned to glance at Annabelle across the room.

Annabelle grinned, probably for the first time in months, and sent a signal with the shift of her eyes and a slight nod. When Julia turned to find out what Annabelle wanted her to see, the receptionist had temporarily stepped into the adjoining room. But the orderly was still hovering.

Just then, a cup crashed to the floor. Annabelle had dropped her tea. "No...no," she said, covering her mouth with her hands and looking contrite. The orderly rushed to clean up the mess. As Annabelle repeatedly said, "Sorry," Julia snatched three sheets of stationery and a pencil from the desk. She pocketed the pencil and shoved the paper under her loose blouse.

Walking purposefully toward her room, she mouthed a silent thank-you to Annabelle. The girl had a smile on her face. *Having a purpose does wonders for the soul,* Julia thought, delighted that Annabelle's little trick had worked out so well.

The next day, in the common area, Julia palmed a precious letter, folded tightly, to her friend. Annabelle passed it to her sister on her next visit, and it went into the mail that afternoon.

Within a few days, Julia's parents arrived for a joyful reunion. "Julia," they cried when they saw her for the first time in years, throwing their arms around her.

"I thought I'd never hear your voices again," Julia said through the tears flowing down her face. "This was all made possible by my friend, Annabelle. I'll introduce you when I can."

They stayed in her room until near the end of visiting hours, catching up on the events of their lives. Her father tried to work out her release, but the administrator of the sanitarium was adamant. It would take her husband's signature to get her discharged. And no one knew where he was, only that he paid her bill faithfully each month by mail.

The following month, her parents visited again with a resolve born of desperation. Her father was determined to get her away from that place, whatever it took. When the orderlies were otherwise occupied, her parents tried to whisk her outside, but the receptionist stopped them. "Julia needs a pass from the doctor to go outside," she said firmly.

Her father whispered, "Run!" and continued to push her toward the door, but the receptionist raised the alarm. A burly orderly showed up out of nowhere. Her father pushed him back and tried to run faster with Julia, but the young man was quicker and wrestled him to the floor. Someone else grabbed Julia and returned her to her room. Her mother stood by, horrified, unable to help. After that, whenever her parents visited, they were guarded closely.

Julia continued praying, and her parents visited almost every month, but her release was impossible without her husband's signature. She may as well have been dead.

Chapter 1: The Stranger in Spencer's Mill

Spencer's Mill, Ohio
Six years later: June 1895

Three young ladies in long skirts and blouses with leg-of-mutton sleeves chatted on the brick sidewalk in front of Link's General Store in Spencer's Mill. They fanned themselves against the heat and the buzzing flies.

"Olivia, did you see how Fannie Barker dressed at the church picnic? Did you see that awful brown thing she wore?"

"Yes, but I don't think her family can afford better. I think the hem had been let down once or twice."

Hattie snickered. "You'd think she'd at least clean her fingernails, even if they're poor."

Olivia's eyes lowered. "You shouldn't be so hard on her. You don't know what kind of life she might live."

Hattie's hand went to her hip. "Olivia, your problem is you're too holier-than-thou. Relax."

Her attention was diverted by the figure of a man riding toward them on an Appaloosa horse. Her eyes widened, and she lowered her voice to a hoarse whisper. "Don't turn around and look; a stranger is coming into town." She pursed her lips and blew a puff of air.

The other two turned to look.

"I said don't look," she hissed.

The young man was riding in from the east, holding the reins loosely, his body swaying in easy sync with the horse's movement beneath him. He was neatly dressed, broad in the chest and square-jawed. The Appaloosa was also striking in its appearance, with a chestnut coat and white hindquarters dotted with distinctive spots. It stepped smartly, its head bobbing up and down.

As the man approached the village marketplace, his eyes scanned the street from side to side. Spencer's Mill was the typical, tranquil small town. Village folks spent their Saturday enjoying the fresh air, shopping, waiting for haircuts at the barber shop, and gathering for lazy conversations.

The three girls ceased their gossiping to watch him. He passed the bakery and neared the general store. When they realized they were staring, they turned to each other in embarrassment.

"Let's keep talking so he doesn't know we were watching him," one whispered.

They kept up an intense conversation but stole glances at him whenever they could.

The rider pulled up to the rail and dismounted, his boots raising puffs of dust as they hit the ground. He carried himself with confidence and tipped his derby hat to the girls.

"Afternoon, ladies," he said with a broad smile, making little wrinkled lines at the corners of his eyes. He opened the screen door to the general store and stepped over the threshold as the girls blushed and giggled.

As soon as he was inside, one of the girls rasped at the other two. "Did you see that? He has a dimple. A *dimple*. I wonder how long he'll be in town."

The stranger rested his hands on the counter and glanced around at the interior. Merchandise of every kind crowded the space, like a dozen other general stores he had seen. Neat rows of canned goods stacked atop each other, baskets of household goods, and other necessities of life lined the shelves. Typical of a general store, the musty air mixed with the aromas of dill pickles, coffee beans, and licorice. Dust particles floated in the air, illuminated by the light streaming through the front window.

"Good afternoon, sir," said the clerk in a white apron, brushing the dusting of spilled cornmeal off the counter. "How can I help you?" Running his fingers through his unruly brown hair, he offered a friendly smile to his prospective customer.

"Good afternoon," the stranger said. "I'm new in town and looking for a room to rent for a while. Can you recommend a place?"

The clerk paused and wrinkled his brow. "Ah, yes," he said. "Spencer's Mill don't have many tourist establishments, but a widow in town rents rooms to folks now and then. Her name is Hilda Steuben. You'll find her on Harding Street. Will you be staying in town long?"

"It depends on if I can find work. The name's Derek March." He stuck out his hand for a shake, and the clerk grasped it.

"Welcome to Spencer's Mill, March. My name's Tucker." The clerk gave him directions to Harding Street. "Mrs. Steuben don't go out very often. She's probably there now."

"Thanks, Tucker."

Derek returned to his horse. The giggling girls were still in the same spot, waiting for another look as he left the store. They pretended to be so engrossed in conversation that they didn't notice him, but he was wise to their ruse. They stole glances at his every move. He grinned, set his hat at a cocky angle for their benefit, mounted up, and turned toward Harding Street.

Upon reaching his destination, Derek strode to the door and rapped. It was a well-kept two-story house in a row of similar homes on a tree-shaded street. He glanced around. *Quiet neighborhood,* he thought. *I like the giant oaks.*

Soon, his knock was answered by a sturdy, middle-aged woman who asked what he wanted. At the sight of her cropped hair, man-style shirt, and long gray skirt, Derek tossed out any idea he might have had about sweet-talking an old lady for extra privileges. This sort looked like she was all business.

"Mrs. Steuben, I'm Derek March. You were recommended to me by the clerk at the general store. I need a place to stay while I look for work."

"Come in, young man, and I'll show you a room. You'll need to pay a week in advance." She peered at him over her spectacles. "You say your name is March? I remember something about a family around here named March, but that was years ago. Are you kin?"

"I doubt it, ma'am. I'm from Philadelphia. I got tired of the city and wanted a quieter life further west. I believe I'll like it here. It's not crowded like the city, but it's still civilized."

"Hmpph."

She led him up a set of creaking stairs to a hallway and through a door opening into a pleasantly furnished room. The single window was framed by oak trim. It was curtained with blue calico and opened to the street. The walls were papered with a subdued flower pattern in the current popular style. The only pieces of furniture were a straight-backed chair, an iron-framed bed with a hand-stitched quilt, and a wardrobe with drawers at the bottom. The home lacked electricity or indoor plumbing, but Derek could overlook those inconveniences. He had lived without them most of his life, anyway.

They agreed on a price that included meals, and then Mrs. Steuben faced him with her hands on her hips. "Here are my rules, Mr. March. No women are allowed in your room. Breakfast is at seven, and dinner will be served at six. If you come in after the kitchen is cleaned up, you won't eat."

Derek liked reading personalities, so he studied her face as she spoke. He thought, *You can tell a lot about a body if you*

9

watch their expressions when they talk. Yes, she's all business.
Derek paid for a week in advance and brought his duffel to his
room.

He examined the room out of habit, carefully opening each
empty drawer of the cedar wardrobe. They were slightly stuck
and had to be coaxed out.

They need waxing, he thought. *I'll run a bar of soap over them.*

He opened the door on the small cubby at the bottom of
the wardrobe. It contained a clean brass chamber pot, ready to
be pulled out for the night.

Curiosity led him to test the comfort level of the mattress by
pushing on it, and he even lifted the rag rug to check for
anything underneath. *Who knows, there might be something
valuable hidden there.* Then he opened his door a crack to check
down the stairs. All was clear.

Once assured of his privacy, he opened his duffel and lifted
out a small wooden box with a lock. It was a beautiful box
crafted of walnut with intricate mahogany and maple inlay
around the top. He removed the gold chain around his neck
that carried a miniature brass key, which he slid into the
keyhole. With a one-quarter turn to the right, the lid sprang
open. He stirred the contents around with his finger to satisfy
himself. It was all there.

Strange, he thought, *it's almost as if I'm enslaved to this box. I
wish I'd never seen it, but I'd protect it with my life if I had to.* He
closed the lid with a click, placed the box in the drawer and
covered it with his socks and shirts. Then he stretched out on
the bed for an afternoon nap. It had been a long ride.

Derek descended the stairs at dinner time and ambled into Mrs.
Steuben's small dining room. The mahogany table with curved
legs was covered with a lace tablecloth, similar to the lace
curtains moving gently in the breeze at the tall windows. They
were glazed with uneven, bubbled glass and were topped off by
arched stained glass windows.

Mrs. Steuben had set places for the two of them and put

bowls of food on the table. Rich aromas mixed and filled the room. Derek would be eating well here.

"We're having chicken this evening," she said. "Come in and take a chair." She said a short prayer of thanks, then handed him a bowl of roasted carrots. "Where do you come from, March?"

Derek smiled and scooped some carrots onto his plate. He slathered them with butter. "I'm here from Philadelphia. Have you been there?"

"Can't say I've ever been that far away from home. What kind of work do you do?"

"I'm good with my hands, ma'am. I can do carpentry, painting, roofing—just about anything. Do you know of anyone needing work?"

"Not right now. Not in Spencer's Mill, anyway. You'll have to get to know people, read the ads in the paper, and maybe even go as far as Lamar to find work. That's fifteen miles back east."

"Yes, I passed through Lamar on my way here. Quite a busy place. Say, tomorrow is Sunday, and I'd like to go to church. I grew up in the Church of the Brethren. Where do you go?"

Mrs. Steuben relaxed her questioning and smiled at him for the first time. "I'm glad you're interested in the things of God. I'm a member of Trinity Chapel. It's pretty similar to the Brethren Church. You can go with me if you like. I'll introduce you."

Derek nodded with his mouth full of fried chicken. "I'd be most grateful."

In the morning, Derek and Mrs. Steuben climbed into her carriage and drove a short distance to the small white church beside the cemetery. Large oaks graced the lawn, and the shrubs were neatly trimmed. The belfry had no bell, which Derek found amusing.

As they walked in together, he overheard a knot of young women discussing his appearance – his dark hair, lively brown

11

eyes, tall stature, and nicely carved features. And there was that astonishing dimple. Derek glanced at them and continued on his way, smiling. *They must think I can't hear them,* he thought in amazement.

Mrs. Steuben introduced him to as many of her friends as she could. They presented their daughters, who somehow happened to be standing with their parents, to make his acquaintance. Few visitors to the church had ever caused as much interest among the young women as Derek March.

After the service, he was introduced to Mr. Joseph Kendall and his lovely daughter, Letitia.

"Mr. March, how do you make your living?"

"I hope to find work here in Spencer's Mill," Derek said. "I'm good with my hands, carpentry, painting, and such. Would you know of anyone looking to hire an ambitious worker?"

"No, but I'll let you know if I hear anything. You're familiar to me somehow. Where have our paths crossed?"

"I don't know, sir. I came here from Philadelphia."

"Hmm…Well, come, Letitia. We need to go home." Kendall walked away with his daughter in tow, looking at the floor and wagging his head. Letitia gave Derek a backward glance and a shy smile.

Derek hoped Kendall wouldn't remember the old news reports. Maybe settling this close to Lamar was a mistake, but being near his old business contacts might be useful. Besides, it was comforting to be in familiar territory. It satisfied his need for stability. Something about the excitement of flirting with danger also appealed to him. He admitted to himself that he lived as if he were above the kind of peril that would make lesser men's knees quake. He believed he was untouchable.

Chapter 2: The Wheelwright's Shop

On Monday morning, Derek emptied his chamber pot and carefully made his bed. He didn't want to give Mrs. Steuben any reason to enter his room. The discovery of that box would jeopardize everything. Satisfied it would remain safe, he went looking for a job. He asked about employment at the local farm supply store and the Rucker Painting Company. Neither business had any work available. Then, against all odds, he found an immediate position at the wheelwright's shop. Mr. Blackburn, the shop owner, needed someone to fabricate spokes and hubs for wagon wheels. Few men in town were skilled at using a lathe, but Derek was eager to learn.

"I'll hire you on a trial basis until we see how fast you can master the process," Blackburn said.

"I learn pretty fast. I think you'll be pleased."

"We'll see. I hope you're as good as you are cocky. I want to build up an inventory before November because the shop is small. You can see it's too small to do the lathe work inside."

"I can see that."

"Working outdoors in the winter is out of the question in these parts unless you're an Eskimo, so we need enough hubs, spokes, and wheels done in advance to fill the orders until spring. I hope to expand the shop next year."

"When can we start?"

"The sooner, the better. Let's get you started now." Over the next two days, Mr. Blackburn gave him a few lessons in mounting the hickory wood on the lathe, keeping the treadle going smoothly and using the spindle gouge to create the shape he wanted. Derek turned out to be a natural, his skills improving every day. By Thursday, he was producing well-formed wheel spokes without supervision and packing them into a crate for winter.

Even though he was new at this job, he already enjoyed it. It satisfied a creative urge in him he had never been able to fulfill. *I believe this is the kind of work I was born to do,* he told himself. In addition, the physical exercise and outdoor activity gave him the fresh air and sun he craved. It was even better when he and Mr. Blackburn developed a mutual respect over the next few weeks.

Derek enjoyed glancing at the people walking by as he worked the wood. Oddly, a striking young woman strolled by frequently and caught his attention. *I wonder why that woman walks by so often,* he thought. *She must live nearby.*

That particular young woman was slender and well-formed, with an untamed mop of red curls that glowed gold when the sun was behind her. He had seen her and her extraordinary green eyes at church. There was something about the girl that signaled she had some interest in him, even though it hadn't been overt. It was something raw that he couldn't put his finger on, as if she were in control. Her presence set his nerves on edge, and he didn't like it. He frowned and pretended not to see her.

The Kendall Yarn Company was a relatively new business in Spencer's Mill, hiring women to spin yarn. They worked in a building behind Mr. Kendall's home on the edge of town, where he stored the fleece sheared from local flocks. The building was long and narrow, with high windows along the sides. The dyed wool came from the carding shack. It was stored at one end of the structure while five women worked at the other. They came daily to spin and gossip, spin and gossip.

Mr. Kendall couldn't get the name March out of his mind. It was hauntingly familiar yet elusive. In a village as small as Spencer's Mill, Kendall was acquainted with almost everyone. Something happened a few years ago, either here or nearby Lamar. He was positive, but the details wouldn't come to his memory.

One day, on his plant inspection, Kendall approached one of the older ladies as she worked at her spinning wheel. Sadie had a disabled foot and came to work on her cane, but she had a lively wit and a zest for life. She was one of Mr. Kendall's favorites. In confidential tones, he said, "Sadie, you're about my age and old enough to remember. Wasn't there something in the newspaper a few years ago about a man named Derek March?"

"That does sound familiar," she said. "I'll have to study on that. If I can remember anything, I'll let you know. Isn't that the name of the young man Mrs. Steuben brought to church?"

"Yes, but there's something about him that bothers me."

"He bothers the young ladies, too," Sadie said with a chuckle. "I've seen how they all look at him and whisper in one another's ears."

"He is right handsome. I wish I had more information about him. He says he's from Philadelphia, but I don't think he's telling the whole truth. I want to know more, should he ever get designs on my Letitia."

Sadie continued spinning. Kendall hoped she would give the problem some serious thought.

Summer days passed as Derek grew increasingly competent at his job. At church a few Sundays later, he was more relaxed. The giggling of the young women didn't stroke his ego as much as it had at first. He had other things on his mind. Now that he had regular employment, he wanted to find a place of his own to live. He was lonely and needed the companionship of a wife to live there with him. It wouldn't be one of the giggling girls; he judged them too immature. He wouldn't rush his decision but didn't plan to drag his feet on it, either.

Derek was proud of his strong-willed personality. He was a man who, once he decided to do a thing, formed a plan and carried it out.

He didn't hear the sermon that day, not that it mattered. Instead, he concentrated on a flaxen-haired young woman of marriage age, sitting with her family just ahead of him. He observed that she had two younger siblings. She was a pretty thing, a possible candidate to be his wife. He spent the time during the sermon planning how he would court her. The first step would be introducing himself after the service was over.

After the final 'Amen,' he leaned toward Mrs. Steuben. "Would you introduce me to that family sitting ahead of us? I don't believe I've met them yet."

"Certainly." She smiled and waited for the Johnsons to file past them on their way to the exit. As Mr. Johnson approached, she put her hand on his arm to delay him.

Johnson was a tall, serious-looking man with dark brown hair parted in the middle and slicked to either side with a frugal application of bear grease. He wore a brown linen vest over his white shirt. His pince-nez spectacles were kept in his vest pocket until he needed them for reading. To finish off his look, his trousers sported sharp creases, giving him the appearance of a businessman, which he was.

"Mr. Johnson, I'd like you to meet Derek March, my new tenant. He recently moved into town. Derek, this is Mr. Joshua Johnson. Mr. Johnson keeps the books for the new Kentmoor Farm Supply Store."

Johnson extended his hand. "Nice to meet you, March. This is my wife, Mrs. Matilda Johnson and our daughter, Carrie. Our younger children have already gone outside with their friends."

Derek shook Johnson's hand. "Pleased to meet you, sir."

Then, he gave special attention to his wife. "Very nice to meet you, Mrs. Johnson," he said. "That's a beautiful necklace you're wearing."

She raised her hand to touch the gold chain carrying a delicately carved pendant. "Thank you, Mr. March. I'm surprised you noticed."

Then he turned to Carrie. "Nice to make your acquaintance, Miss Johnson."

He waited for a reaction, but she only nodded and said, "Same to you." It was a disappointment, to be sure, but he thought there would be time to get to know her better. The prospect of a challenge stimulated him.

On the way home, clouds partially covered the sun, bringing some relief from the late July heat. The horses swished their tails to swat the flies as they trotted down the road. Mrs. Steuben pointed out the few Monarch butterflies flitting about the milkweed along the roadside.

"How old is Miss Johnson?" Derek asked.

"Don't hold me to it, but I believe she's eighteen," was the answer. "She's a lovely girl, isn't she?"

"Yes. Is she keeping company with anyone?"

Mrs. Steuben smiled. "No, but if you're interested in her, you'll have to take your time. Her father dotes on her and is quite protective. He's discouraged all the other young men up until now."

Derek nodded thoughtfully. *I'll take that as a challenge.*

Chapter 3: An Intrusion

The following week, Derek attended church again with Mrs. Steuben. He sat quietly and respectfully but didn't believe what the pastor said, as he had in his younger days. He would like to think that God was still there, but when he prayed, his prayers rose no higher than the crown of his hat. Derek was convinced that God had either turned His back or never existed. *A real God would have never let me lose so much in that card game. Look how it ruined my life.*

As the pastor droned on, Derek inspected his fingernails and reflected on his childhood. His parents had been firm believers in God and had taken him to church every week. They said his prayers with him every night and helped him memorize Bible verses. Even now, he could say all the right things to make people believe he was devout, but to him, they were empty words that he only used to gain social acceptance.

He folded his hands in his lap and fidgeted until the end of the sermon. As he filed out with the rest of the congregation, he was greeted by several people. He became aware of the presence of the red-haired girl behind him. She followed him and Mrs. Steuben to the carriage under a spreading oak tree beside the church.

"Mr. March," she said in a voice rich with an Irish brogue.

He turned to face her. She stood inches away from him and

extended her hand. "I dinna get to meet ye before. Me name is Dolly Rooney." Her eyelids closed lazily over her catlike green eyes and opened again, and a chill went through him.

Mrs. Steuben stood back, watching with her hand on her hip, giving the girl a disapproving stare. "We need to be going so the ham doesn't burn, Derek."

"Nice to meet you, Miss Rooney," said Derek, quickly mounting the carriage. Dolly stood where she was, smiling at him. He wondered what her smile was meant to convey.

As they drove from the church, Mrs. Steuben said, "Hmmph. What was that tart up to?"

Derek shrugged. "She just wanted to be friendly."

"More friendly than was proper, I'd say."

Derek took a breath. "Just so you'll know, she's been sauntering by the wheelwright's shop during the week. She makes me uncomfortable. I won't be taking her up on her invitation."

"And an invitation it was, that's sure."

"So it's ham for lunch?"

"No, we're having stew."

Chapter 4: Courting Carrie

Over the next few weeks, Derek became adept at other processes besides lathe work. He learned to manufacture the hub from a hickory log and heat the metal to band the hub. He chiseled out the mortises to accept the spokes, fashioning the rims and attaching the metal tires.

As he pedaled on the lathe, it hummed steadily. He applied his chisels to the wood, and curly shavings flew back at him. Sawdust stuck to his clothes, filled the cuffs of his pants, and coated the ground. He enjoyed the earthy aroma of freshly cut wood filling the air, even though it sometimes made him sneeze.

Once the hub was fashioned, he sanded it smooth, then turned his attention to installing the metal bands. His ball-peen hammer made sharp, rhythmic taps that echoed off the surrounding buildings. He inspected his work and smiled with satisfaction, loving the job and the atmosphere.

"March, I need to leave to run an errand," Blackburn said. "Can you watch the shop for me? Take care of any customers who come in."

"I'll do that, sir." Derek was pleased to be gaining the confidence of his employer.

About two months had passed since he got to town, and Carrie was on his mind. He assigned himself a target date on the calendar for visiting her. When that day arrived, he rode to Carrie's house after work to seek out her father. Approaching the address he was given, he surveyed the home's exterior. Standing two stories tall, it was a larger house than he expected, given that the parents and only three children lived there. It was well cared for, and the grounds were nicely groomed. At his knock, Mrs. Johnson opened the door for him.

"Is Mr. Johnson in?" he asked.

"Yes. He's out back on the porch swing, reading. I'll take you there."

He followed her through the house, noting the bare pine floors, worn furnishings, and tidy rooms. They went out the door onto the porch. The youngest daughter, five-year-old Cynthia, sat on a tree stump with a book.

"Josh, Mr. March is here to see you."

Engrossed in his book, Joshua Johnson marked his place with his finger, raised his eyes, and peered at Derek over his pince-nez.

"Mr. Johnson, may I have a word?"

Johnson put his book down and stood to shake his hand. "Have a seat in the rocker over there, March. Did I get your name right? Now, what can I do for you?"

Derek sat in the rocker and leaned slightly forward to fold his hands between his knees. "I'll come right to the point. I'd like permission to see your daughter once a week. What I have in mind is sitting on the porch swing and talking for an hour or two."

Johnson chuckled. "I don't mean to make light of the situation, but before we get into a serious discussion, I need to point out that she still has a younger brother and sister at home. You probably wouldn't get much privacy on the porch."

March smiled. "I don't see that as a problem."

"I'd like to know your intentions."

"Of course. I'm at the age where I need a wife, but I want

21

the right one. I'd like to get acquainted with your daughter as a friend and determine if we would be a good match. I should know in a week or two. If our personalities don't fit together, I'll stop seeing her before her affections become involved."

Johnson's eyebrows raised. "That's unusual thinking, March. Don't you believe two Christian people are always a good fit for each other?"

"It's tempting to think that, sir, but history doesn't bear that out. My parents were devout Christians but bickered continually at home. I don't want to live a life like that."

Johnson nodded. "What is your financial standing?"

"I'm working at the wheelwright's shop, learning a lot from him. He pays me a good wage, and I'm putting aside savings to buy a house. I already had some savings before I got here, so I'll be able to buy a small home soon."

"That's admirable for someone your age. I appreciate a man who knows what he wants and has a plan for his life." He lowered his eyes briefly to consider his response, then fastened his gaze on the younger man. "You're more mature and ambitious than Carrie's other suiters, and you're in church every Sunday. Those are positive signs to me. Under those circumstances, you may ask her if she would agree to see you…on the porch, for now, as you said. You understand I'm giving my permission for only one visit. We'll see how it goes."

"Thank you, sir."

"She's in the parlor reading if you'd like to ask her."

Derek smiled and nodded. As he had been told, Carrie was lounging on the burgundy Chesterfield sofa, casually reading a Charlotte Brontë novel. Derek approached her.

"Miss Johnson, may I speak with you?"

The girl glanced up from her book to see Derek standing awkwardly, both hands grasping the brim of his felt cap in front of him.

"Have a seat, Mr. March."

"No, thank you. I won't be long. I just spoke with your father. He's granted me permission to see you once a week for a conversation on the porch if you're agreeable."

Carrie hesitated but couldn't stop her eyes from sparkling. "What evening do you have in mind?"

"Are you available Friday evening? I could come for a visit after dinner, say about seven o'clock, and we could have some time to talk then."

"All right, Mr. March. I'll expect you Friday at seven."

He grinned. Carrie stood and walked with him to the door, closing it behind him.

As he mounted his horse, he still wore a smile. He pushed his hat back on his head. The second step of his plan was accomplished. She was a beautiful girl, and he was a patient man. He would take his time. If he found Carrie suitable, eventually, he would ask her to marry him. She must be a woman with a pleasant personality, without being argumentative or nagging. And she must have a soothing voice, not a shrill one. He couldn't stand piercing, nagging voices like his mother's.

Carrie watched out the window until he rode off, then crossed the parlor and examined herself in the wall mirror, pleased with her reflection. She had come a long way from being a headstrong tomboy, skinning her knees and risking her neck. She had become a lovely young woman.

Thoughts swam through her head. *When I first met him at church, I wasn't free to talk to him because Papa was standing right there. Now, I'll have my chance, but I'll have to keep my head on my shoulders. This may lead to something serious.*

She returned to the sofa but left her book unopened. As she snuggled into the crook of the couch's padded arm, her eyelids fluttered shut, and her imagination took flight. She daydreamed about living in a cozy little cottage decorated with gingerbread trim. She would be married to a strong, handsome husband who adored her. There would be a cooing baby on her hip. It was such a pleasant image that she drifted off into a nap until her mother disturbed her.

"Carrie, it's time to start supper. I need some help in the kitchen." The voice sounded distant, but she roused enough to realize it was her mother only a few feet away. She shook herself awake.

"Yes, Ma." She rose and went to the kitchen to help prepare the meal. She pulled plates from the sideboard and set the pine table for five as her mother peeled potatoes at the sink.

"Mama, what do you think of Mr. March? Papa gave him permission to call on me."

"He's a handsome man, isn't he? And very charming. He always seems to have the right thing to say. But be cautious, daughter. The fact that he has no family in town is a disadvantage because we don't know what kind of people he comes from. It takes a long time to get to know someone, seeing them in various situations. How does he handle stress? How does he handle someone disagreeing with him? You need to find out those things. Who knows? There may be a marriage proposal in your future. You need to know those things before you're married. Afterward, it's too late."

"I like what I've seen so far."

"That's a start, but you haven't seen that much. Just be careful. Snap those green beans, will you, dear?"

Carrie tied her apron over her dress and went to the kitchen counter. She rinsed the beans and snapped off their ends, but her mind was not on her work.

The next day, she could hardly wait to talk to Lizbeth Reese. Lizbeth was her aunt according to the family tree—her mother's youngest sister—but Carrie was the older of the two by a few days. The young women were more than aunt and niece; they were best friends. They had been playmates since they were babies.

Carrie finished harvesting the ripe vegetables in the garden and gathering the eggs, then spoke to her mother. "Mama, I'd like to take the carriage to visit Lizbeth."

Matilda smiled. "I think I know why, but first, I need your

The Man With a Mask

help canning the beets. If you help me with that first, you can visit Lizzy in the afternoon."

Taking care of the beets took longer than Carrie had hoped, and it was a seven-mile ride to Lizbeth's house. Carrie decided to make a short visit anyway. She hitched up the carriage and took the long drive. Lizbeth's home was in a large mansion at the end of a long driveway lined with maple trees. She lived there with her mother, Susannah, and stepfather, Christian Wolf, who were Carrie's grandparents. Christian was a well-known attorney whose office was in Lamar, another eight miles east.

Upon her arrival, she found Lizbeth in the middle of a knitting project, a winter scarf forming one stitch at a time. The wooden knitting needles clacked steadily.

"What a pleasant surprise, Carrie. Hold this ball of yarn while we talk, will you?"

"Sure." Carrie picked up the fuzzy wool and turned it steadily, feeding yarn to Lizbeth's nimble fingers.

"I have some news," Carrie said, wiggling her eyebrows.

"What is that? And why do you look so mysterious?" Lizbeth stilled her needles to listen to whatever could be so momentous.

"Mr. March is going to come calling on me this Friday."

Lizbeth's mouth dropped open. "How did you manage that one, Miss I'm-Not-Interested?"

Carrie giggled. "It wasn't anything I did. It was his idea. He talked to Papa."

"Where is he taking you?"

"No, it's not like that. We'll just talk. We'll sit on the porch swing and get acquainted."

"That sounds boring. Such a handsome man...."

The look in Lizbeth's eyes told Carrie that her imagination had taken her on a side trip. She laughed. "Come back down to the ground, Lizzy. Maybe he won't like me. If he doesn't, I'll suggest that you might be someone to call on."

"Not much chance of that. I'd say congratulations are in

order."

"Don't be silly. I don't even know him yet. Mama warned me about being careful around someone when we don't know his family. I think she's right."

Lizbeth gave her an impulsive hug. "Good luck, Carrie. This could be something special."

"It could be." Carrie sighed deeply and decided to admit her feelings. "You know, when I first laid eyes on that man, something leaped in my heart. I thought how nice it would be to spend the rest of my life with someone like him."

"You and all the rest of us girls. Don't start planning the wedding yet. Any number of things could happen to prevent it."

"Yes, but I'll pray that God will work it out if he's the right one."

Smiling brightly, Carrie crossed her arms and hugged herself. Lizbeth wagged her head with a grin and resumed knitting.

Chapter 5: A Father's Concern

Joshua Johnson realized the day would come when a young man would sweep his daughter off her feet, but he planned to control the process as much as possible. He spent time in prayer, asking for wisdom and guidance.

It occurred to him that he should check out young March as thoroughly as possible. Information about him may be scarce since he said he was from Philadelphia, almost another world away from Spencer's Mill. But it wouldn't hurt to drive by the wheelwright's shop to see if he was doing well. Maybe he could talk to his employer privately sometime and ask his opinion.

He went to the barn and saddled the horse. He planned to approach the wheelwright's shop in no hurry so he could take a good look. He hoped no one there would notice him, but if they did, he would stop and have a neighborly chat. If they questioned why he was in that neighborhood, he would pretend to be on an errand to see one of his company's customers. He realized his plan was a little deceitful, but it wouldn't do to let Derek know he was on a spy mission.

Down the street they went, Joshua Johnson and his horse, passing the wheelwright's shop at a slow canter. He prepared to peer into the open shop door, but it was unnecessary. An open fire was ablaze in the vacant lot next to the shop, and smoke filled the air. The burning wood popped and snapped as ash and sparks rose. At that moment, Derek was carefully feeding a long, narrow steel band into the flames. His shirt was drenched in sweat and clung to his body. He reached into his pocket for a handkerchief to wipe his brow, then leaned briefly on one of the two water barrels beside him. He happened to glance toward the road as Johnson passed by.

"Mr. Johnson," he called with a grin and a wave. "Do you have time to see what I'm doing?"

Johnson turned toward the vacant lot and dismounted. "I can take a minute. That looks interesting. What are you doing with that steel in the fire?"

Derek explained with a gleam in his eye. "See that wheel there on the ground? This steel band is the tire that will go around the outside of it. As soon as the metal gets black-hot, I'll take it out of the fire and wrap it around that wheel. Then, I'll throw water on it. As it cools, it shrinks and holds the whole tire in place. Guaranteed never to come off. I don't know why I get so excited about this." A broad grin covered his sweaty face. He brushed away the stray hair sticking to his cheeks and forehead.

"Have you been doing this long?"

"Only a few weeks. I started by learning to turn spokes on the treadle lathe. Then, my skills expanded. I love this job."

Johnson grinned at him with admiration. "I had no idea about that process. I must be getting on with my errand, but I'd like to come by when I have more time. I'd like to watch you put the tire around the wheel, then throw water on it. There must be an enormous amount of steam that billows up."

Derek laughed. "Oh, yes, there is. You have to stay out of its way to avoid getting burned. You'll have to come by. It's pretty impressive." He mopped his brow again.

As Johnson rode away, Derek poked the fire with a long stick, waiting for the steel to turn black.

He's not afraid of work, thought Johnson. *That's a point in his favor. Just to be sure, I'll check the county criminal records and send a telegram to Philadelphia asking for information.*

A father was responsible for checking out his daughter's suitors, and he intended to be as thorough as possible.

.

Chapter 6: The Romance Begins

Carrie's 1895 wall calendar hung in the bedroom she shared with her little sister, and she made a precise "X" over the day's square each night as she went to bed. She awoke with anticipation at first light on Friday. This was the day that Mr. March would come calling.

The decision about which dress to wear was a major consideration. She had already consulted with Lizbeth. They had decided on the blue one, but she wanted to try all three before making her final choice.

She sat in front of her mirror, examining her image. Then she picked up the boar bristle brush with the silver plated handle and went to work on her hair. She brushed it up and held the curls in place with clips. Then she changed her mind, removed the clips and brushed it down again without making a decision. She would have all day to think about her hair.

Her mother called. "Carrie, please come to the kitchen. I need you to make breakfast for Papa. I want to pull the weeds in the garden before the day gets too hot."

Carrie came back to reality. "Isn't Alvin doing the weeds?"

Alvin was the youngest of her three brothers, the only one still living at home.

"He'll do the vegetable garden, but I have special herbs and flowers I want to take care of myself. Besides, you need to practice cooking."

Carrie smiled. Who knows? She might be married soon and need to know her way around a kitchen. She went downstairs, tied an apron over her dress, and cracked some eggs into a cup. She was busy at the cast iron stove when her father entered.

"Good morning, Carrie. Are you making coffee?" He took a chair and opened the newspaper at the table.

"I'll get that in a minute, Papa. I'm still heating the skillet for the eggs."

"You ought to get the percolator going first. Coffee takes longer than eggs. You want the coffee to be ready when the eggs are done. Remember that. One day, you'll have a husband." His face was behind the newspaper so she couldn't read his expression.

"Yes, Pa." Her jaw dropped when he turned the page, and she spotted his smile. This was the first time he ever mentioned the time when she would be married.

Papa's respect for me has moved up a notch, she thought and straightened her shoulders. She opened the burlap bag of coffee beans and scooped some into the grinder, grasping the hand crank and giving it a few vigorous turns.

"I went by the wheelwright's shop this week," he said.

"Do we need a new wheel?"

"No. I was checking on that young man. He's excited about his job and seems to be doing well."

"Why did you do that?"

"Just watching out for you."

Carrie flushed with embarrassment that he had done such a thing, fervently hoping that Derek didn't realize he'd been spied on. She measured the ground coffee into the percolator basket, slipped it onto the center stem in the percolator, and filled the pot with water. Snapping on the lid with the glass bubble, she put it on the stove to boil, then spooned a chunk of bacon fat from the icebox into the iron skillet. As the eggs cooked, she splashed hot grease over them as she had seen her mother do. It didn't take long before the whites were firm, the yolks were still fluid, and the edges of the egg were browned, crunchy and curly. Perfect. She tilted the heavy iron skillet and slid the eggs onto a plate.

The bubbling in the percolator caught her attention, and she glanced at the glass knob. Dark, rich coffee spurted into it, sending its aroma wafting into the air. She took it off the stove, poured a cup for her Pa, and placed it in front of him with the eggs. He leaned in and took a whiff of the steam rising from the cup.

"That smells delicious. Would you bring me a slice of bread to sop up that yolk?"

She got yesterday's loaf of bread, cut a slice, and put it on his plate. Then she brought the butter dish to the table. "Anything else?"

"No, that's fine, Carrie. Thank you. Are you going to join me?"

"Yes, in just a minute."

She put an egg in the skillet for herself. When it was ready, she sat down with him at the table and bowed her head for a silent prayer of thanks.

Carrie speared a piece of steaming egg white with her fork and raised it to her lips. The hot morsel in her mouth tasted of bacon. Delicious. She could please a husband with this kind of cooking. "Do you have a busy day ahead of you, Pa?"

"Yes, I have to calculate payroll and write the invoices for orders going out tomorrow. I'll be working all day at the office." He put his fork down and drained the last of his coffee. "Would you get me another cup, please?"

She poured more coffee for him and one for herself, carefully preventing the dark grounds in the bottom of the pot from flowing into the cups.

"Thank you. Now let's talk about Mr. March," he said, his

tone becoming serious.

"What about him, Pa?" She turned her attention to her father's face.

"He may be the right man for you, but he may not be. I know you're excited about his visit, just as any young girl would be. But be careful, daughter. If he makes any improper advances, it means he doesn't respect you. You don't need a man who cares more about his wants than your needs. Since we don't know much about him, just be careful, will you?"

"Yes, Pa, I will. I won't disappoint you."

Joshua rose from his seat and kissed Carrie's forehead. "Thanks for breakfast." It was a short walk to the Kentmoor Farm Store, so he headed out to his office on foot.

That was quite a talk. Carrie couldn't imagine a man as charming as Derek March being a problem for any girl, but she would follow Pa's advice.

The day dragged on, one long hour after another. Carrie's mind was on her hair and dress as she worked with her mother cleaning the house.

Alvin had irresponsibly played ball with his friends while wearing his best clothes. He had ripped his shirt and put grass stains in his trousers, so Carrie was assigned to do the mending. Her mother scrubbed the trousers clean with lye soap in one tub of water, then Carrie rinsed them in another tub and wrung them out. She was grateful they were prosperous enough to own a wringer attached to the side of the rinse tub. Outside, she hung her brother's britches on the line to dry. The day was perfect for it: sunny and breezy.

As she worked, her mind wandered. Alvin would no doubt be punished for that indiscretion. Father's sentence would be carried out privately, so she may never know the details. She wished Alvin would learn to behave himself.

Mother was wise enough and young enough to remember what it was like to be a girl. As she emptied the wash tub, she asked, "Carrie, would you like me to help you fix your hair before supper?"

"Mama, I would love that."

Later that afternoon, as promised, she brushed Carrie's hair and clipped it into an artful updo. It accented her slender neck. "You look lovely, dear."

The girl checked the mirror, and tears came into her eyes. "Thank you, Mama." Her look was almost regal, making her feel like a princess. The blue dress would be perfect with her blonde hair.

Evening came, and the supper dishes were washed and put away. Outside, the skies were clouded over and threatening rain. Carrie rushed into the backyard and pulled Alvin's dry trousers off the line. A light mist came down with a cooling breeze, and the world smelled fresh.

Afterward, she fussed over every detail in the parlor, stashing a stray newspaper into the magazine rack and dusting all the furniture. She straightened the books on the bookshelf and tidied the sheet music on the old Straube piano. Everything needed to be perfect when Mr. March arrived. Then she slipped into her blue dress.

"You look beautiful, dear," her mother said. "Now, wait in your bedroom. When Mr. March comes, Papa will answer the door and call you to the parlor. You don't want to appear too eager."

Carrie obediently went to her room, sat on her bed, and fidgeted. She would rather have been waiting in the parlor where she could peer through the windows. She would have preferred privacy in her bedroom, too, but Cynthia was there playing with her dolls.

"Look at my doll, Carrie. I braided her hair for her. Isn't she pretty? And Mama made a new dress for her. Don't you like it? It's pink with blue stripes, and it has lace on the pocket." Cynthia had many dolls and wanted to have a tea party with Carrie.

"Not this time, Cynthia. Please. I'm busy thinking."

When there was a knock on the door at seven o'clock, Cynthia was still prattling on.

"Hush," Carrie warned her sister.

"Why?"

"Oh, Cynthia, please be quiet. Your dolls are pretty, but I want to hear what they're saying in the parlor." Her ears strained to know what was going on. Scraps of male conversation floated upstairs to her room, but it was too muffled for Carrie to understand the words. She wondered what they were discussing.

Cynthia shrugged and pretended to pour tea for a doll party.

Eventually, Papa called, "Carrie, Mr. March is here to see you."

When Carrie descended the stairs into the parlor, Derek's eyes widened. "Very pretty."

She smiled at him. "Mr. March, it's good to see you. How are you?"

"I'm fine, thank you, Miss Johnson. And you?"

"Fine, thank you."

Carrie's mind went blank. She didn't know what to say next. She was relieved when her mother rescued the awkward moment. "Why don't you show Mr. March the swing on the porch, and I'll bring some lemonade and cookies for you."

"Thank you, Mama. Mr. March, would you like to come outside?"

Derek opened the screen door, allowing her to go through first. She raised her eyes to his, lingered for a second, and smiled as she passed through the doorway. "Thank you," she said.

Oh, my. That must be what people mean when they talk about flirting. I'd better stop it.

The two seated themselves on the swing, allowing a suitable distance between them.

"You look lovely," he said.

"So do you." They both laughed when she realized how inappropriate her words were. "I'm sorry. I didn't mean...."

35

She folded her hands in her lap and shut her mouth.

"Maybe we should start over. My name is Derek."

"My name is Caroline. You may call me Carrie. Everyone does."

He stuck out his hand, and she shook it, an awkward accomplishment from a seated position beside him. "Nice to meet you, Carrie."

She blushed.

"I don't know much about you except that you're very pretty. What do you like to do?"

"I like to read and discover new things I didn't know before. I like to cook and knit. I don't like canning beets." She turned her hands over and showed him her pink-stained fingers. He chuckled. "What are your interests, Mr. March?"

"I do wish you'd call me Derek. But my interests? I like to travel. I like working with my hands and creating things." His eyes were bright, with wrinkles at the corners as he talked enthusiastically. "I like making things of wood and metal. I like being around people, but mostly, I like the companionship of a few special people. You know…people I can feel comfortable with and be myself without putting on airs."

Carrie's mother stepped onto the porch with lemonade and a plate of cookies with icing, which she placed on a small table beside the swing.

"Thank you, Mama."

The sweet aroma of warm sugar cookies filled the air, and Mrs. Johnson disappeared into the house.

"Have a glass of lemonade, Derek. And help yourself to a cookie."

Derek grinned and took the cold lemonade with a sprig of spearmint. He chose a cookie from the plate. "I think I'll have this big one." He ducked his head and gave her a shamefaced smile.

"Don't look guilty, Derek. That big one was just for you." Carrie smiled and held her cookie self-consciously in her lap. "What you said sounds a lot like me. I don't mind being around a crowd of people for a short time, but then I want to go home. I have one favorite aunt who is my age. Her name is Lizbeth. We're best friends. And I have several other friends, but I'm most comfortable with Liz. I know she'll always be there. We've known each other since we were babies. I can be myself around her...Yes, I understand what you were saying."

Derek took a bite of the sweet cookie and immediately followed it with a swig of lemonade. His eyes squinted, and his mouth puckered from the tart lemons.

Carrie laughed. "Maybe we should have had a glass of milk instead of lemonade."

He smacked his lips. "Wow."

When Derek recovered, he asked, "If you like reading, did you ever go to the library in Lamar?"

She smiled. "Some of my friends told me about it, but there never seems to be a good time to go. I think that would be wonderful, to be surrounded by dozens of books and be able to choose which one you want to borrow."

"No, not dozens. It's hundreds of books. Hundreds. Maybe I could take you there someday."

Carrie's eyes lit up. "Do they have mystery stories?"

"Oh, my, yes. They have every kind of story. And they have books on history, geography, and any subject you're interested in. They probably even have some knitting books. You can spend hours there without realizing how much time has passed."

Carrie's eyes danced. "That sounds wonderful."

The conversation got easier as the evening progressed, and Carrie became curious about Derek's past.

"Did I hear you're from Philadelphia?"

Derek squirmed in his seat. "That's where I spent most of my time. I've been to many other places, too, because I couldn't resist the passion for traveling. I've been back east and up in Michigan to see the Great Lakes. And Chicago—now there's a place to visit. You ought to ride the elevated train."

"You've had an interesting life, then. Why did you decide to come to boring old Spencer's Mill?"

"I'm getting older. I'm twenty-seven now, and it's time I settled down. I've saved almost enough money to buy a house, and I'm looking around here to find something appropriate. I plan to find a wife and raise a family."

Carrie lowered her head to hide the blush coming over her face. She didn't know what to say.

Derek's voice softened, and he spoke gently. "Carrie, look at me."

She raised her eyes, and he continued. "Why are you embarrassed? It may be something you and I may want to think about eventually. Or we may not. We may find out that we don't like each other and go our separate ways. That's something that a body ought to be certain about. In the meantime, don't be embarrassed. You're of marrying age, so I would be surprised if you didn't think about it."

She took a deep breath, relieved at his understanding. She made a bold statement. "So far, I like you."

His lips curved into a dazzling smile, showing off his dimple, and he nodded, gazing at her.

Their conversation flowed as the hands of the clock ticked forward. Finally, he checked his pocket watch. "I'm sorry to end the evening, but I must go, Miss Johnson. May I call on you again next Friday?"

"I would like that. But please call me Carrie."

They shook hands like they were wrapping up a business deal, and he left.

Carrie picked up the glasses and the plate of extra cookies and went inside. Both parents were reading at the kitchen table, just a few feet from the door.

"How did it go, dear?"

"Just fine, Pa. He's quite a gentleman. He didn't make any improper advances. He wants to see me again next week."

"What did you talk about?"

"Pa."

"I want to know."

"All right. We talked about many things. The most interesting was talking about the library in Lamar. I've never been there, but he says they have hundreds of books. You can choose whatever you want and even take it home to read."

"Yes, I've been there. It's an amazing place. I'm glad he's an intellectual fellow who likes to read and increase his knowledge."

"He seems like a nice young man," her mother said. "Exactly how old is he?"

"He says he's twenty-seven."

"So he's nine years older than you. He's old enough to be responsible for a wife."

Carrie lowered her eyes. She didn't want to talk about this. "We're not considering marriage."

Her father laughed, a deep, hearty laugh. "Maybe not, but I'll bet you're both daydreaming about it."

At a loss as to how to respond to that, Carrie rose to go to her room. "I need to go to bed. I'm tired."

As she went, she wished she could talk to Lizbeth. There was so much to share. She pulled her blue dress over her head, brushed off the cookie crumbs, and hung it in the wardrobe. She checked her hair in the mirror. Her lovely hairdo had been disturbed by taking off the dress. *Might as well take out those clips tonight,* she thought. She slipped into her nightgown and took her hair down.

Bowing beside her bed, she prayed, "Heavenly Father, thank you for sending Derek into my life. Please give us both wisdom to know what to do."

She rose and checked on Cynthia, asleep in the next bed, surrounded by rag dolls. Then she slipped under the sheet, hugged her pillow, and drifted into a pleasant slumber.

Chapter 7: A Blooming Relationship

On Sunday, Carrie learned there wasn't much privacy in Spencer's Mill. A group of young women stood in a circle outside the church talking in undertones until Carrie approached; then, they said nothing.

Lizbeth must have spilled everything I told her, she thought. The group broke up, and some of them approached Carrie to ask about her evening with Derek. It seemed that her friends either clamored for details or were jealous and avoided her.

"There's not much to tell," Carrie said. "We sat on the porch swing. We drank lemonade, ate cookies, and talked. That's about it."

"Come on, you can tell us," said one. "Did he kiss you?"

"No, we didn't even hold hands."

"That's a relief. Then maybe I still 'ave a chance."

Carrie chuckled. "Maybe you do."

The girl hoping to have a chance was Dolly Rooney. Since her family arrived from Ireland, nearly everything she did made the other young women suspicious of her. She used her red hair and Irish accent to flirt aggressively with the men. Carrie wondered why she did that. Didn't she have a plan for her life that included settling down with one good man? At the rate she was going, she would end up a dance hall girl with a questionable reputation, supporting herself any way she could and never being able to attract a decent husband.

After the service, Derek approached Carrie from behind and tapped her on the back. "Good morning, Miss Johnson," he said, smiling.

Carrie couldn't help the grin that brightened her face. "Good morning, Mr. March." She noticed some of her friends observing that exchange and nodding at each other knowingly.

The week went by slowly. The wait was almost excruciating for Carrie. She had her eye set on Friday night.

"Mama," she said one day in the kitchen as she dried the dishes. "I wish Friday night would come early."

"When I was your age, Grandma used to warn me about wishing my life away. I'll pass that on to you. Enjoy each day as it comes."

"That's good advice, but hard to take sometimes."

Her mother smiled. "I was your age not so long ago. I know what changes are taking place in your heart and mind. I want you to know that. This is an exciting but dangerous time in your life. Let me emphasize the word *dangerous*. Your whole future depends on what happens in the next few months. So I'm watching over you from a distance, giving you enough room to make independent decisions. But I'm ready to step in to help if you start to slip and fall. And I'm praying for you."

"Thank you, Mama." She was genuinely grateful for that. She didn't want to be responsible for independent decisions of such magnitude yet. At her young age, she didn't have any practice.

For Carrie's part, she was conscientious about keeping up with her daily chores but still found time to visit Lizbeth on Thursday. The girls talked about Derek.

Carrie urged Lizbeth not to say anything to anyone else. "If you tell other people what I'm telling you, so help me, Lizzy, I'll never tell you another thing. I want to keep this a family matter for now."

"I promise to keep my lips sealed. I apologize for sharing so much information last Sunday. It's just that I was excited for you."

"You're forgiven." Carrie turned a smile on her and gave her a reassuring pat on the shoulder. "By the way, I didn't see Grandma when I came in," she said. "Is she home?"

"The last I saw her, she was in the backyard tending her flowers."

"Does she know about Derek?"

"Yes, I admit I already told her."

"I think I'd like to go say hello."

The two girls walked outside. They found Susannah lounging at a small bistro table near the zinnias, fanning herself and drinking tea. She swatted at gnats while honey bees buzzed among the goldenrod.

"Carrie," she said, "come sit with me." She reached out to hug her. "I haven't seen you for a while. How are you doing, and how is that young man you're seeing?"

Carrie blushed. "I'm doing fine. The young man is fine, too. We're just at the talking stage, and if we decide we don't like each other, we'll stop spending time."

Susannah laughed. "Whose idea was that? What if one of you likes the other, but their affection isn't returned? That's when things get messy. Here, sit with me...Lizzy, would you go in the house and bring out some tea for Carrie and yourself?"

Lizbeth returned to the kitchen on her errand, giving Susannah a chance to talk privately with her granddaughter.

Carrie took a chair and leaned toward her grandmother with a smile. "So far, we both like each other, but it's early. How would I know if the time came to break off the relationship?"

"That's a hard thing, Carrie. Be on the lookout for anything that's off about him, strange statements he might make, or beliefs that contradict yours. I'm not talking about the minor things, like your favorite color is blue and his is red. That's not important. I'm talking about you want to be a follower of Jesus, and he doesn't. Or maybe there is something in his background that's suspicious."

"So far, I haven't seen anything like that. He goes to church every Sunday. He wouldn't do that if he didn't want to follow Jesus. He's respectful of me; he respects Papa and Mama; he's employed by the wheelwright and works hard...No, I haven't seen any bad signs...at least not yet."

Susannah reached over and took Carrie's hand. "A word of wisdom, dear. Not everyone sitting in a pew is committed to following Jesus. Some want to learn more before deciding, while others are there only to socialize. So, take your time and evaluate Derek's motives. I want you to know that I'm praying for you to make the right decision. God's hand is on you. You're a level-headed girl, so I'm sure you'll be fine."

"Thank you, Grandma."

Lizbeth returned with two more glasses of tea, and the three settled in for a pleasant chat.

At Mrs. Steuben's house, Derek sat in his room with the box on his lap. The lid was open, and his fingers traced a path through the contents. *Maybe it's time to turn some of this into cash. I know a man in Lamar who might help me with that. But dealing in Lamar may be too dangerous. There was that fellow in Wapeka...."*

There was no need to rush into anything. He hadn't yet found the house he wanted. He had spent several evenings riding his horse up and down the streets of Spencer's Mill without finding any suitable home for sale. Finally, he sent a telegram to Oliver Hardin, a local real estate specialist in Lamar, saying he was interested in a two-bedroom in Spencer's Mill. By the following day, he had received a reply. Mr. Hardin would be in Spencer's Mill on Thursday. He had two houses he could show him.

The next day, Derek approached his employer. "Mr. Blackburn," he said as he sorted through the hickory logs stored in the back of the shop, "I've been looking for a house to buy because I've decided to settle down permanently in Spencer's Mill."

"I'm glad to hear that, March. I can use you long-term here. Have you had any luck finding anything you like?"

"No, sir, not yet."

Blackburn raised his finger. "I have a friend in Lamar, a fellow named Oliver Hardin. He's well-known in the area for his knowledge of local property. He owns quite a few parcels himself. You should contact him."

Derek chuckled. "I already have, and I want to talk with you about that. He'll be in Spencer's Mill on Thursday and would like to show me two houses. Could I have enough time off Thursday to see what he has?"

Blackburn grinned. "You don't waste a minute, do you? Yes, look at the houses. It shouldn't take more than a couple of hours. I can spare you that long."

"Thank you, sir."

Now, Derek would have to do some fast thinking. He had enough cash for a large down payment, but how could he safely get the rest? He had at least until Thursday to worry about it, but then he may have only a few days to take action.

Thursday arrived, a hot, muggy August day. Derek went to work and turned spokes on the lathe until Hardin arrived at noon.

"Are you ready to go look at houses?"

"Yes, sir. Let me tell Mr. Blackburn I'll be back later."

Derek spoke to Blackburn, then climbed into Hardin's carriage. "I'm sorry I'm so hot and sweaty, sir. This is not how I like to dress when I do business."

Hardin brushed it off. "We do what we have to do. I've gone to look at houses in the same condition myself."

This man will be easy to work with, Derek thought.

Hardin slapped the reins, and the horse started with a little jerk of the carriage. "The first property is one I bought from a couple who recently inherited another house out of town. They wanted a quick sale on this one. It was in rough shape, so I did a lot of work. I had to knock down the old fireplace and build a new one. I put in a new kitchen pantry and painted the walls in every room. Of course, you'll probably want to put in some wallpaper. But it looks pretty good now, and there are other improvements I'll explain when we get inside. We'll see how you like it."

"Where is it?"

"It's not far from the downtown shops. I'll show you where it is."

A few minutes later, in a residential area within walking distance of the general store, Hardin parked the carriage in front of a frame house that had been repainted, including the fence around the yard. It had a front porch under roof and plenty of skillfully sawn trim around the porch and gables. The decorative gingerbread had become very popular. It had been painted white like the picket fence.

Oliver lingered in the carriage for a minute, letting Derek take in the view. "I didn't cut that gingerbread myself," he said. "That takes too much time. I hired a fellow with one of those fancy fretsaws. He did a good job, didn't he?"

Derek nodded and leaned forward in his seat in anticipation.

"Let's go in," Oliver said. "This house has the two bedrooms you requested: a cellar, a stable out back, and another storage building. In addition, I've wired it for electricity and installed plumbing. The plumbing works now, and the electricity can be hooked up as soon as the town puts up the poles, which should be within a year. It has all the latest conveniences."

Derek whistled. "I may not be able to afford all that. We'll have to discuss the price."

"Come in and look around. Then we'll talk about it."

Hardin unlocked the door with a large brass key from his oversized ring. Derek marveled that he picked the right one without having to try several. They entered the parlor. It was

45

spacious and bright with a large fireplace and gave off the aroma of fresh paint. The parlor led to the kitchen with a new pantry. Off the hall, there were two bedrooms with a bathroom between them. Derek chuckled to see the bathroom with an actual toilet, porcelain tub, and sink. What luxury. Most people in the village could only wish for something like this.

Derek's heart leaped when he thought of living there with Carrie. He took a deep breath. "Tell me what you're asking for it."

"It's a fair price, considering all the features. I'm asking a thousand dollars."

Derek cocked his head and tried to conceal his yearning for the house while he struggled with the price. "That's more than I planned to spend. Where is your other house?"

"It's a little further out, on Hope Street. Let's go have a look."

They climbed into the carriage. As the horse clip-clopped along, Oliver gave Derek a brief history. "It was originally a log cabin but sat abandoned for a few years. I bought it six months ago and gave it a new 'skin,' so to speak. I paneled the outside so it looks like a more modern house. It has a large fireplace, a new kitchen, and two small bedrooms. No electricity or plumbing has been installed yet, but they could go in later. You'll see that it's quite cozy, well suited to a bachelor or a newly married couple."

"Any outbuildings?"

"There's an outhouse, of course, and a barn in the back with a stall for one horse. The well pump is out back, too."

"No pump in the kitchen?"

"No, the water still has to be carried."

They turned onto Hope Street, which had only two houses, both on the north side. The first house was a larger clapboard house, and the second was a little house that sported a newer and cleaner look. The word that came to Derek's mind was 'basic.'

"We're looking at that second house, the smaller one,"

Oliver said.

"What about the other house on the street, the one we passed on the way to the small one? What kind of neighbors live there?"

Oliver laughed. "It's vacant now since the lady who owned it died. She was a character, into everybody's business. Her children want to sell it, so we're negotiating a price. They loaned me the key, so I think they'll accept my offer. But it needs some renovations."

"When do you think you'll have that one ready?"

"It probably won't be until around Thanksgiving."

"Well, let's take a look at the small one."

The house was located in a wooded area. Hardin said, "The house comes with three acres, but much of the land is useless since it's often swampy in wet weather. Still," he said, "there's enough good land in the back for a vegetable garden and chicken coop."

Derek liked the look of it from the outside, but the inside was a step down from cozy. With two bedrooms carved out of the space, it was tight, not allowing for much furniture.

"I don't think this one is big enough for a small family, but tell me what you're asking."

"This one will go for $625. You say you have a family?"

Derek shook his head. "Not yet…I like the area, but the tiny size of this house almost makes my chest hurt like I can't get enough air. It makes me feel squeezed. I'm not in a big hurry. What do you think you'll ask for the one next door where the neighbor died?"

"Let's go look at it," Oliver said. "We can walk over. I plan to tear out the kitchen, build a new pantry, replace the roof, and paint the rooms."

"Will you put in electricity?"

"I could, depending on the buyer. You're talking an extra hundred."

They arrived at the front door, and Oliver found the key on his ring. They stepped inside. When they pulled back the heavy curtains, sunlight flooded the room.

"This is a good-sized parlor," Derek said.

"Come see the kitchen."

The kitchen had a bare pine floor with a water pump inside. Derek frowned. "I can see why you're building a new pantry. This one is in sad shape, with doors sagging on the hinges. Some of the plaster walls have been damaged, too. They need patching and painting."

"Yes, I'll do all of that."

"The bedrooms are both a good size. The larger one is big enough to carve out a bathroom if one wants to go to that expense. What will you be asking for this house?"

"This one will be about eight hundred when it's finished," said Hardin.

"So with electric wiring, this one would be nine hundred. I could get that first house you showed me for an extra hundred."

"Yes," Oliver said. "But this house comes with more land. It has four and a half acres, most of it tillable."

"But the other is more convenient to shopping for my future wife and within walking distance of my job. Let me think about this. I need to weigh the options before I make my choice."

"Of course. I'll take you back to the wheelwright's shop now. Send me a telegram when you figure out what you want."

On the way, Derek wondered about financing options. "Do you ever take a down payment and monthly payments until it's paid off?"

"That's called a land contract. I never have before. I use the profit from one house to buy the next, so I like to deal in cash. What did you have in mind?"

"I may not be able to get the cash together all at once. It may take me another thirty to sixty days to liquidate my assets. I could probably come up with eight hundred dollars right away to put on that first house."

Hardin's eyebrows raised. "Eight hundred dollars is

substantial. I may consider something like that. Let me give it some thought. On the other hand, you could take out a bank loan."

The two men shook hands before parting, and Derek returned to his work. That first house near the shopping area could be where he and his wife would spend the rest of their lives. He whistled a tune cheerfully and threw himself into making enough spokes for another wheel.

That evening, back in his room at Mrs. Steuben's house, he lifted his box out of his drawer. *I wonder how much I could get for this piece.* He held up a large rectangular step-cut emerald hanging on a silver chain. Small diamonds surrounded the emerald. He laid it over his forearm to admire it. *Maybe I should start selling something less recognizable.* He pulled a gold bangle bracelet from the box and turned it over.

There was a knock on the door that startled him. With his heart pounding hard, he closed the box as quietly as possible and shoved it into his drawer. "Yes?"

"Mr. March, supper is ready. Are you coming downstairs?"

"Yes, thank you, Mrs. Steuben. I'll be right down." *That was a close one.*

The next day was Friday. Derek longed for the workday to be over so he could visit Carrie. At quitting time, he rushed home, bathed, and changed into clean clothes before Mrs. Steuben had the evening meal ready.

"My, you look snazzy," she said. "Are you going somewhere tonight?"

"Yes. I'm calling on Carrie Johnson."

Mrs. Steuben beamed at him. "She's quite a prize. I've known her since she was a mere kiddiewink. What does her father say about that?"

"I asked his permission first. He agreed."

"That's good. You know how he dotes on her. I wouldn't want to be in the shoes of anyone who did her harm."

Derek glanced at her from the corners of his eyes as he

swallowed a mouthful of roast beef. He smiled and wiped his mouth with his napkin. "We haven't been seeing each other very long. We agreed that we're just getting to know one another."

"Hmph. That sounds like unrealistic thinking. You must not know much about women."

"Why do you say that?"

"Every woman of a certain age is looking for a husband. I'm sure Miss Johnson is no exception. You need to handle her emotions carefully."

He nodded thoughtfully and kept eating. He wanted to finish quickly so he wouldn't be late for his date with Carrie.

"Would you like to take some of those zinnias out in front of the house to give her? Pick a half dozen and bring them in here. I'll put them in a spare vase, and you can take them to her as a gift." She reconsidered. "No, pick just five. An uneven number makes a more attractive arrangement. And bring in some of the greenery with them, too."

"Mrs. Steuben, that is both unexpected and generous. I'll go get them right now." He went outside to the flower patch and chose five perfect zinnias in pink, orange, purple, yellow, and white to present to Carrie. He took them into the house where Mrs. Steuben was busy cleaning a spare vase. She made an attractive arrangement and tied a ribbon around the container.

"I'm getting to like you, Derek. But don't expect favors like this every day." She wore a crooked grin.

He smiled. "Yes, ma'am. And thank you." He took the flowers and made his exit.

Arriving at the Johnson home, he knocked on the door and waited. Mr. Johnson answered as before and invited him in.

"Thank you, sir. I brought some flowers for Carrie."

"She'll be ready in just a moment. Have you had a good week?"

"Yes, I have. I'm in the middle of turning enough spokes for a back wheel for John Reese's carriage. His son drove it over a rock and cracked the rim. He doesn't want to take a chance on a weak wheel. He wants the whole thing replaced."

Johnson's eyebrows raised. "Is there a difference between making a front wheel and a back wheel?"

"On a carriage like Reese's, there is. They're different sizes. He has fourteen back spokes but only twelve in front."

"I never realized that."

"Isn't he related to you? Isn't he the fellow that owns the Crust and Crumb Bakery?"

Johnson nodded. "Yes, and Katie's Buffet with it. He's my wife's brother."

"I've never met him, but I understand he's a fine man."

"None finer, but we don't see each other as often as we should. Let me call Carrie. Carrie! Mr. March is here. Don't keep him waiting."

Carrie made her entrance down the stairs in a turquoise-colored dress that complemented her skin and hair. Derek stood to greet her.

"Carrie, you look beautiful. Here, I brought you some flowers."

She beamed at him, her heart dancing. "Thank you, Derek. I'll set them here on the coffee table where we can all enjoy them. Would you like to sit on the porch again?"

"I would."

Derek held the swing and stopped it from moving while Carrie sat, arranging her dress. Then he took the space beside her, closer than before. She folded her hands and smiled, lowering her head shyly. Derek looked at the long line of her neck and fantasized about kissing her there. But if he did, he would be throwing away the relationship he wanted to build with her. Her father would kill his plans without thinking twice.

They sat quietly, looking over the garden and chicken coop. The squash and pumpkins had blossomed.

"Have you done anything interesting since last Friday?" she asked.

"Yes, I did. I looked at houses."

Carrie's eyebrows raised. "Why did you do that?"

"I'm ready to buy a house and settle down. I want one big enough for the small family I may have eventually."

Carrie didn't blush this time. "Did you find anything you like?"

"I looked at three of them. My favorite was the first, and it's near the general store. Would you like to walk over and peek through the windows? It may not be the one I end up with, but it's the one I want if I can meet the seller's price."

Just then, Mrs. Johnson stuck her head out the door. "Would you two like a cup of tea?"

"Ma, Derek invited me to take a walk with him. Could I go?"

Matilda smiled. "How long do you plan to be gone?"

Derek answered her. "I thought we could take an hour."

"I'll check with Mr. Johnson."

Matilda came back with an answer in just a moment. "Papa said an evening is not an appropriate time to walk together since this is only your second date. It would be better to do it in daylight. You should wait and do that on a Saturday."

Derek's jaws clenched. His plans were being thwarted, but he quickly hid his irritation, hoping the women hadn't noticed. He put on the mask of a polite gentleman, then turned to Carrie.

"Next week, I'll pick you up on Saturday morning instead of Friday night. Would that be acceptable? I'll try to borrow a carriage from Mr. Blackburn, and we'll take a ride. Maybe we could have a picnic while we're out."

"I'll speak to Mr. Johnson about it," Matilda said, disappearing from the doorway. A moment later, she was back. "Mr. Johnson has agreed to that plan."

"Thank you, Mama."

Derek's irritation was raised again. *Once we're married, we won't have to get his approval for anything,* he thought.

His eyes followed Mrs. Johnson's back as she returned to the kitchen and closed the door.

Carrie turned to Derek. "What can you tell me about the house?"

Derek recovered his composure. "It's very advanced for 1895," he said. "It has a lovely front porch, a new kitchen, and two bedrooms. The rooms have been freshly painted."

"What makes it advanced?"

"The plumbing. It has an inside bathroom with a tub and one of those fancy toilets that flush water down the pipes. It's also wired for electricity, ready when the town puts in the poles."

Carrie gasped. "Are you serious? I thought those conveniences were only for the larger cities. Can you afford something like that?" Her ears turned red. "Begging your pardon because that's none of my business."

He smiled. "I told you I'd been saving money."

"I can't wait to see it."

They spent another hour in the swing together, talking about everything and nothing. At the appointed time, Derek rode his horse back to Mrs. Steuben's rooming house.

The week passed slowly for Carrie, but inevitably, Saturday morning came. Carrie believed she had aged a year since she had seen him.

This time, she was dressed in a pink cotton print dress and had packed some sandwiches, cheese, and cookies in a basket with a canteen of lemonade. She waited for Derek in the parlor, seated near the window. The grandfather clock behind her ticked slowly.

It was nearly ten o'clock when he arrived, and her father met him at the door. After some small talk, Derek and Carrie said goodbye. He helped her into the carriage he borrowed from the wheelwright, and the two headed toward Derek's favorite house.

Carrie's eyes were full of life, and she chatted excitedly. Derek only smiled and nodded occasionally as the words poured out her mouth. "I'm sorry, Derek. I can't seem to stop talking."

He gave her an amused grin.

They rode along, enjoying the pleasant weather and one another's company until they reached the house. Derek pulled the carriage in front and tied the horse to the rail. "This is it."

"Oh, look, it has gingerbread trim on the gables and porch. I love gingerbread on a house."

Derek grinned. "Come up on the porch. You can look through the window and see how spacious the room is and how the sun lights it up." He ran to her side of the carriage, took her hand, and helped her down.

Carrie walked to the porch window but couldn't see inside very well because her reflection in the glass blocked her view. She shielded her eyes with her hand and rested it on the glass. "Now I can see much better," she said. Sunlight flooded through the side window. "I've never seen a more beautiful parlor. Look at the fireplace. It's framed in oak with beautiful carvings on the mantel. Imagine this room with a rug on the floor and comfortable furnishings."

"Come around to the side. I'll boost you up so you can look into the kitchen." At the side window, she was too short to see inside. "I'll kneel here, and you can stand on my knee. Don't worry about falling. I'll hold you."

Carrie realized this was pushing the bounds of their new relationship but decided to allow it. *What would Papa think?* she wondered, but she wanted to see inside the house. She waited as he dropped to one knee and steadied her as she stepped up onto his other knee. She leaned on the side of the house and shielded her eyes while he steadied her by holding her hand.

"Look in there, Derek. What a beautiful kitchen. What a joy it would be to cook in such a place." She dropped lightly to the ground, and he stood.

"I thought you'd like it. Now come with me to the other side. You can see the larger bedroom from there."

They went to the other side of the house. He offered his knee, and she stepped up without hesitation. "Look at the size of that room. And the floors. They're oak, aren't they? I overlooked the floors in the other rooms. Were they oak as well?"

"Yes, I believe so."

"And it has a built-in closet. I've never seen anything like it. You don't even need a separate wardrobe taking up floor space."

"Not unless my wife has a large selection of dresses." He grinned at her. She pretended not to hear, but the pink blush on her ears betrayed her embarrassment.

She stepped down off his knee. "The woman who lives in that house will be so blessed."

They locked eyes for a moment. She so wanted to be the one living there with him.

"Let's find a place to enjoy our picnic," she said.

"I'd like to go to the river. We could have a picnic under that big oak."

"That sounds perfect."

They spread a blanket beside the river under an oak tree. Carrie unpacked the lunch, and they enjoyed their sandwiches while listening to the bubbling water. Some distance downstream, a boy stood with his fishing line in the water. They watched, excitedly hoping for his success, as he pulled out a bluegill. He managed to get the flopping fish into his bucket.

"He'll have fish for supper," Carrie said.

"I used to fish when I was a boy. But it's been years...." Derek lost himself in his memory for a few seconds, then came back to the present. "Did you ever fish?"

"Oh, yes," Carrie said. "Papa used to take me with my older brothers. But I preferred to sit on the bank with a book while the boys did the fishing."

After their lunch, they climbed back into the carriage. On the way back home, he took her hand. She didn't resist. "I'd like to sit with you in church on Sunday."

She pursed her lips. "Wait one more week. If you did that,

and then changed your mind about me, it would be an embarrassment. I want us to be sure first."

He took a moment to look at her. *Maybe she's not as sure as I am. Perhaps I need to give her more time, even though I would give anything to make her mine right now.* "As you wish. I don't want to cause you any discomfort."

"Thank you, Derek. You're a real gentleman."

She invited him to sit in the swing when they reached the house. "Would you like a cup of tea, and we'll rest for a few minutes before you go?"

"That sounds pleasant."

Carrie went into the kitchen. For the few moments that she was gone, Derek had time to think. He was sorry about what he had done to Julia, but Carrie would be different. He vowed to himself that he would love and cherish her and treat her with respect. He would work hard to be an excellent father to their children.

I hope Julia is happy in the sanitarium. It would be easier to move on if I could be sure she was happy there. Then, shocked that thoughts of Julia had intruded on his time with Carrie, he returned to the present. *Where did that thought come from? Will I never be able to leave the past behind and start fresh?*

Carrie returned from the kitchen. She sat beside him, quite close, and they sipped their tea together, basking in one other's presence and watching butterflies play in the wildflowers.

The question at the back of Joseph Kendall's mind had nagged at him since he met Derek March at church in June. He was confident he was familiar with that name. Then, one night, as he drifted off to sleep, he sat bolt upright in his bed.

So that's where I know that name, he thought. A few years ago in Lamar, the wife of a man named Derek March disappeared. What was her name? Let's see...I think it was Julia. No one ever found out what happened. It was suspicious, the way she vanished and the way March moved out of town immediately after that. I wonder if she's even alive...I wonder if it's the same man. It's possible there could be two men with the same name.

Kendall was a man who despised gossip. He lectured his wife and daughters whenever they talked loosely about someone. He was familiar with the damage that could be done to an innocent man's reputation by loose talk, to say nothing about the loss of respect for the person doing the gossiping. He hated the very thought. So he decided to keep his lips sealed until he had proof that this Derek March was the same one whose wife had gone missing. It would be a burden he must carry. *Thou shalt not bear false witness,* he reminded himself. He tried to get back to sleep but found himself tossing and turning all night.

Chapter 8: Meeting the Relatives

Carrie and Derek decided to meet again on Saturday rather than Friday the following week. That would appease her father and give them more time together. Derek complied with Mr. Johnson's strict rules—for now—but longed for the day he could claim Carrie as his wife.

He rode to the Johnson home on horseback, talking to the horse as they traveled. It snorted and shook its head. Since he hadn't been able to borrow a carriage from Mr. Blackburn, he suggested to Carrie that they take a walk. The weather was cooler than usual. The skies were a brilliant blue, and gossamer clouds floated overhead.

"I'll pack a picnic lunch so we don't have to return to the house when we get hungry," Carrie said. When she started for the kitchen, Derek held her back.

"Let's have lunch at Katie's Buffet, the restaurant beside the Crust and Crumb Bakery," he said. "I hear they serve soup you can't get anywhere else, and they have a salad bar. My friend says you can make your own salad and put whatever you want in it."

Carrie laughed. "That's my uncle's bakery and restaurant,

but I've never eaten there. That would be fun. And if my aunt and uncle are there, I'll introduce you."

"Bring a basket with you. We may see something at the bakery we want to buy. I hear their apple pies are the best for miles around. We could bring one back to your house and share it with your family."

Carrie retrieved the basket and told her parents that she and Derek might be gone until after lunch. Mama held her peace while Papa warned her to return no later than two o'clock.

The couple left the house on foot, chatting happily.

As they walked, Agatha Brown, an elderly member of Trinity Chapel, came riding by in her carriage and stopped to offer a lift. "Miss Johnson, how nice to see you. Would you like me to take you and your friend wherever you're going?"

"Thank you, Mrs. Brown," Carrie said. "That's very nice of you to offer, but we're just out for a walk."

"It's no trouble, really. I'd be glad to take you to save you some time and shoe leather."

Carrie turned her best smile toward Mrs. Brown. "We're enjoying our walk so much I would hate to cut it short. But maybe you could make the same offer the next time you see us. We may take you up on it then."

Mrs. Brown sighed. "All right. Well, enjoy yourselves." And she continued on her way.

As her carriage proceeded up the street, Carrie grinned at Derek.

"You know what just happened, don't you?" She giggled.

"No. What?"

"Mrs. Brown wanted to give us a carriage ride to meet you and pump you for information about yourself. Her reputation as a gossip is legendary."

The twisted grin on Carrie's face told Derek that it amused her, but he thought he might have just escaped a dangerous situation. He didn't want information about himself getting around. If the truth got out—even though he didn't think it would—it could mess up his plans. No—it could mess up his life. A puff of air escaped his pursed lips, but he kept his thoughts to himself and recovered his good humor.

He reached for Carrie's hand. She pulled it away. "Derek, please. We're in public. I'd rather do that privately."

"Really? You'll let me hold your hand on your back porch?" He gazed down at her, his eyes twinkling.

"Of course, Mr. March. But don't you tell anyone else." She flashed him a smile and turned her head.

Things are coming along nicely, thought Derek with satisfaction.

They walked by the post office, the barber shop with its red and white striped pole, and the doctor's office. They reached the business area of town with time to spare before lunch and decided to look around the general store to check out the new merchandise. Several customers were there shopping, including a friend of Carrie's she had known in school. The girl approached.

"Carrie Johnson, is that you? I haven't seen you since school." She addressed Carrie, but her eyes flitted to Derek.

"Hello, Mavis. Yes, it's me. I'd like you to meet my friend, Derek March. Derek, this is Mavis Dearing, an old schoolmate."

"Nice to meet you, Miss Dearing."

"Oh, it's Mrs. Corning now. I married Elias."

Carrie did her best to conceal her shock. She had never cared for Elias and thought he was a bad fit for Mavis. There was something off about him. His ideas about life were skewed. He was generally suspicious and thought everyone was out to take advantage of him. Carrie wanted to avoid commenting on that unfortunate match, afraid she would say something embarrassing.

"Please say hello to Elias for me," she said.

"I will. Say, do I remember you from somewhere?" Mavis asked, shifting her attention again to Derek.

Derek took a breath. "I swear there must be someone

around here who looks like me," he said, "but I'm from Philadelphia."

"Maybe it was a look-alike. Well, Carrie, it was good to run into you again. We'll have to get together and catch up on each other's lives."

Carrie said that would be nice and was relieved to end the conversation. Mavis took her basket of purchases and left the store.

"How well do you know her?" Derek asked.

"Not well. I went to school with her, but we were never close friends. And I was always uncomfortable around Elias. He was just…well…different."

"What do you think of me? Am I different?"

Carrie thought for a moment. "You're certainly different from Elias." She chuckled, and Derek grinned at her.

"I'll take that as a compliment."

"That's the way I intended it."

They continued browsing through the articles in the store and came to a section with ladies' makeup and accessories. Derek was fascinated. "You're so lovely, Carrie. Do you use any makeup?"

Carrie's voice dropped to an uncomfortable whisper. "Shush, Derek. I use a little, and so do my friends, but if our mothers found out…It's something Christian girls are expected to avoid, but I've read the Bible, and there's nothing in there against it."

"What about the verse where Paul said to let not your beauty be the plaiting of hair? I forget how it goes exactly."

"It was Peter, not Paul. He said, 'Whose adorning let it not be that outward adorning of plaiting the hair, and of wearing of gold, or of putting on of apparel…'" Yes, I know the verse. Don't you think he was cautioning women not to depend on outward beauty alone but to also be beautiful on the inside?"

"I certainly hope so. I enjoy looking at a beautiful woman."

Carrie's eyes snapped up to his. He took note of the frown on her face and laughed.

"I don't want to look at all of them, just one. You. And I would like to buy you a gift, Christian girl."

"I don't need a gift, Derek, but thank you anyway."

"I want to buy you a rabbit's foot brush to put on a touch of rouge. Would you use it if I bought it for you?"

Carrie had long wanted to try one, knowing some of her friends had them. The temptation was too much. She smiled shyly and nodded.

"Here's a little basket with a few rabbit's foot brushes. Choose the best one, Carrie, and use it in good health."

He focused on her as she timidly reached into the basket, sorted through the small supply, and chose the one she liked best. She held it up for Derek's inspection. "What do you think of this one?"

Derek grinned. "It's perfect, and if it will help you feel your best, it's my joy to give it to you. Of course, I don't think you *need* makeup. But I've heard tell that people of the fair sex enjoy enhancing their beauty. So let's go pay for it."

He took her by the elbow and led her to the cashier. Reaching into his pocket, he pulled out the necessary coins and handed them to the clerk.

Carrie dropped the brush into her purse. "Derek, I don't know how to thank you. That was very generous."

"You can pay me back later."

Her forehead wrinkled in confusion at that surprising comment. "Oh? What do I owe you?"

"You owe me the honor of your presence as often as your father will allow it. And I want you to think of me every time you use it." He grinned impishly at her.

Carrie relaxed, and she returned his smile. "Mr. March, you will find that I am a person who pays her debts."

"Ready for lunch?" he asked. "Let's go next door and see if your aunt and uncle are there."

Carrie and Derek walked next door to the Crust and Crumb Bakery, planning to take the inside entrance to the restaurant section. The heady aromas of yeast bread and cinnamon filled the air. They were greeted by Gracie Reese, Carrie's cousin, on duty as the hostess.

"Carrie, how long has it been since we've seen each other?" She stepped forward and gave Carrie a hug around the neck.

"It's been a while, Gracie. This is Mr. Derek March. We're here for lunch. Are your Ma and Pa here?"

"Ma's in the kitchen baking, as usual, but Pa's out running an errand. I'll get you seated in the restaurant, then tell Ma you're here. I'm sure she'll want to see you. And Mr. March, I'm pleased to meet you."

He nodded. "And you, Miss Reese."

She led them to a table, put menus before them, and went to tell her mother who was there.

As they studied their menus, Katie Reese breezed into the restaurant side of the bakery. She was a petite, brown-haired woman in a white apron stained with the ingredients of years of baking. "Carrie, how are you?" she asked, hugging her niece.

"Fine, Aunt Kate. This is my friend, Derek March. We came for lunch."

"Mr. March, a pleasure to meet you. You came to a great place to eat. I hope you enjoy soup and salad. Choose your soup and give your order to Gracie, then you can go to the buffet and build your salads. By the way, Carrie, how are your parents? It's been too long since we've been together."

"They're just fine. I'm sure they'd love to get together with you. I'll tell Mama you asked about them."

"Good. I need to get back to the kitchen. Lovely to see you, Carrie. And you, Mr. March."

Kate returned to the kitchen, leaving Carrie and Derek to browse their menus. Carrie decided on the cream of potato and cheese soup, while Derek chose the Cincinnati-style chili with beef. He had never heard of chili before and wanted to try it. They gave their orders to Gracie and stepped to the salad buffet, filling their bowls with lettuce, spinach, tomatoes, and a delicious variety of other vegetables. A variety of dressings were available in labeled cruets.

As they returned to their table, John Reese entered and greeted the couple.

"Uncle John, I'd like you to meet my friend, Derek March."

John studied Derek's face a bit longer than was comfortable for Derek. "Your name is somehow familiar, Mr. March. Do you live in Lamar?"

Derek opened his mouth to answer, but Carrie jumped in. "Derek is from Philadelphia. He grew up beside a river. It was probably another March family you're thinking of. Derek has moved to Spencer's Mill and plans to buy a house here."

"Yes, I'm probably thinking of some other family. Welcome to Spencer's Mill, March. Good to meet you." He thrust out his hand, and the two men shook.

John retreated into the bakery, and Gracie brought their soup with fresh buttered rolls.

Derek fidgeted with his fork. "Carrie, I don't think your uncle likes me."

"Of course he does, Derek. Why wouldn't he? He doesn't know you well enough to dislike you."

Derek ate his lunch with little conversation.

After a few minutes of silent contemplation, Carrie spoke. "Derek, my heart is troubled, but I'm not sure why."

"Maybe my discomfort over your uncle's question is spilling over to you."

"Did I do wrong to say what I did?"

"No; thank you for intervening. It's just that so many people think they've known me at some time or another. I'm stumped as to how to respond." He wagged his head. "Forgive my blue mood. I should snap out of it. Tell you what, let's buy a pie from the bakery when we're finished here. We'll take it back to your house and eat it there."

As they left the restaurant and bought their pie in the bakery section, she called back into the kitchen, "Goodbye, Aunt Kate and Uncle John." When her aunt and uncle entered the sales room to say their goodbyes, Carrie didn't detect any suspicious attitude from Uncle John.

Outside on the brick sidewalk, she turned to Derek. "I don't see how you thought Uncle John didn't like you. He seemed friendly enough to me."

"Yes," Derek admitted. "I must have been mistaken the first time."

Two days later, John Reese visited the new Kentmoor Farm Supply Store, where his brother-in-law, Joshua Johnson, worked in the back office. The new store was located next to the old, established stores. It was a larger facility with plenty of parking space for horse-drawn wagons in the front and a loading area in the rear. John found his brother-in-law's office in the back of the store and tapped gently on the door frame.

"Do you have a minute, Josh?"

Joshua looked up from his work. "John, how good to see you. It's been a long time. Come on in and have a seat."

The two men shook hands, and John laid his hat on Joshua's desk as he took the straight-backed chair.

"Are you here to buy something from the store, John? What can I do for you?"

John frowned and brushed a piece of lint from his sleeve. Then he looked John in the eye. "How well do you know that young man Carrie is seeing?"

"We've known him for three or four months now, and he's become like part of the family. Exceptional young man. He's hard-working, respectful...we haven't found any fault in him."

"Have you checked out his family? Maybe looked him up in the public records?"

"His family is in Philadelphia, so we're at a disadvantage. But I've checked the public records in this county, and I telegraphed the police in Philadelphia to see if he had a record there. Everything came back clean. Why do you ask?"

"I can't put my finger on it. He made me vaguely uncomfortable. But if you've checked him out, well, facts are more reliable than feelings. Maybe I read him wrong. Still, Joshua, I'd watch him closely if I were you."

Williams

"John, I can see you're very concerned, but we haven't detected any fault in him."

"Well then, I'm sorry to have brought this up. I hope you weren't offended."

"No problem, John. I appreciate your watching out for Carrie. It's a blessing to know that family can be depended on."

"I've bothered you enough, so I'll get on with my errands. Good to see you again, Josh. Please tell Matilda I miss her."

John picked up his hat and left, leaving Joshua with an uncomfortable feeling. He reflected on the young man's relationship with Carrie, about the activities they pursued together, and the conversations they had. He came up with nothing that should bother him, but still, he felt unsettled. *It's probably of no consequence. I'm probably having doubts only because John suggested it. Still, it won't hurt to question Derek more closely.*

On Friday, in anticipation of Derek's arrival at seven o'clock, he sent Carrie to her room and told her to wait a little longer than usual.

Derek arrived promptly for his date with Carrie. Mr. Johnson answered the door and welcomed him in.

"Carrie's running a little late," he said. "Have a seat."

Derek chose the chair opposite the sofa where Joshua sat and prepared to wait.

"I've never talked to you about where you grew up, Derek. Carrie said you lived in a cabin on a river. That sounds like an idyllic childhood."

Derek shifted his weight in the chair. "It was, mostly."

"Was it a big cabin?"

"It was big enough, but there were only three of us."

"Tell me about the kinds of things you did. Did you have many friends?"

"I had a few friends," Derek said, "but we lived away from the city, so we didn't have that much contact with people." *I'm being interrogated,* he thought. *I wonder why. I thought my*

66

relationship with Mr. Johnson was solid.

"But you would have had to go into town to buy supplies. Did you go with your mother?"

"My Ma didn't go into town except on rare occasions. When I was little, we had a fire in the cabin, and her face had been burned. There was heavy scarring on one side, so she didn't like people to see her face. She mostly stayed home."

Joshua's eyes softened. "How dreadful. That would be even more horrible for a woman than a man. I can see why she didn't go into town. How did you survive?"

"Pa did a lot of hunting, and we fished. Ma had a big vegetable garden and kept chickens. We did all right."

Joshua observed him closely to see if he was lying, but he didn't spot anything that indicated dishonesty. "I forget what Carrie said the name of that river was."

Derek paused. "When I was a boy, I thought of it as a river, but maybe I should have used a more accurate word. It was more like a stream. See, our cabin sat back from it about thirty feet, and when I laid in bed at night, I could hear the bubbling water flowing downstream. I don't think it had a name, but it flowed into the Delaware River. And train whistles blew in the distance. It was a haunting sound. I loved it." He lowered his head, smiled, and nodded. "Yes, I loved that sound."

Joshua's mind was stuck on the tragedy Derek described earlier. He wagged his head. "Your poor mother. I had no idea. But it seems that you had a pretty good childhood anyway."

"I did."

"Just out of curiosity, what were your parents' names?"

"Uh…Thomas. My father's name was Thomas. And my mother was Sylvie. They're both gone now. They're buried on that plot of land by the river…er, stream."

Mr. Johnson checked his pocket watch. "I wonder what's keeping Carrie. Carrie! Don't keep Derek waiting."

He must have been satisfied with my answers, Derek thought. *What caused his suspicion all of a sudden?*

Carrie emerged from her bedroom, wondering what had

taken so long.

Seated on the porch swing, Carrie bubbled with excitement. "My brothers are coming for Sunday dinner, and you're invited." Her eyes were bright. "I haven't seen them for months."

Derek's heart sank, but he tried to hide his unease. "And you said their names are Herbert and Francis?"

"Yes, Herbert is the oldest, and Francis is a year older than me. They work in the oil business. Francis has a job in the corporate office, and Herbert works on the well pumps, keeping them in good operating condition."

"That must be a dirty job." Derek thought if these fellows worked in Lamar, they might have heard of him. He wondered if he should feign illness on Sunday and send a message to church with Mrs. Steuben that he wouldn't be able to make dinner with the Johnsons. Or he could tell Carrie that a rush order came in for wagon wheels, and he had to work Sunday. He didn't know if she would believe that. He scooted slightly closer to Carrie and took her hand, trying to think of the right thing to say, but his thoughts were interrupted.

"I baked a cake today with butter icing," she said, turning her face toward his.

Their eyes locked and held. He didn't care about the cake; she was so beautiful. "It's good that your parents are sitting on the other side of that door, or you would be in trouble."

She giggled. "I'll get you a piece of that cake. Would you like a cup of tea with it?"

He smiled and pulled away from her. "That sounds good."

She rose and went into the kitchen to slice the cake and brew the tea. Derek sat on the swing alone, fretting about the brothers he would meet. When she returned, Derek said, "Carrie, I don't think I should come to dinner on Sunday. You need some family time with your brothers."

Her eyes widened, and she put her hand on his face to turn it toward her. "No, Derek, you must come. They want to meet you, and I want you to meet the rest of the family."

He sighed. He should have waited until Sunday to send a message that he wasn't coming, but it was too late. "If it means that much to you, I'll be here. But they may not like me."

"Of course they will. Then it's all settled."

Sunday arrived. Derek fussed over his appearance before stepping into Mrs. Steuben's carriage. He wanted to make his best impression on two prospective brothers-in-law. "What do you know about Carrie's brothers, Francis and Herbert?" he asked her.

"They're nice young men...hard workers, and honest. They look out for their sister."

"They'll be at the Johnsons' for dinner today, so I'll meet them for the first time." His nervousness showed in his bouncing knee.

Mrs. Steuben smiled. "Don't worry, Derek. You'll do fine."

Derek tried to relax during the church service but couldn't sit still. He ran his hands through his hair. He rubbed the back of his neck. He crossed and uncrossed his legs. *I'm surprised the brothers aren't here,* he thought. *They must be making the drive from Lamar this morning. What will I say if they ask me about my past? I hope I don't have to lie to them like I did their father. Thomas and Sylvie. I'll have to write down those names so I don't forget them.*

After church, he drove home with the Johnsons, as usual. Francis and Herbert were there, lounging in the parlor. They were big, strapping young men with broad smiles and outgoing personalities. Other than that, they looked nothing alike. Francis had dark hair, but Herbert's head was covered with a copper-colored, naturally curly mop. Derek judged them both to be in their early twenties, a few years younger than himself.

When the rest of the family arrived home, the boys jumped up and ran to their mother first, squashing her in a double hug.

She laughed and hugged back. Then, the boys shook hands with their father and greeted their sisters and little brother, excited to be home. Last, they turned to Derek.

"And who is this fellow?" asked Francis with a grin.

Carrie stepped forward. "I'd like you to meet my friend, Derek March."

Francis took Derek's hand in his big hand and nearly crushed it. "Good to meet you, Derek. We already know a lot about you, thanks to Carrie, who can't keep her mouth shut. You can call me Frank. That's what my friends in Lamar call me. Saves time. You say only one syllable instead of two." He grinned.

Derek liked him despite his angst. "Nice to meet you, Frank."

"And this is my brother, Herbert. You can call him Herb."

Derek chuckled as he shook Herb's hand. "Same reason, I suppose?"

"Naturally. Come on, Derek, let's you and me and Herb play a little football in the backyard while the women get dinner ready."

Surprised at what personable fellows these were, Derek followed them outside. He reminded himself to be careful about what he said. He couldn't afford to let down his guard.

Herb had a football, and they tossed it among themselves to warm up. They decided to begin their football game by pitting Herb and Derek against Frank, the larger brother. Herb kicked the ball to Frank, who tried to run the ball to the far end of the yard, avoiding Herb and Derek. He managed to knock his brother down. Derek kept up with him, pace for pace, but couldn't stop him. As Frank reached the designated goal, he slammed the ball to earth and bounced it into the air in a victory dance.

Herb slapped Derek on the back. "You all right, old man?" he asked.

Derek wiped the sweat from his brow with his sleeve. "Aw, come on, I'm not that old. I'll bet I could run that ball right through the two of you brothers."

"Hey, Frank, did you hear that challenge? Let's take him up

on it. You and me against the old guy."

Derek grinned and took his position opposite them.

Herb kicked the ball, and Derek leaped into the air to snatch it. He cradled it in the crook of his right arm, then ran at the brothers. He hoped to slip between them, but he wasn't successful. Frank reached out and tackled him hard. Derek hit the ground. Pain shot through his knee as he tumbled fast, losing his grip on the ball. It bounced away.

"You got me," he said, panting. "I hate to admit it, but I think my knee is hurt."

"I'm sorry, man," Frank said as the brothers helped him to his feet. "I didn't intend to hurt you."

"It's fine, Frank. Just one of the risks of playing football."

"Seriously, Derek, I'm real sorry."

Herb teased. "He's probably faking it to get Carrie's sympathy. She'll fawn all over him."

Frank and Herb snickered at that joke, and Derek took it as intended. He limped to the house with his arms over the brothers' shoulders, through the kitchen toward the parlor. "I can't sit in there. My trousers are dirty."

Carrie watched drop-jawed as Derek made his way through the kitchen. She entered the parlor with a dishtowel in hand. "What happened to you?" She rushed to the sofa and put the towel down so he could sit. She inspected the blood and grass stain on his trousers. "You need to clean that cut and get it bandaged. Herb, do you have a pair of trousers you could loan Derek until he gets his washed?"

"I may have." Herb turned to check his supply of clothes.

Carrie sat next to Derek. "Do you know how to get that stain out? I can give you some instructions. Really, tell me what happened."

Derek glanced at Frank and Herb, grinning. "You were right." Then, to Carrie, he said, "Your brother knocked me down, and I twisted my knee. Walking is painful, but I'm sure it will get better."

Carrie's hand went to her chest. "I'm sorry you're hurt.

Wait, I'll get a cold cloth to put on your knee. It'll make your pants wet, but keep the swelling down."

The brothers choked back their laugh and poked him in the arm. As soon as Carrie disappeared into the kitchen to get a wet cloth, they snickered. "Make the most of it while you can, brother," said Frank.

The meal and the rest of the afternoon passed pleasantly. Derek thought being part of that family would be even better than he thought. His only regret was his scarred past. When it was time for him to go home, Herb volunteered to take him in their carriage.

Along the way, Herb said, "I don't know if you're aware, but Carrie is crazy about you. She can hardly talk about anything else."

"That's good to know. I feel the same about her."

"Are you going to ask her to marry you?"

"I plan to, but I have to wait until the right time. I don't think your father will let her go so easily."

"Well, he likes you, too. I wish you the best of luck. I think you'd make a good addition to the family. But we might want to lay off the football games before somebody gets hurt worse." Herb chuckled at that.

They reached Mrs. Steuben's house. "Thanks for the ride home, Herb. I hope to see you again soon."

"Same here, Derek. Take care."

Derek went upstairs to his room, excited about his great day with two future brothers-in-law. But soon, his old guilt crept back in, bringing a headache. It wouldn't leave him alone. He was full of regret about the jeweler and what he had done to Julia. If only he could find a way to overcome his past. It would be wonderful to be a part of the Johnson family with a clear conscience, but he might as well forget that. He would have to bear his burden silently, taking care that no one ever found out.

Chapter 9: Preparing to Raise Funds

Derek struggled with an intense desire to buy that house from Oliver Hardin. Owning a home like that would boost his status in town. Carrie had already expressed her excitement; she would love to live there. The property would be within his reach if he could sell more items in his box, but it would need to be done discreetly.

He came up with the idea of going to Toledo to find a buyer. No one there would recognize any of his jewelry. Now, he only needed a cover story for going that far. He decided to invent a dying relative. He had told plenty of lies to a lot of people, so one more wouldn't matter. It wouldn't make him suffer any worse guilt because a lie wasn't as bad as the other sins he had already committed. A man does what he has to do to get what he wants, and he wanted Carrie and that house.

"Mr. Blackburn," he said the next day at work, "I have a sick aunt I need to attend in Toledo. The doctor says she's near death, and I'm her only living relative. Can you let me take a week off? I would go by train, take care of her needs, and return by the following week."

Blackburn cringed. "An entire week? Our business increased after you began adding to our production. I would hate to lose you for a week, especially since it's September already, and there's not that much time left that you can work outdoors."

Derek pressed him. "Please, Mr. Blackburn. I wouldn't ask, but she doesn't have anyone else. And according to the telegram I received, her health is fading fast."

Blackburn sighed heavily. "All right. You've proven yourself valuable here…but I suppose I could spare you for that long. When do you plan to go?"

"I'd like to go on Saturday and return by the following Saturday. I need to go soon. I don't know how much longer she'll live."

"All right. Try to make another two hubs before you go, but don't chisel out the mortises. We don't know how many spokes we'll need until an order comes in."

"Yes, sir. I can do that. And thank you."

Derek was satisfied that his plan was coming together. He was confident that if he asked Carrie to marry him, she would say yes, even though they hadn't been seeing each other very long. She would make a splendid wife. And he was going to buy that perfect house for her. All he needed to do was get rid of some of that jewelry.

Then he had a sudden thought. If he had a wife, he would need to be rid of all of it. He couldn't afford the possibility of her finding it accidentally and asking questions. If he could sell it all, it would give him a healthy bank account for the future. A wife would be less likely to find out about that.

But there was a problem. Who would have enough cash to buy that much stolen jewelry? And if he sold it in a single lot, would someone recognize it as coming from the burglary in Lamar? There was that risk, and he would need to think it through with a clear head.

The Johnson family had invited him to dinner on Wednesday night, so he would tell Carrie he must be away for a week caring for a sick aunt. It was gratifying to know that she would be heartsick to see him go. But when he returned, he would buy her that house. He hoped Hardin would not find another buyer before he could get his cash together.

When he knocked on the Johnson door on Wednesday evening, Mr. Johnson invited him in. Soon, dinner was on the table. He and Carrie sat beside each other, occasionally touching hands surreptitiously under the table. He smiled to see that she was wearing a bit of rouge on her porcelain skin. It made her even more attractive. *So she's able to use her rabbit's foot brush.*

Her face wore a glow when she was near him.

Derek turned to Mr. Johnson. "I received some unfortunate news today. My Aunt Enid in Toledo is desperately ill, and I'm her only living relative. She needs me to help get her affairs in order."

Carrie's face fell.

"I'm sorry to hear that, Derek," said Mr. Johnson. "When will you be leaving?"

"I sent her a telegram saying I could be there Saturday evening. I'm going up by train. Depending on the situation, I may be back within three or four days, or it may be as long as a week."

"Will we be together Friday night, then?" asked Carrie. Disappointment showed in her eyes and the crease in her forehead.

Derek smiled at her. "I wouldn't miss it for the world. After I leave work, we'll have dinner together and take an evening drive in the country. Does that meet with your approval, Mr. Johnson?"

Johnson hesitated. "I think that will be all right. You've been seeing each other for a while now. Just be mindful of my rules, and don't be gone long."

"The air is cooler at night now," Carrie said. "I'll bundle up. Riding in the chilly air will be like a hayride, won't it?"

Friday night arrived. After dinner, Carrie wrapped herself in her warm woolen shawl and climbed into the borrowed carriage.

Derek lit the kerosene headlamps, jumped in the carriage with her, and they traveled down the road, enjoying their peace and privacy.

"Let's go talk by the river," said Derek.

"That sounds nice."

A few moments later, they pulled into a spot where the moon was reflected perfectly on the surface of the dark, flowing water. They sat together silently, hand in hand, listening to the constant chirping of the crickets in the night. The privacy was intoxicating.

"I wish this would go on forever," Carric said. "The atmosphere is perfect, and so is the company. Isn't it beautiful?"

Derek's heart pounded wildly. He ached to sweep her up in his arms and show her the kind of love she had never known, but he couldn't destroy his chance to have her as his wife. Things would have to be taken slowly.

"It is beautiful," he said. "It's like where I lived as a child, on the banks of a river. We had a cabin there. It was so peaceful. I miss that."

"Then there are rivers in Philadelphia?"

Derek's reverie was interrupted, and he came back to the present. He shifted his weight. "Yes."

"What was the name of your river?"

Derek took a moment to answer. "I never thought of the river as having a name. We just called it the river."

"Oh." Carrie paused, then continued with her next question. "Do you have brothers and sisters?"

"No, I'm the only child in my family. I missed the give-and-take of siblings. But you have three brothers and a sister. You're very fortunate."

They sat quietly in the moonlight, huddled together for warmth until it was time to return to the house. Derek was miserable, having to restrain his longing. His heart hammered in his chest. Finally, he gave in to his impulses. He put his arm around Carrie to draw her closer, then kissed her passionately. He didn't expect the reaction he got.

She hammered on him with her fist and pulled away abruptly. "Stop that, Derek," she cried. "What do you think you're doing?"

His mouth flew open. "Don't you think you're being prudish? I thought you loved me."

"I...I.." Tears flowed, and she buried her face in her hands.

Even through his anger and hurt, he reached out in compassion and put his arms around her. She allowed that and sobbed against his chest.

He didn't know what to think. He didn't want their last night for over a week to end this way. But it was too late to go back and do it differently. He returned Carrie safely to her home, untouched, and went to his room at Mrs. Steuben's house to sulk.

Chapter 10: The Trip to Toledo

The following day, Derek stood alone with his black valise, waiting to board the train to Toledo. Uniformed porters pushed luggage carts to the baggage car, bumping unevenly over the wooden platform. Their metal wheels made the platform vibrate like a drum. The other passengers mingled about, laughing and talking among themselves excitedly. The large, black locomotive, followed by the coal car, loomed nearby on the rails like a living thing, hissing steam, while the engineer in his blue and white cap climbed up to take the controls.

Derek was nervous, and his stomach was in knots. He was about to collide with his past, having to deal with stolen goods. And Julia was in Toledo. He hadn't decided whether to check on her. But this trip was unavoidable if he were to get on with his future. Otherwise, he wouldn't be doing it. His valise contained his revolver, a few clothes, and most importantly, his wooden box. His knuckles were white around the handle of the valise; his whole future was in it.

As the conductor sang out, "All aboooard," the passengers queued up and began climbing the steps into the Pullman coach. Derek took his place in line and attempted to enter, but a large lady squeezed ahead with a hat box and jostled him back down on the platform. He tried it again.

He hoped he could get a seat where no one wanted to chat with him. He wasn't in the mood, so he sat by a window and put his valise between his feet. He slumped with his cap pulled down over his eyes, crossed his arms, and tried to sleep. But the train was nearly full, so a gray-haired gentleman in a business suit disturbed his nap.

"Pardon me, sir," he said. "Empty seats on this train are getting scarce. Would you mind if I took the seat beside you?"

"Not at all," Derek lied.

When the stranger tried to put his luggage in the overhead, he tripped and bumped Derek, who removed his cap and opened his eyes to see what had happened.

"So sorry," said the stranger. "I didn't mean to disturb you."

"That's all right."

The man extended his hand. "My name's McCard."

Derek was obliged to shake his hand. "Nice to meet you, McCard. I'm March."

The stranger took his seat. "Is this a pleasure trip for you?"

"No, it's business." Derek noted how the man was dressed. "You're on a business trip, too?"

"Yes, I'm meeting with a prospective customer in Chicago. The fellow wants to build himself a steam automobile to test an engine he designed. He's planning to go into manufacturing if his test is successful. That's where I come in. I represent Dunlop Tires. If I can sell him the tires for his first auto, and he's successful, there's a good chance that many orders will follow as he builds more automobiles."

"Interesting. I wish you well."

The stranger opened a newspaper. Derek pulled his hat over his eyes and tried to nap again. He needed to make up for his fitful sleep the night before.

Three hours later, after a stopover in Florissant, the train pulled into the station in Toledo. In the middle of a nap, Derek was awakened by the train's deceleration. The brass bell on the engine clanged, the wheels screeched on their iron track, and steam billowed from the underbelly of the train with an insistent "psssssssst." The passengers grabbed their luggage from the overheads and filed off.

Derek shielded his eyes against the sun and waited for a Hansom cab. His first stop would be a hotel, where he could safely stash his valise while he did some research. He needed to find out where he could sell his pieces. He thought the best place to nose around would be a pub. Information flows easily with ale.

He whistled and motioned to a cab coming his way and asked the driver to take him to a reputable hotel. He ended up at the Grand Maumee by the river. The Grand Maumee wasn't a posh establishment, but that was fine with Derek. He didn't want to fritter his money away on this trip.

"Would you wait while I get a room and deposit my luggage? I'll want to be taken to a pub."

"Yes, sir, I can do that."

Derek didn't take long to check in and stash his belongings in his room. He went back outside and asked the cabbie where he could get a drink.

"What kind of pub do you want? Do you want entertainment or just a place to tip your glass?"

"I want someone to talk to over my ale. Entertainment might make conversation easier."

"There's a two-block stretch where you could find about five pubs. I'll drop you there, and you can take your pick."

The driver let him off in an area of saloons with an atmosphere of partying. Fast, competing music from different pubs floated out to the sidewalks. Men whose dress revealed varying occupations walked through the doors. Some of them were with friends, but others went in alone. On a Saturday night, there would be entertainment: dancers and singers of varying quality. And there would be ale. Lots of it.

Derek decided to try the Lion's Eye Tavern first. It was patronized by men who worked on the docks, rough men who could make their way around the back alleys. The tavern was dim with cigarette and cigar smoke. Sweaty men dressed in stained, faded work clothes sat on stools at the bar or at tables. The only women present were employees, either waitresses or singers. At one end of the bar, a band played on a makeshift stage, accompanying a hard-looking woman with an average voice and above-average enthusiasm.

Derek took a leather-padded stool at the bar and ordered a pint. He struck up a conversation with the man on the next seat.

"Is this a good place to get a drink?"

"If it wasn't, I wouldn't be here." The irritable man lifted his glass and downed it.

"I guess that was a foolish question. My name's March." He stuck out his hand.

The stranger shook it indifferently and peered at him through red-rimmed eyes. "You're not from around here, are you?"

"I haven't been here for a while. Have you lived in Toledo all your life?" As soon as he asked that question, Derek realized that wasn't the best way to revive the conversation.

"Yeah. Bartender, get me another one." The bartender obliged. The man sat with both hands around his drink. He was drinking something harder than ale, but Derek couldn't identify it. A lit cigarette glowed in the ashtray beside him, sending a narrow stream of smoke curling toward the ceiling.

The two sat in silence for some time, nursing their drinks. Derek didn't know how to get to his point smoothly. Finally, he thought, *If I'm going to get any information from this fellow, I'll have to ask it plainly.*

"Say," he said, "if somebody had some stuff to sell, where could they go around here to unload it?"

The man turned his unshaven face toward him, and his brow creased. His eyes drilled through Derck. "Are you a cop?"

"No, of course not. I'm just trying to raise a little money to get back home."

"Go ask someone else. You don't look like you belong here, anyway."

Derek paid his tab and slid off his stool in defeat. *I handled that badly,* he thought. *I'll have to try another bar.*

The next pub down the street was O'Shea's. He walked into the dimly lit establishment a little wiser. *At least I know what not to do,* he thought. The acrid smell of cigarette smoke burned his nostrils. Thankfully, there were currently no rowdies in this bar. Only the hum of voices, laughter, and the clinking of glasses met his ears. An occasional boisterous guffaw rose above the general noise level.

This time, he searched for a seat close to the entertainment, thinking a different approach may be more successful. He found a table with four chairs and only three men sitting there.

"Is this seat taken?" he asked.

"No. You're welcome to join us. The more, the merrier." Judging from the slur in his speech, this fellow was an early arrival.

"Sit down, friend," said another. "What's your name?"

"Thank you. The name is March."

"Nice to make your acquaintance, March. I'm Bradley. My friends here are Peterson and Milkins. You did say that was your name, didn't you, Milkins?"

Milkins nodded and tossed back a drink.

"Good to meet you," Derek said. "What kind of entertainment do they have here?"

"Top notch. A chorus line of the prettiest girls you ever seen."

Peterson let out a spirited laugh. "The more you drink, the prettier they get."

Derek laughed along with him, even though the joke was stale from being retold so many times. When the barmaid came by, he ordered a pint of ale. Soon, the band, dominated by a snare drum, a trumpet, and a slide trombone, struck up a rousing number. A line of chorus girls pranced onto the stage arm in arm, dressed in scanty outfits accessorized by mesh stockings, red high heels, and tall feathered headdresses. They kicked to the music. The clientele erupted in cheers and catcalls, and the liquor flowed.

As the evening progressed, conversation at the table grew more comfortable. Secrets were shared, and the drinking men felt like pals. One of the men talked about a problem with his boss. Another had a bitter complaint about his wife, and the other three men fed him all kinds of poor advice.

Finally, Derek leaned forward and confidentially told the other men he was in a financial bind. "I racked up some gambling debts; I'm in big trouble."

"Man, the worst thing you can do is to try to win it back gambling. Don't even think about that. You'll end up dead in an alley."

Another man asked, "Do you have anything you can sell to get the money? Guns, or anything?"

"I do have some stuff, but I wouldn't want it to get around that I had it. I'd have to find a buyer that would be tight-lipped. You know what I mean?"

The men sat back in their seats, nodding. Derek thought they probably knew precisely what he meant. Peterson leaned over to him. "I can give you the name of a guy, but you didn't hear it from me. You got it?"

Derek leaned forward eagerly. "I understand. I never heard what you're about to tell me."

Peterson lowered his voice. "Guy's name is Turk. That's probably not what his mama called him, but that's all I know him by. He has a place called Value Discount, and I'll give you the address. But don't talk to nobody but Turk. You got a piece of paper?"

Derek searched his pockets. "I have a hanky. You can write it on that."

They borrowed a pencil from the barmaid, and Peterson wrote the address on the cotton handkerchief. "Don't lose that, man. Remember, you're talkin' to nobody but Turk."

"I can't thank you enough," Derek said. "This could save

my life." He stuffed the handkerchief in his pocket and spent another half hour with his new friends, talking about nothing important and watching the chorus line. Near midnight, he paid his bill and left.

Sunday passed uneventfully since the Blue Laws kept the businesses closed, but on Monday morning, Derek woke refreshed and enjoyed a hot breakfast at a nearby restaurant. He had a decision to make about the jewelry. *Should I try to sell it as a lot, or would it be more profitable to sell it a few pieces at a time?*

He decided to take only a few pieces at first to see if Turk would give him a reasonable price. He slid the chosen pieces into his pocket and went to the hotel lobby to ask for directions to the Value Discount address. Fortunately, it was within walking distance.

The weather was cool and cloudy. Derek struck out at a comfortable pace and was at his destination within half an hour. This area of town didn't appear to be as safe as the area around the hotel, so this may be the place he was looking for. The outside of the stores were run down and neglected, with missing paint and wood decaying at the ground level. Bird droppings and an occasional bit of trash littered the ground in front, mixed with weeds popping up wherever they found a place to root.

He stepped inside. The walls were lined with firearms and glass cases with merchandise that people in financial straits could do without: jewelry, china dolls, silverware, and small tools, among other things. He approached the counter.

"I'd like to speak to Turk," he said.

"You got him." He was a heavy man of about fifty with a cigar hanging from his thick lips. His head was balding, and his fingers were stained yellow from the tobacco. "Whaddaya need?"

"I have some pieces I'd like to sell." He reached into his pocket and pulled out the gold bangle, a diamond and ruby ring, and an elaborate diamond necklace.

A twitch in Turk's eye revealed he was impressed with the jewelry, but he was otherwise practiced at hiding his emotions. He chewed on his cigar. "Where did you get this stuff?"

"Out of town."

"Good enough." He pulled his loupe from his pocket and inspected the stones, ensuring the mountings were tight and the settings were solid gold. "I'll give you fifty dollars."

"I want a hundred."

"Look, buddy, I have a business to run. I can't pay top dollar."

Derek was prepared to haggle. "I can't let it go for nothing, either. And fifty is nothing."

"I'll go fifty-five." He fingered the diamond necklace.

"I'll take ninety-five."

"Sixty."

"Ninety-two."

Turk moved the pieces around on the countertop. "All right. I'll go to seventy, but that's it."

"Not good enough, Turk, but I'll do you a favor and come down to ninety."

They argued back and forth, neither trusting the other. They finally settled on eighty-two dollars. Derek turned over the three pieces and stashed the cash in his pocket.

"I have more," he said. "Are you interested?"

Turk peered at him. "Let's go to my office." He jerked his head to indicate the direction. It was a small space with a beat-up old wooden desk. It had a glass wall that gave him a view of the shop. Once inside, he waved Derek to a seat and closed the door.

"How much stuff do you have?"

"I have ten times as much as that."

Turk took a deep breath. "I don't want it all at once. I could buy it over time, so I don't raise any suspicions."

"I'll only be in town until Saturday. Then I'm going home."

"Where's home?"

Derek dismissed the question with a wave of his hand. "It doesn't matter."

Turk thought. "I'll take a look at it. Bring it in tomorrow. I'm not making any promises. And if I were you, I'd come in a taxi and have a pistol for protection. There are pickpockets and muggers out on the street."

Derek nodded. "I'll see you tomorrow."

Alarmed about the pickpockets and other folks of evil intent, he walked back to the Grand Maumee Hotel with the equivalent of two months' pay in his pocket, feeling less confident about his safety. Whenever his route crossed an alley, he slowed his pace. He tried to peer into the shadows before walking past it. He stared into the face of every person on the sidewalk, suspecting them of wanting to rob him.

A block before he reached the hotel, a leather goods shop provided some slight relief. Derek stopped in and bought two money belts to carry money and jewelry. They would be safer strapped around his waist, covered by his shirt and coat.

The hotel was a welcome sight. He climbed the stairs to his room and stretched out on the bed. He was worn out. It wasn't even noon, but he was emotionally exhausted and desperately lonely. He would love to talk to Carrie about his experiences here, but that was unthinkable. And heaven forbid that Mr. Johnson should find out. No one must ever know what he was doing in Toledo.

Without warning, his conscience reared up again. He hated it invading his day. Why couldn't he keep it under control? It demanded that he relive his past sins, and he was compelled to obey. *I'm responsible for Julia being in that sanitarium. Maybe I would feel better about it if I checked on her to make sure she's being cared for. Should I go there, or should I leave her alone?*

He finally decided he should visit the sanitarium without her knowledge. *I'll make inquiries, satisfy myself that she's well-fed and comfortable, and then leave. No one can accuse me of being hard-hearted. I take my responsibility for her seriously. Don't I pay that bill every month without fail? But I'll feel better when I know she's well. I'll go after I get some rest and calm my nerves.*

With that decision made, Derek opened the box and checked on the remaining jewelry. He removed the smaller pieces and placed them in one of the money belts. The eighty-two dollars and more jewelry went into the other belt, and both went around his waist. His shirt bloused out and disguised his stash.

He shut the box lid over the rest of the jewelry with some relief and slid it under his mattress. Then he bunched up the quilt to disguise the lump it made.

His hands trembled, and sweat poured from his brow. *What is wrong with me? How did I ever get into this mess? God, where are You? Why have You abandoned me?*

He dropped to his knees on the floor in despair. He thought about pleading for forgiveness from the Almighty but had second thoughts. Why would God answer the prayers of someone who had done what he had done? He would have to live the rest of his life relying on himself. All he wanted was a quiet life with a woman who loved him, who would bear his children and take good care of him. Was that too much to ask?

He was too tired to go out. He tried to lie on his bed, but the lump was in the wrong place. He searched under the mattress with his hand and pushed the box to one side. Then he lay beside it. He was nearly asleep when there was a knock at his door.

"Who is it?" he called.

"It's the chambermaid. I'm here to change your bed."

Derek gasped. He never thought of someone coming into the room and finding his box. He opened the door a few inches. "Ma'am, would you do me a favor?" He held out his hand, offering a Liberty silver dollar. "I'll be here until Saturday morning, and I won't need you to come in all week. Can you handle that?"

Snatching the dollar, she smiled, revealing a missing tooth. "I can. Enjoy your week." She slipped the coin into her bodice and moved down the hall, humming cheerfully.

Derek exhaled slowly through pursed lips and tried to calm

his quaking knees. That was close. His whole life could have been destroyed in a heartbeat. If she had come in and found the box, she would have either stolen the jewelry, leaving him with no way to buy a house, or she would have called the police. That would have been even worse. He would be locked up for years for what he did or maybe hung for murder. Sweat covered his face and hands.

He would have to think smarter. Much smarter.

He took a few deep breaths, then bunched the quilt over the box again. Any chance of resting had been destroyed. He might be able to burn off some nervous energy by going out. He tucked his pistol into his belt and left his room. But before he went downstairs, he folded a scrap of paper into a one-inch square and slid it between the door and the doorframe. If anyone entered his room in his absence, he would find the paper on the floor when he returned.

He left the hotel and hailed another Hansom cab.

"Take me to the Maplewood Sanitarium," he said. "I'll want you to wait for me while I'm inside. It won't take long."

"Yes, sir." And away they went. It would be at least a half-hour drive. That left Derek plenty of time to think, but he found that he didn't want to. He tried to empty his mind and concentrate on the rhythmic clip-clop of the horse's hooves. He tried to enjoy the passing scenery, but the crime he committed replayed in his head for the thousandth time.

He remembered the overwhelming boom of the pistol shot that assaulted his eardrums, the hot smell of gunpowder after he fired, and the panic that gripped him as the shopkeeper's face registered shock as he fell. He remembered the victim lying in a spreading pool of blood, then stepping over the legs of the dead man to get to the jewelry cases. And the surprise of his life: catching a glimpse of Julia's frightened face in the shadows when he fled and the sick feeling in his stomach. He didn't even stop for her; he ran for his life.

He told himself that had it been during the war, the shooting would have been justified. *It was either his life or mine,* he thought. But on a deeper level, the guilt ate at his soul. It had been his choice to rob a jewelry store. But why had it gone so wrong, so fast? Why couldn't the jeweler give him what he wanted? Just a few pieces. But no, he was compelled to protect his assets with his life. So Derek had to shoot him, then took it all. And why was Julia there? That was something he never expected. He shook his head to eliminate those thoughts.

He wondered what Carrie was doing. He missed her.

The cab pulled up at the sanitarium, and Derek hopped out. "Please wait for me," he told the cabby. Walking to the front door and pulling it open, he strode to the front desk. He inhaled the scents of bleach and urine. At least they were trying to keep the place clean.

"I want to inquire about one of your residents. Can you tell me how Julia March is?"

"Mrs. March is doing well. She's sitting right over there." She pointed to some women playing cribbage at a table guarded by a large orderly. Julia's back was to him. He barely recognized her since her hair had grown long and was wound into a disheveled bun on the back of her head. Loose strands of dark hair hung down her back and onto her shoulders. He was gratified that at least she appeared healthy.

"Would you like to go say hello?"

"No, thank you. I just wanted to make sure she was well."

"Can I tell her you were here, Mr.---?"

"Uh...Harper. Mr. Harper. No, you don't need to mention it. Thank you."

He made a quick exit and told the cabby to take him back to the Grand Maumee. The cab couldn't turn around without going around the loop end of the driveway. They made their U-turn and passed the doors of the sanitarium, going in the opposite direction. Derek glanced over to see Julia staring at him with her hands pressed against the window, her mouth forming a scream. He averted his eyes, wishing he had never looked that way.

He slept late on Tuesday morning, having had a rough night. He had been awakened several times, his mind filled with images of Julia screaming. He was sorry he had gone. He wanted desperately to go home and be done with this cursed mission but still hadn't accomplished his primary goal: selling all his jewelry except the two pieces he had reserved for Carrie. For her, he kept a modest sapphire necklace and a gold wedding band.

It was nearly ten o'clock when he was prepared for the day. He had a sweet roll and coffee at the restaurant beside the hotel, then returned to his room. Strapping on his money belts, he tried to hide the box with the rest of the jewelry under his coat. A worried-looking man stared back at him from the mirror. No one would be fooled that he had nothing under his jacket, but at least it would be difficult for someone to grab his valuables and run.

Last, his revolver went into his belt. He hoped he didn't need it. With all his other baggage in the way, it would be tricky to reach quickly.

Rather than walk into that part of town, he hired another Hansom cab and was delivered to Turk's door. He walked in, checking every direction to ensure he was safe.

"Good morning, Mr. Smith," said Turk. "Let's go into my office."

The two men entered the glassed office without saying another word and seated themselves at the desk. Derek pulled out the box first, setting it aside. He opened his shirt and took the jewelry from his money belts one piece at a time, laying it all on the desk. Then he pulled the key from the chain around his neck and opened the box. Turk's eyes nearly bugged out.

"You're wondering where I got this," Derek said. "It was willed to me by my late father, a jeweler."

"Of course," said Turk. "If we can agree on a price, I'll have to store this in my safe and sell it in small amounts so the police don't get suspicious. Don't you think that would be the best plan?"

Derek nodded, and Turk's lips twisted into a knowing grin. "Since I'm taking a risk here, I can't offer you top dollar. You understand that."

"Look it over and tell me what you can give me."

"This will take a while."

"I'm in no hurry."

Turk left once to help a customer, then returned to his desk. He tallied up what he was willing to pay.

"Six hundred for the lot."

"I need eight hundred."

"That's impossible. I'm not J.P. Morgan. I'm prepared to give you four hundred from my safe today, but I'll have to go to the bank for the rest. I could have it tomorrow if you sold me the lot for seven hundred. You're stretching me."

Derek sucked in a breath and took a moment to think. "I can see that you want these pieces. If you give me seven-fifty, you have a deal. And I leave only four hundred dollars' worth with you until you have the rest of the money."

The dickering went on until they settled on seven hundred twenty dollars. They sorted through the jewelry and agreed on what was worth four hundred. Turk paid Derek, who put the money and the unsold merchandise in his belts. He tucked his empty box under his arm and returned to his hotel.

Another day gone, thought Derek. *At least I have four hundred dollars I didn't have before, but I feel like I'll never get this deal settled. I want to get back to Spencer's Mill in enough time to get rid of this horrible feeling. There's an evil cloud over me. I don't want to infect Carrie with this black mood. What kind of man have I become?*

He stretched across his bed at the hotel, trying to decide whether to return to see Turk tomorrow or look for someone else. He stared at the ceiling and fidgeted. He didn't have the heart to return to the tavern and seek out another fence. He decided to stay in. Remembering that he had passed a bookstore on his walk, he returned, bought a book to read, and spent the evening in his hotel room.

That night, he dreamed he was in a rowboat with no oars, waves tossing him to the right and to the left, rocking him from bow to stern. The sky was black with heavy storm clouds. He screamed for help, but no one answered. When he awoke, he realized his dream mirrored his mental and emotional state.

Wednesday arrived. Half the week was gone. It had been a miserable experience so far. Derek's plan was to sell the rest of his merchandise to Turk. He hailed a cab and drove to the Value Discount store, asking the cabbie to wait for him.

He found Turk polishing the glass on the display case as he walked in. Another customer was in the store, so Derek browsed the shelves of merchandise without acknowledging his relationship to Turk. An astonishing variety of items was on display, including an ornate silver mirror with a matching hairbrush for a lady's dressing table.

Derek picked up the mirror and brush, inspecting them closely. *I wonder if Carrie would like these pieces.*

Once the customer left, Derek forgot the mirror and brush set and approached Turk.

"Did you get the money?"

"Come into the office. I couldn't get it all. I could only get a hundred."

Derek's heart sank. His plan to be done with this headache was squashed. The men sat down to decide what Turk would take for a hundred dollars. He wanted to pick out the best pieces.

"I'm unwilling to give up the best and have only lesser value pieces to sell."

"Why?" Turk demanded. "If you keep the lesser pieces, you can attract buyers with less money. You can probably sell them faster that way."

"If you believed that, you'd take the lesser quality pieces."

"That's not true. I have a store; you don't. Buyers with cash know they can come here any time and find something valuable. If they don't come today, they'll come later. Their timing don't matter to me. But you—you're pressed to sell immediately."

"I'm still not watering down the quality of my collection. If we can't agree, I'm leaving the store without selling you anything."

"Where are you staying if I come up with the rest of the money?"

"I'm staying in a safe place. I'll come back tomorrow and see if you want to buy more…if I have anything left."

As soon as Derek stepped outside, Turk hurried to the door. Derek spotted him as he watched the cab leave, so he told the driver to go in another direction. He didn't want Turk to know he was staying in one of the riverside hotels. "It's a good day for a drive. I'd like to see more of Toledo."

The cabby nodded and took him on a tour of the lakefront.

The pleasant curving road afforded him a view of trawlers bobbing about at their docks with fishermen patching nets. He found that the endless splashing of Lake Erie's gray waves on the sandy shore soothed his spirit. Even though a fishy aroma filled the air, the cool breeze was refreshing.

He chatted with the cabby about the shipping business. They talked about changes taking place in the city and about national politics. He found that the cabbie's view of politics lined up with his own, and a camaraderie grew between them. When Derek got hungry, he spotted a clam shack ahead, across the road from the lake. The coffee he had for breakfast wasn't enough to keep him going.

"Please stop here," he said to the driver at the back of the cab. "I'd like some lunch at this little restaurant." As he climbed out of the cab, he turned to the driver. "Say, I know you haven't had lunch, and I don't like eating alone. Would you care to join me?"

The cabby grinned. "I've never gotten an invitation like that from any other fare, but I'll take you up on it. You realize that's not the fanciest place in town."

"My stomach doesn't care. Come on." He waved his hand

toward the little shack.

The cabby chuckled and accompanied Derek inside. It was a greasy little cafe with five tables, none of them occupied. A frazzled-looking woman with braided graying hair took their order for clam chowder and coffee.

"I can't get this where I come from," Derek said.

"Where's that?" the cabby asked.

"Indianapolis." Derek was desperately weary of lying to disguise his identity and where he was from. He was glad it would soon be over.

"What are you doing in Toledo?"

"My Aunt Enid is sick. I'm helping her take care of her affairs."

"She must have things to sell. Were you able to get that taken care of at the Value Discount place?"

"No, I still have some work to do. I just don't know where to go."

"I might be able to help you." The cabby's voice lowered. "I have some…uh… gentlemen who come to me when they have things to sell, if you know what I mean."

"What kinds of things?"

"Mostly things they don't want to publicize. I only keep this cabby job so people don't wonder where I get my money. I'm kind of a go-between. I buy things; then I have contacts who take them off my hands."

"That sounds like a lucrative business."

"Usually. Once in a while, I lose a little scratch, but mostly it pays well."

Derek leaned back and studied the cabbie's face. *Upon my word, this man is a fence.*

Looking around the room to ensure they were alone, he leaned toward his lunch companion again. "I need someone who'll pay me a fair price."

"All we can do is look at what you have."

Derek had a flash of realization. He was now in more danger than ever since the cabby had the address where he was staying and knew that he had valuable merchandise. He could easily be robbed in the middle of the night. He must make a sale quickly.

"How much cash do you have available? I'd need it today. Do you have five hundred?"

The cabby whistled. "Really? You have that much?"

"You'd have to take a look. We can't do it here. And I want you to know that I have my revolver with me. It's not that I don't trust you. I don't trust anybody right now."

"I understand that. We'll need a private place to do business. I have a place a couple of miles from here. We could do it there."

"No, I'd rather do it at my hotel. I don't know anything about your place."

"Do you have the stuff in your room?"

"Yes. We can look at it there if you have the cash." Derek thought he could move to another hotel if the fellow didn't buy all his jewelry.

"I'll drop you off at the Grand Maumee. Then I'll pick up the cash and come find you. What's your room number?"

"I'll wait for you in the lobby, and we'll go to my room together."

Derek swallowed hard. *I feel like I'm doing a balancing act, like those crazy fools who crossed Niagara Falls on a wire. Will this life of deception never end? All I want to do is settle down with Carrie, forget the past, and live a normal life.* He thought his head would explode.

The cabby dropped him off and quickly left without mentioning how long it would take him to return. Derek retrieved his book from his room, settled into a worn chair in the lobby, and prepared to wait.

Surprisingly, the cabby was back within forty minutes. He strode into the hotel, smiling. Derek rose from his chair and invited him to climb the stairs to his third-floor room. He checked for his little paper wad and found it still in place. *No one was in the room. That relieves my mind.*

95

Unlocking the door, he motioned the cabby to go in first. Derek followed him, then smoothed the sheet on his bed for a place to lay the jewelry. "Did you bring the money?"

"Yes. And I want to tell you that I have a pistol, too."

"Fair enough." Derek unbuttoned his shirt and pulled the jewels out of his money belts.

The cabby's eyes grew wide. "So that's where you were keeping it. Smart idea." He fingered each piece. "Are these genuine? They look like good quality settings."

"Of course they are. If you look closely, you'll see the jeweler's stamp pressed into each piece. You don't use solid gold, then mount paste jewels in it."

"Where did it come from?"

"I got it out of town. No one here will recognize any of it."

"Indianapolis?"

"Yes."

The cabby took his time looking over each piece. "You say you want five hundred? I can't go that high."

"What do you have in mind?"

"I wouldn't give you more than three hundred."

The inevitable dickering began, and they settled on $370.

"Would you throw in those money belts so I could carry the jewelry back with me?"

"I can give you one of them. I need the other one. You can buy more at the leather goods shop...Oh, I forgot about the box. Would you be interested in that fine box with its key? I don't need it now. Let me show you how it works." He slipped the key from around his neck and inserted it into the keyhole. He turned it a quarter turn, and the lid popped open. "I'd let it go for five dollars, and you know that's a deal."

The cabby pursed his lips and ran his fingers over the inlay. "I do have a use for that box, but not for five dollars. I'll give you three."

"Four."

"Three-fifty. Take it or leave it."

Derek took it and was relieved to be done with the box.

That meant Carrie would never see it, and she would never ask questions about it. The thought made him smile. He brushed a little dust off the top and handed it to the cabby.

The cabby took it and tucked it under his arm. "Thanks, friend. Good luck with whatever you're doing next. If you ever need me again, hail a cab and ask for Aggie."

"Thanks, Aggie."

The cabbie put as much jewelry as he could into one money belt, then stuffed the rest into the deep pockets of his trousers. He tucked the empty box under his arm. The two men shook hands, and Aggie was gone.

Derek was covered in sweat. He longed to ask for God's help like his mother taught him, but he didn't think God would pay attention. He yearned to talk to Carrie and gain some sense of normalcy. It had been a horrible day, the second worst day of his life.

He packed his belongings in his valise, checked out of the hotel, and moved to the Riverside Hotel down the street. He would be going home tomorrow.

Tomorrow would be better.

Chapter 11: Going Home

After breakfast on Thursday morning, Derek took his valise and got a cab to the train station to buy a ticket to Lamar. There was a train leaving at one o'clock in the afternoon. Counting the stop in Florissant, it would probably arrive in Lamar at about four o'clock. That would leave him time to get his horse from the livery stable and be back in Spencer's Mill by seven. But that would be after dark. Since he was carrying all that money, it may be better to spend the night at the Lamar Hotel.

Yes, he thought, *if I stay in Lamar tonight, I can put my money safely in the bank tomorrow and go by Oliver Hardin's place. I can ask if that house is still for sale. I can't wait to tell Carrie.*

The train ride home was better than the ride to Toledo. Derek was relaxed. His money was safely strapped around him under his shirt. He had accomplished his goal and was looking forward to seeing Carrie again.

After a good night's sleep at the Lamar Hotel, he woke energized and had a leisurely breakfast at the Old English Tea Room. The omelet and bacon tasted like the best he'd ever had. While he enjoyed his coffee, he picked up a newspaper. Scanning the want ads on the back page, he learned that a local gentleman had a carriage for sale. He drained his coffee cup, took the newspaper with him, and mounted his Appaloosa. He was a mile from the address in the ad.

"I've come to see about the carriage you advertised," he told the seller.

"Let's go out to the barn. It's in good shape; you'll see that, but you might want to put on a new coat of paint. It's served me well for several years."

Derek inspected the carriage closely, squishing the horsehair upholstery to test the comfort level and checking the paint for chips and dings. "This is an interesting red crown painted on the back," he said, running his fingers over the surface. "I like that and the painted spokes. It's something not everyone else has."

"Yes, I had a talented friend do that for me since my last name is King. The crown makes it less likely that someone will want to steal it since it's so easily recognized."

"Good idea." Derek found the carriage perfect for a man getting ready to take a bride. They agreed on a swap: Derek's valuable horse for the carriage and a brown mare. Derek said goodbye to his beautiful Appaloosa, giving its nose one last pat, and drove away in his new carriage with a good-tempered horse.

Banking laws had changed recently. In response, the First Ohio Bank became the First National Bank. It now had two extra teller windows to handle the business of a burgeoning population. On Friday morning, Derek walked in to deposit the proceeds of his jewelry sales.

The teller's eyebrows arched. "That's quite a large deposit, sir."

Derek had anticipated some questions being raised. After all, nosiness and gossip were the local pastimes. "Is it too large?"

"Oh, no. But begging your pardon, where did you get all this money?"

Derek was ready with an answer. He wore a solemn expression. "My Aunt Enid died and left it to me. Very sad. She was a special lady, and now this is all I have left of her."

"I'm sorry to hear that, sir. My condolences."

"Thank you." Derek was amazed that he wasn't bothered at all after that lie. Maybe he was finally getting his conscience under control.

The teller processed his deposit and made the notation in his bank book with the new balance.

Derek left the bank and drove to Oliver Hardin's house. Elated after getting his cash safely into the bank, he was eager to buy that house. He rapped on the door.

Oliver pulled it open while the hinges squeaked in response. "May I help you? Oh, it's you. Come on in, March."

"Thank you. I came to tell you I'd like to look at that house again. This time, I'd like to have my fiancée with me."

Oliver brightened. "Congratulations. Who's the lucky girl?"

"Her name is Carrie Johnson. Do you know her family?"

"Oh, yes. Her Grandfather Reese was my mentor before he passed away several years ago. Fine family. When would you like to show her the house?"

"I'll see her tomorrow and tell her about it. Would you be available in the morning to let us in?"

"I have another appointment, but I'll tell you what. I'll loan you the key. You and your young lady can look at it tomorrow and leave the key on the kitchen counter when you're done. I'll use my spare to get in and pick it up."

Derek grinned. "Thank you, sir. I think she'll like it."

Smiling, Oliver patted him on the shoulder as he made his exit. "I hope so."

Derek took a few deep breaths. The evil presence he had experienced over the past week was evaporating. Things were beginning to feel more normal. He mounted his carriage and took the long ride back to Spencer's Mill.

Chapter 12: The House

Derek arrived at Mrs. Steuben's house late in the afternoon.

"Derek, welcome home," she said, beaming at him. "You're back early."

"Yes, ma'am. Sadly, my aunt died. We had just enough time to take care of her affairs."

"I'm sorry about your aunt. It's good to have you back. I didn't expect you for dinner, but it's early enough to add some extra to the pot."

Later, she served a meal of fried perch, pickled beets, and boiled potatoes. They ate together, chatting happily.

The following morning, Derek drove to the Johnson house to surprise Carrie. When she opened the door to his knock, her eyes lit up.

"Derek. I can't believe you're here. How did things go in Toledo?"

"I was able to spend a couple of days with Aunt Enid, but sadly, she passed away on Tuesday. While I was there, I took care of her affairs, so there were no loose ends. She left me some money. I want to use it to buy a house. She would like that."

Carrie's hand went over her chest. "I'm so sorry about your

aunt, but grateful you were there for the end. Do you still have to sell her house?"

"No, she lived in a rental. And her passing was to be expected. She's much better off now, being in heaven with Jesus and the rest of her family."

"Sit here on the Chesterfield, Derek, and I'll get you a cup of tea. Grief isn't an easy thing to deal with."

She went to make tea, leaving him to sit on the sofa with his head down. He was ready to change the topic when she returned with two cups.

"Thanks to Aunt Enid's generosity, I have enough money to buy my house now. Would you like to see the inside?"

"Where is it?"

"It's the one I showed you before. The one near the general store. If you come with me now, I'll show you the inside. I have the key."

Carrie hurried into the kitchen to ask her mother if she could go. Excited conversation from the kitchen reached Derek's ears, and he smiled. Life was returning to normal. He told himself that the only lies he would ever tell Carrie would be about things in the past. No lying about anything in the future. He made himself that firm promise, believing he had enough self-control to carry it out.

Carrie returned with a grin. "Mama wants to go with us. Do you mind?"

"Of course not," Derek said. "I'd like to hear what she thinks about it, too. Fortunately, I just bought a carriage, so there's room for all of us. Come on; I'll show you."

The three of them walked outside to the waiting carriage.

"Derek, did you say you just bought this?" Matilda asked. "This is very nice." She ran her hand over the top of the door.

Carrie walked around the carriage, examining it. "That's an unusual crown on the back. And look how the spokes have been painted red and yellow. But your beautiful Appaloosa— where is he?"

"I hated to let him go, but he was part of the trade. This

horse is better suited for pulling a carriage or a wagon. I wanted to be able to take passengers with me." He winked at Carrie, who blushed and smiled. They all climbed into the carriage with the red crown on the back.

Carrie patted the smooth horsehair upholstery on the seat. "This will last for years, Derek."

"That's what I hope."

They drove to the house renovated by Oliver Hardin. As they approached, Derek explained the features. He led them up the stone-lined path, slid the key from his pocket, unlocked the door, and motioned for Carrie and her mother to go inside.

Carrie walked in and gasped. "Derek, this is more beautiful than it looks from the outside. Look at all the light coming through the windows. And look how big this room is. Look at the beautiful oak floors. This will be the parlor, won't it?"

"Yes, this is the parlor. It's not a mansion, but it's big enough for a small family. Look, there's a place to put a Christmas tree by the fireplace in that corner."

Her mother took in the size and quality of the house with widened eyes. She ran her hand over the fireplace bricks. She fingered the push buttons on the wall that were ready to turn the electricity on and off as soon as the village put up the poles.

Derek smiled. "Let me show you the kitchen and the two bedrooms." They walked through the house, imagining where furniture could go.

Derek pushed another door open. "And here is the bathroom. It has a tub, and the contractor even installed a toilet. It's connected to a septic tank buried behind the house."

Carrie's hand covered her mouth. "I am amazed. No one else I know has this luxury."

Matilda turned to Derek. "This is wonderful. God has really blessed you."

Derek nodded, but that comment struck a raw nerve. He didn't believe God had anything to do with it. He cocked his head. Someone was laughing very close, almost like it was inside him. It was a mocking kind of laugh. "Did you hear that?"

"Hear what?" Carrie listened but didn't hear anything.

"I didn't hear anything," Matilda said.

"Hmm. I must have imagined it." No, he was sure he *didn't* imagine it. It was the devil or one of his minions mocking him over the irony of Matilda's remark about being blessed by God. He was being mocked as a man condemned. He tried to shake off that feeling as if he could change his destiny by the force of his will. He had been told that Jesus would forgive anything, but he didn't believe it. How could He forgive a murderer? How could He forgive a man who locked his wife in a sanitarium? Neither of those things could be confessed if he were to live a normal life.

When they left the house, Carrie had a thought. "Derek, do you have some time?"

"For you? Yes. What would you like?"

"I'd like to pick up Lizbeth and show her your house. Would you mind?"

He grinned. "Not at all. We can do that."

"You'll have to do that tomorrow, dear," her mother said. "That's three or four hours round trip by carriage. If you wait, she'll be in town tomorrow anyway for church."

Derek turned to Matilda. "I won't have the key tomorrow. I promised to leave it inside the house for the owner to pick up this afternoon."

"I'm sorry," she replied. "Carrie, you know that Papa would say it's improper for an unengaged couple to spend all day together."

Carrie lowered her head in submission.

"That's disappointing," Derek said, anger rising. His nostrils flared, and he cracked the reins harder than necessary. But he masked his emotions the best that he could as he turned the carriage back to the house. His desire to spend the day with Carrie was burning inside him, but he would have to give it up for now.

Matilda looked at him in surprise. "Derek, I can see you're

ups—"

He interrupted her. "May I still come tomorrow after church?"

Matilda nodded. "Of course. You can have Sunday dinner with us."

Derek nodded and drove mother and daughter back home. After dropping them off, Derek returned to the house he wanted. He walked through it slowly, taking his time, testing the windows to make sure they opened smoothly, opening pantry doors, and fantasizing about a life there with Carrie. Time with her would help him relieve his sadness, but that wasn't an option. Her Pa had too many rules. He pounded his fist on the kitchen counter to relieve some bottled-up emotion.

After a few minutes, he reluctantly left the key as promised and locked the door behind him. Then he took a lonely drive by the river where he had spent such a warm time with Carrie. His heart ached. He needed her companionship. He needed to touch her. He wondered if it was too soon to ask her.

Later that evening, Matilda and Joshua went to their upstairs bedroom together. The oil lamps cast a warm glow over the room. The temperature had dipped, so Matilda closed the window before undressing, thinking the quilt would feel good tonight. Joshua removed his cufflinks in front of the mirror as she pulled her nightgown over her head. She slid under the covers and waited for her husband to finish his routine, putting on his nightshirt and finally placing his boots beside the bed, just so. He extinguished the lamps, fluffed his pillow, and climbed in bed beside her. The moon was visible through the window.

"I had to slow down the romance today," Matilda said. "Carrie wanted to drive to Lizbeth's house with Derek and bring her back to Spencer's Mill. She wanted Lizbeth to look at the house he intends to buy. It's such a long distance, halfway to Lamar. It would have taken at least three hours round trip in the carriage, and then I suppose they would have wanted to return her home. So I told them it was improper for two unengaged people to spend the day together."

Silvery moonlight illuminated Joshua's face. He grinned and the corners of his eyes wrinkled with amusement. "I wish I could have seen the expression on his face. How did he take that?"

"Actually, I think he was pretty frustrated. But he didn't try to challenge me or argue me out of it. He accepted it more or less gracefully."

Joshua was still grinning. "I remember how it was to be a young man in love. My own response might not have been so agreeable. So yes, that is impressive."

The two lay in silence for a while, but Joshua couldn't sleep. "Matilda? Are you still awake?"

"Umf," she answered.

"Did you see any sign of a temper?"

"Not really." She turned over to face him. "Like I said, he was frustrated, but I wouldn't call it a temper."

The next day after church, Derek went to the Johnson home for Sunday dinner and found another guest there. Lizbeth had been invited to stay. Carrie hoped to show her the house after the meal.

"Lizzy, Derek is buying something special, and I'd like you to stay so you can see it with us."

"What is it?"

Carrie grinned. "It's a surprise, something special, like I said. I don't want to tell you until you see it yourself." She warned her younger brother and sister not to say anything to Aunt Lizzy. There wasn't much danger of that since they hadn't been interested enough to listen to details.

The inviting aromas of meatloaf, mashed potatoes, and buttered corn filled the house. Dinner was served on time, but Carrie was eager for it to be over. She was impatient to clean up the kitchen.

"I'll help," Lizbeth said and grabbed a towel. They managed

the job at record speed.

Derek sat casually chatting in the parlor with Carrie's father until she was ready to go. Then he helped the ladies into the carriage, and they headed off. A few minutes later, Carrie pointed at the house as they approached. "Derek is going to buy that house. Would you like to see the inside through the windows?"

Lizbeth put her hand to her mouth. Her eyebrows raised, and she beamed at Carrie. "It's beautiful! I love that gingerbread trim." She admired the scrollwork decorating the gables and the pierced balusters lining the porch. They hopped out of the carriage to get closer. As the girls followed Derek, Lizbeth poked Carrie in the ribs with her elbow, then tilted her head toward her and grinned. Carrie stifled a giggle.

They stared through the front windows and remarked on the large parlor, the amount of light, the fireplace, and the expensive flooring. Derek described the rest of it in detail.

"Congratulations, Derek," Lizbeth said. "This is a wonderful house, the most up-to-date I've seen in Spencer's Mill. For the size of it, it certainly has all the luxuries."

"I haven't bought it yet, but I hope to close the deal soon. Attorney Wolf is drawing up the papers, but he says there's some hitch in the title. He doesn't think it will stop the sale, but there will be some delay. He'll let me know when it's ready to close."

Lizbeth giggled. "Attorney Wolf is my stepfather. I'll ask him to hurry it along."

They returned to the Johnson house, chatting excitedly all the way. Upon their return, Carrie's little sister Cynthia listened to the animated talk. Innocently, she asked, "Carrie, are you going to live there with Mr. March?"

Carrie blushed deeply. "Cynthia, that's not a proper question to ask. Go find Mama and ask her why."

Cynthia skipped out of the room to find her mother while Lizbeth did her best to choke back a hearty laugh. Derek stood by with a wide grin. Carrie chanced a glimpse at him from the corner of her eye, then averted her gaze. Her blush was still hot on her face.

Lizbeth, still giggling, said she must be leaving. "Thank you for the tour of the outside of the house. Maybe one day I'll be able to visit the inside."

Derek smiled. "I hope so."

After Lizbeth's departure, Derek wanted to spend time on the porch swing. The two of them sat there for the rest of the afternoon, talking, laughing, and sitting closer than they had previously.

The following Sunday at church, the pastor announced that a community barn dance was being held next Friday at the Wilkinson barn. There was quite a stir among the young people. The Wilkinsons had the largest barn around. Carrie's heart throbbed with the hope that Derek would invite her.

Her hopes were realized after the sermon when the Johnson family climbed into the carriage to go home. Derek approached her father.

"Mr. Johnson, may I have a word?"

Johnson turned to him, amused. "What is it, March?"

"I would like permission to take Carrie to the barn dance with me."

"You may ask her, but it's her decision."

Derek lifted his eyes to Carrie, sitting in the back seat of the carriage, eagerly waiting to hear what her father had to say. She wore a broad smile and raised eyebrows. Derek stepped closer to the carriage. "Miss Johnson…"

She turned her face away and fanned herself, still smiling. "Yes, Mr. March?"

"If you're not busy next Friday night, would you accompany me to the dance?"

"And if I said no?"

His mouth turned into a sly smile. "Then I would have to go alone and dance with every girl there." He wiggled his eyebrows.

"Well, then, I guess I had better go so you don't make a silly fool of yourself."

"I guess you had better." They both chuckled.

She became more serious. "Of course, I'll go with you. What time will you pick me up?"

"I'll be there at seven, as usual. Wear something pretty so I won't be embarrassed to be seen with you."

She snorted. "I have a dress that I wear to mop the floor. It has only one patch on the backside."

"Caroline." Her mother's eyes opened wide at her use of the word 'backside.' "Remember, you're a lady."

"Sorry, Mother."

Derek stifled a laugh. "I'll see you Friday evening." He patted the side of the carriage in parting before rejoining Mrs. Steuben.

It was another long week while Carrie again planned her dress and hair. She spent time with Lizbeth, who advised her to wear the turquoise frock with the ruffled bodice and clamshell buttons.

At seven o'clock on Friday night, Carrie was ready when Derek knocked on the door. They said their goodbyes to her family and drove to the Wilkinson barn, where the fiddle music was already going strong as they approached. The barn was packed with people of all ages who enjoyed dancing. The caller for the square dance had come all the way from Lamar for the evening.

Derek and Carrie took their place in the quadrille of square dancers. The couples at the head and foot of the square danced into the center while the couples at the side waited their turn, tapping their toes and clapping to the music. When it was their turn, Carrie and Derek danced toward the center.

"They must square dance in Philadelphia," said Carrie, amazed he did the steps so well.

"Spencer's Mill isn't the only place where people square dance."

They returned to their positions, and the caller called out a *do-si-do*. Carrie and Derek faced each other while Derek crossed his arms. They moved in clockwise circles, passing right shoulders while Carrie swished her skirt. They continued their circular movement until they were back to back, Carrie keeping her dress in motion the whole time. Four beats later, after their left shoulders passed, they again faced each other. They were having a great time but needed to rest. This was a strenuous dance, and Carrie wasn't accustomed to it.

They found chairs to catch their breath. "I'll get us something to drink at the punch table," Derek said and rose to cross the room.

As he poured two cups of punch, he sensed someone's presence beside him.

"Mr. March?"

He glanced over to see the tousled red hair glinting in the light of the oil lamps and those green eyes staring at him. He nearly dropped a cup.

"Miss Rooney," he said.

She wore a red dress with a low neckline, a form-fitting bodice, and a string of pearls around her neck. "I 'ave a request, Mr. March. I want to dance with ye this evenin'."

He turned to face her. "Not me. Any other man here would like to dance with you, but I'm with Miss Johnson. My intentions toward her are serious, and I don't want to jeopardize that by dancing with someone as attractive as you. I don't want to arouse her jealousy."

Dolly laughed, a low, throaty laugh. "That's quite a compliment." She punctuated her next sentence by jabbing a finger at his chest. "I'll see you later."

With a whirl of her red dress, she turned and strode away. Derek followed her with his eyes, then turned toward Carrie. She was watching intently from across the room. His heart sank. *Now, what do I do?* he wondered. *Is this going to cause trouble?*

He forced a bright smile and walked toward Carrie, weaving his way through the crowd. Unknowing, he sloshed punch across the sawdust floor. When he put a dripping cup in Carrie's outstretched hand, her eyes narrowed. "Oh, there's punch everywhere," she said, flapping her free hand to shake the wetness off her fingers.

"Sorry," he said, giving her his handkerchief to dry her hands. She noted that something was written on it but tucked that curiosity in the back of her mind to ask about it later. She had something else more pressing now.

"I see you made a friend," she said.

Derek sighed. From his experience with other women, he realized this comment was only an opening remark to a more extended conversation.

"She likes me, I guess. But I want you to know I have no interest in her. She's not the kind of girl I want to settle down with."

Carrie paused, then asked the question uppermost in her mind. "Have you decided if you like me?"

Derek looked into her face with his eyebrows raised. "Can't you tell?"

"I mean, am I the type of person you would settle down with? Maybe not me, of course, but someone like me."

"Why not you?" he asked.

She hadn't expected that question and stammered her answer. "I…I don't know."

He sighed. Conversations like this could lead to a trap he couldn't escape. "Yes, Carrie, someone exactly like you. How does that make you feel?"

She smiled with relief. "Like dancing," she said. A banjo accompanied the fiddle in a bright jig.

"Finish your punch, and let's join the crowd on the dance floor." He took his stained handkerchief and mopped his brow, relieved that the topic had ended successfully.

Soon, another square dance started, and the couple entered the quadrille, chatting happily. There was a do-si-do, then an

Allemande left. Derek let go of Carrie's hand to change partners in the Allemande, and there was Dolly Rooney, smiling with her face close to his. He couldn't wait until the next Allemande.

As he danced with Dolly, he glanced at Carrie to see who she was with. He could see her eyes over the shoulder of her partner. She returned his gaze. *Oh, no,* he thought. *She saw me with Dolly again. I need to get her out of here.* He let go of Dolly's hand and went to his next partner.

When the dance ended, he took Carrie's hand and pulled her to the side. "You know it wasn't my choice to dance with Miss Rooney. She wormed her way into our quadrille."

Carrie's mouth turned into a crooked smile. "You can't deny you were having fun."

"Oh, I was," he said dramatically. "And what about you, dancing with that dashing George Pitt? He's had his eye on you for a long time."

She burst out laughing. "George Pitt is at least sixty years old and has a red nose and a belly hanging over his belt from too much beer. Besides, Mrs. Pitt would go after him with her umbrella if he showed any interest in anyone else."

Derek grinned. "Why don't we get out of here? We could drive down to the river and chat where it's quiet."

"Maybe we could go for a few minutes. I don't want to be late getting home. It's best to keep Papa happy."

They left the barn and drove down the lane to the river to sit and rest. It was pleasant, but Derek sensed that Carrie was tense, probably thinking of what happened the last time they were there. After a short time, she began to fidget. "You should take me home now, Derek. Thank you for a lovely evening."

"That's not what I want to do."

"I know."

He drove her home. As they said their farewells, they shared an innocent hug.

Over the next four weeks, Derek became a regular dinner

guest. He was now sitting in church with the Johnson family, and everyone assumed there would be a wedding in the future.

In the meantime, Derek completed the sale of the house. He and Oliver Hardin went to Christian Wolf's law office to transfer the deed.

"Mr. Wolf, I want you to put the deed in the names of Derek March and Carrie Johnson March."

Christian sucked in a breath. "Derek, you're not married. That's a generous impulse on your part, but I strongly counsel you against it until you're married. Has she agreed to marry you?"

"No, I haven't asked her yet, but I feel strongly that this is the right thing to do. Is there a law against it?"

"No. It's just not wise. Even though Carrie is my granddaughter and would benefit from this, you're my client, and I must look out for your best interest. Her name could always be added later if you get married."

"Mr. Wolf, if there's no law against it, I insist on including Carrie's name with mine. And I'd appreciate it if you kept it a secret. I only want to protect her if something should happen to me."

Mr. Wolf leaned back in his chair. "What do you think might happen to a man your age?"

"An accident, maybe, or some terrible virus. It happens." He didn't mention getting arrested or being condemned to hanging.

Christian sighed and did as his client asked. "I hope you don't eventually regret this decision, son."

Derek went on the lookout for used furnishings around town so he could move in. One of the church families offered a feather bed they didn't need after the death of an elderly parent. He ordered some linens from the general store, hanging some sheets over his bedroom window for privacy. Another family had an old, weathered dining table in their barn they said he could have. But he had no other furnishings, and sources in

Spencer's Mill were limited. He needed to go to Lamar, where there were furniture stores.

One Wednesday during dinner, Derek asked Mr. Johnson's permission to take Carrie to the library in Lamar on Saturday. Carrie turned to him in surprise and delight.

Mr. Johnson had a mouthful of food and a fork in his hand. He swallowed, leaned back, and wiped his mouth with a napkin. "We'll discuss it in the parlor after dinner."

Derek nodded and dropped the subject. He still resented his plans being subject to the whims of another person, but things had been going well lately. He thought he had a pretty good chance of getting approval.

When the meal was over, Carrie and her mother went to work cleaning up the kitchen. Alvin and Cynthia were sent outside to entertain themselves, and Derek sat in a wing chair across from Mr. Johnson, who lounged at one end of the Chesterfield.

"So you're asking to take Carrie to the library on a day's jaunt."

"That's not the most important thing I wanted to ask you," Derek said. He spoke in low tones to avoid having Carrie and her mother hear what he had to say. His knee bounced, and his heart pounded.

"You can relax, Derek. I think I already know what it is."

Derek swallowed and gathered his courage. He couldn't guess the answer to the next question. "I'd like your permission to ask Carrie to marry me."

Johnson sighed. He adjusted his spectacles and licked his lips. "I wish we could have met your people to get some idea of the family you're coming from…but truthfully, we have come to think of you as our family. You're a hard worker, you're even-tempered, and you love my daughter. You treat her with respect. You even own your own home. That's a big head start for a young husband."

Derek held his breath and kept his gaze on Mr. Johnson.

"I can't think of any reason why I should deny you. I think

you'll make a fine husband for my Carrie. But if you ever hurt her, I want you to know you'll answer to me. To be fair, Derek, you need to know that I have a certain amount of anxiety over this step in Carrie's life. I would like to keep her young and innocent forever, but that's not God's plan."

Derek believed him. "Yes, sir. Thank you, sir. I'll take good care of her." A grin spread over his face so wide that his eyes turned to slits. His dimple deepened. He leaped out of his seat and crossed the room to shake Mr. Johnson's hand. Then he sat beside him and spoke in conspiratorial tones. "Here's my plan. I want to take her to Lamar, visit the library, then take her to that new Italian restaurant. She's never been to either place. I'll ask her to marry me at the restaurant."

Johnson smiled and nodded. "That will make it special for her." Then he took a deep breath. "You know I love my daughter and will do everything in my power to protect her. If I hear of you treating her improperly, I'll make your life miserable."

"I understand that, sir. You said that before. And even if you weren't making that point, I think too much of Carrie to do anything like that to her. I honor and respect her."

"As long as we understand one another. Yes, you have my blessing, and I hope you have great fun on your trip. I've often thought about taking her to the library and introducing her to those great stacks of books, but there seems never to be enough time. I'm glad you're going to do what I never did."

Derek couldn't stop grinning.

Johnson said, "I won't mention this to her and spoil the surprise, but I'll tell her mother."

"Thank you."

In a few minutes, Carrie entered the room, drying her hands on a dish towel. "Are you ready to sit on the porch for a while, Derek?"

"I sure am. I'll be right there."

Carrie returned to the kitchen, filled a plate with apple-cinnamon turnovers she had made earlier, and placed it on the table beside the porch swing. Then she brought out two mugs of milk. When Derek stepped onto the porch a minute later, she asked, "What did Papa say about going to the library?"

Derek had a twinkle in his eye. "Your Pa gave me permission to take you to the library in Lamar on Saturday."

Her eyes lit up. "Oh, Derek, that's so exciting. I've wanted to go there for a long time. I must say, I'm surprised that he gave permission. His attitude must be changing."

When the hour grew late, Derek rose. They were still in the privacy of the porch, and she stood to see him out. He turned and put his hands on the sides of her face. She was beautiful in the moonlight. "I want to put my arms around you and hold you close to me for just a moment. Would you let me do that?"

Carrie caught her breath. Her eyes darted around to see if anyone was watching, then whispered hoarsely, "Yes."

Derek wrapped his arms around her, and she melted into him. Her arms reached around his back, and her face fit into the hollow of his neck. He held her for a moment, kissed her forehead, and left.

Carrie sat stunned in the porch swing with her heart pounding wildly. She didn't know what to think, so she relived the loving embrace over and over. It was so different from the rough kiss he had forced on her at the river. It was tender and sweet. She would like to spend more time in his arms.

Her mother stuck her head out the back door.

"Coming inside, Carrie? It's late."

"Yes, Mama."

"Bring the empty plate and mugs with you."

When Derek arrived home, he opened his dresser drawer and moved his socks to the side. The money belt was still there, untouched. He opened it and took out the two pieces he had refused to sell. One was a silver chain with a small teardrop sapphire and two tiny diamonds that would nestle against her chest. He had also withheld a ring, a simple gold band that he would put on her finger.

His thoughts went unbidden to Julia. He hadn't been able to be this generous with her, but at least now she had a place to live and didn't need to worry about ever going hungry. He told his conscience he had done the best he could for her. Now, it was time to move on.

Chapter 13: The Proposal

Early on Saturday morning, Derek's boots hit the porch at the Johnson home, and he rapped on the door. Carrie opened it, dressed in her prettiest frock. Derek smelled the aroma of corn and coffee coming from the kitchen. He smiled. The family was eating fried cornmeal mush, his favorite, for breakfast.

"Come in, Derek. I'm almost ready to go." He stood near the door while she went to finish combing her hair.

Mr. Johnson walked in from the kitchen, wiping his mouth on a napkin. "You remember what we talked about?"

"Yes, sir. It's been on my mind all week." Derek flashed a grin at Mr. Johnson, who returned his smile.

"The family is in the kitchen having breakfast. Would you like to join us?"

"If Carrie has already eaten, I'm eager to get on the road. I want to have enough time at the library before we go to the restaurant. That's where I'll ask her."

Johnson nodded. "Carrie ate a light breakfast early, so she'll be ready when she gets her hair brushed." He turned and walked back to his mush and coffee.

Derek waited in the parlor restlessly, shifting his weight

from one foot to the other. He checked his reflection in the wall mirror while listening to muted voices in the kitchen and the occasional scraping of chairs on the wood floor.

In a few minutes, Carrie came from her bedroom. Her parents left the kitchen and came to see them off. "Have fun today, you two, and Derek, don't forget what I said."

"No, sir, I won't."

"'Bye, Mama! 'Bye, Papa! 'Bye, Alvin and Cynthia!'"

As the couple left the house, her siblings rushed to the window to wave goodbye to their sister.

Derek and Carrie were off. The carriage took a left turn toward Lamar.

As they drove into the countryside, Derek asked, "Move over here closer to me, will you, Carrie?"

She slid on the seat until she was pressed up against his side. He wrapped an arm across her back and rested his hand on her shoulder. "Beautiful day, isn't it?"

"It's going to be a little cool for September. By next month, we'll need to bundle up even during the day."

They rode for a few miles past the lush, wooded areas, then into the farmland.

"Carrie...did you ever decide if you like me?"

Impishly, she replied. "Mr. March. Do you have doubts? I thought you were a self-assured kind of man. The first time you came to church, you tipped your hat at a jaunty angle when the young ladies were around. I was certain you did that for their benefit, and I said to myself, 'Carrie, that man is a self-assured kind of man.'"

Derek's face reddened. "All right, Carrie. You just caught me blushing. I don't do that often. You got me."

She bent forward in gales of laughter, then turned toward him. "Yes, I like you, Mr. March." She batted her eyes teasingly.

"I've never seen you this...this...silly. Maybe fun-loving is a better term. I'm not sure I even know you."

"Then let me introduce myself. You may call me Miss Caroline." She tilted her head at him and raised an eyebrow.

119

His mouth turned up teasingly. "And you may call me 'Sir.' And you'd better get your face farther away from mine, or something will happen that your Pa wouldn't like."

She couldn't get the grin off her face. "Yes, your lordship."

He grabbed the reins with both hands. As they rode along, he glanced at her continually, and she returned his attention with flirtatious looks.

They arrived at the library in high spirits and stepped out of the carriage. He took her hand and pulled her toward the door. "Come along, now, Miss Caroline. It's time to broaden your horizons."

They stepped through the doors of the library, and Carrie sucked in a breath. The walls were lined with bookshelves. Even more were stacked in the center of the room.

"Derek, there must be a thousand books in here. Where do you start?"

"Let's start by walking along the rows and seeing what they have."

Carrie found a section of books on needlework. "I want to stay here for a few minutes and browse, Derek. Do you mind?"

"No, go ahead. I'll keep looking. I thought if they had something on woodworking, I'd like to read that." He went off to another section. After some time passed, he went back to find her. She was engrossed in a cookbook.

"Look at all these recipes for foods I never knew existed." Her eyes were filled with wonder. "I'd like to try some of these dishes."

"It's time for us to go have some lunch. Why don't you check that book out? We'll bring it back in two weeks." He had two selections under his arm that he wanted to take with him.

"All right. But if I'm allowed to take two, let me also take this book with crochet patterns." She reached to the shelf behind her and grabbed the volume that had caught her attention earlier.

They took their choices to the desk, where the librarian checked them out. "I'll see you back in two weeks," she said.

Derek and Carrie returned to the carriage and slid their books under the seat for safekeeping.

"Where are we going for lunch? I didn't pack a picnic."

"I didn't want you to. We could go to the Old English Tea Room. They have good food, but it's an older restaurant. Would you like to try something different? We could go to Martinelli's and have some Italian food. They just opened up."

"I'm up for something new, but I won't know what to order."

"A customer at the wheelwright's shop said they have good lasagna. We'll both order that."

"I don't know what that is."

"Do you trust me?"

She giggled. "I don't know if I should, but yes, I do."

He smiled and glanced at her from the corner of his eye.

He didn't know why, but that answer bothered him. As they drove to the restaurant, Derek was preoccupied with her response. *I know what it is,* he thought. *Her high standards are part of what makes her the woman she is. I don't want her to trust me so much she lets me lead her down the wrong path. That would spoil her.* This would be something to think about later.

Martinelli's Restaurant was on a side street where Carrie had never been. One other couple had already been seated for lunch and were looking at menus. It was a small place with barstools at a wood bar and several tables in the dining area covered in red and white checkered tablecloths. Salt and pepper shakers sat on each table, along with wine bottles in raffia holders. Each bottle held a candle that had burned down and dripped over the bottle in colorful layers. The effect was festive. The whole place was painted red, white, and green.

A dark-haired gentleman with a mustache and a white apron led them to a table. He lit the candle between them.

"We don't usually light the candles before twilight, but you two look like you might enjoy a little romantic atmosphere." He blew out his match while Derek grinned. "Now, sir, may I take your order?"

Derek took charge. "I was told you have good lasagna."

The waiter stretched to his full height. "Sir, we have excellent lasagna, the very best this side of Italy, and that includes all those presumptuous restaurants in New York and Philadelphia."

"Then we'll have two, and bring us something to drink."

"We have a lovely house wine."

"That will be fine, but we would also like some water with a slice of lemon."

"Yes, sir. Coming right up."

He made a slight bow, turned smartly, and walked away.

"Derek," Carrie whispered. "I never drank wine before."

"That's why I asked for water. You can taste the wine. But even if you like it, sip it slowly between bites of lasagna, and don't drink a lot. You're not used to it. I don't want to take you back to your Pa in a tipsy state."

She put her elbows on the table and clasped her hands under her chin. "This will be a new experience."

"Trust me?"

"I probably shouldn't, but I do."

Derek had a second stab of conscience, and he turned serious. "I don't want you to feel that way, Carrie. Never trust me to the point of violating your principles. Never. Promise?"

She was startled at the turn in his mood. "Yes, I promise."

"You don't have to drink the wine."

"I'd like to taste it. But if I like it and start drinking too much, you'll tell me when to stop?"

"Yes, I will."

The waiter returned with their water and placed two empty wine glasses before them. When he released the cork on the wine bottle, Carrie jumped at the unexpected pop and smiled apologetically at Derek. The waiter poured a little into their glasses and left the bottle on the table.

Derek raised his glass. "To new experiences," he said.

Carrie tilted her head. "What do you mean?"

"Raise your glass, Carrie. We touch glasses when a toast is given."

She raised her glass the same way he did. "Toast?" Her eyebrows were knit in confusion. "Are you talking about a slice of bread in a skillet?"

"No. I said, 'To new experiences,' and that's called a toast. Let's try it again."

He lowered his glass, setting it firmly on the table, and she followed suit. Derek raised his again and said, "To new experiences." Carrie raised hers and touched it to his glass, making a little clink.

"Well done," said Derek with a smile, sipping the wine. The waiter stood from a distance, watching the scene play out. He wore an amused smile and winked at Derek.

Carrie sipped her wine and made a face. "It's sour. It needs sugar."

Derek laughed. "That was just the first sip. It gets better with each taste."

"I would hope so." She squeezed the lemon slice in her water and took a drink.

Shortly, their lasagna was brought to them on china plates. Carrie was amazed at the layers of steaming pasta, which she had never seen before, stuffed with rich tomato sauce and herbal flavors she couldn't identify. It had crumbled sausage and lots of cheese melted in. A bit of lettuce was tucked at the side for color.

"This is beautiful," she said. Her eyes were as large as quarters.

"Taste a bit of the corner. Blow on it first; it's hot."

"We need to say grace first, Derek."

He stopped short, then bowed his head along with her. "Can you say the prayer for us, Carrie? My mouth is full."

She grinned, then said a prayer of thanks. "Now we can eat." She forked the corner of the lasagna, blew on it, and lifted it to her mouth. Her eyes grew large again. "Oh, my, I've never tasted anything like this before. This is wonderful. Do you suppose the library would have a book with this recipe?"

He grinned. "Maybe. We'll have to look the next time we go."

They worked on their lasagna in silence, having mouths too full to talk. Carrie tried another sip of wine. It was better this time, so shortly, she had another.

"I understand now. It does get better with each sip."

He nodded, his mouth still full.

She giggled. "Why do people want to drink something that tastes so bad at first?"

Derek swallowed and scratched his temple. "I never thought about that."

She stopped halfway through her meal, not able to eat it all. She took one last sip of wine, then drank some water.

"I can't eat any more, Derek. You take your time. I'll enjoy the flickering candle and let my stomach settle."

After finishing his lasagna, he set his plate aside and patted his stomach. "Now, Carrie," he said. "Give me your hand."

She reached across the table to him. He could almost see question marks in her eyes.

"You may not have realized it, but I bought that house for you if you'll have me. Will you marry me?"

She nearly knocked over her glass of water. Her chin dropped, and she stared at him with wide eyes. Then, slowly, a smile lit up her face. "Yes, Derek, I will. My sincere wish for these past few months has been for you to ask me that very question."

He closed his eyes in relief and gripped her hand. "I will be honored to be your husband. I promise to take good care of you, Carrie. And I have a gift for you."

He stood, walked behind her chair, and drew the necklace from his shirt pocket. He placed the stones loosely against her throat and fastened the silver chain behind her neck. To Derek, the sapphire and diamonds were right where they belonged.

"That necklace was made for you, sweet Caroline. It's been waiting to be worn at your throat."

"Thank you, Derek." She fingered the necklace and raised the pendant to inspect it better. When she realized what it was, she sucked in a breath.

"Derek, this is too expensive!"

He smiled and took his seat. "I'll not buy things like that as a habit, but this is a special occasion. You deserve something beautiful. We'll show your Ma and Pa when we get back."

"Wait, Derek. We don't want to go too fast with this. I believe Pa would want to be able to give his permission. You'd better ask him about marrying me first, not tell him. Here's a plan. When we return to the house, I'll thank you for a nice time, then go to my bedroom. You take it from there."

Derek chuckled. "I didn't realize you had a sneaky side. That would have been a great idea if I hadn't already asked him. Waiter, could we have our check?"

Carrie rose from her chair. "Really? You already asked him?" She walked toward the door like she was on a cloud. "Is this real?"

"Yes, Miss Caroline. It is." Derek paid the bill, took his fiancée by the arm, and left the restaurant.

The following two hours were spent in giddy delight. They discussed wedding plans and shopped in the stores, looking at furniture, linens, and kitchen supplies. They didn't buy anything since they may be getting wedding gifts. They would go shopping again after the wedding.

The trip back to Spencer's Mill passed quickly since there were plans to make. Once they were out of Lamar's populated area and into the country where no one was around, Derek pulled the carriage to the side of the road.

"Carrie, I really, really want to kiss you."

She leaned toward him and melted into his arms. After lingering in the kiss, she sat with a crooked smile and fanned herself. "That's enough of that. We don't want it to lead to anything dangerous."

"The dangerous part will wait until after the wedding."

Derek grinned all the way to Carrie's house.

Chapter 14: Making Plans

Upon reaching the Johnson house, the two of them went inside. Carrie took her library books in with her. Her father sat in the parlor reading while her mother knitted a sock.

"Did anything special happen today, daughter?" Joshua had a twinkle in his eye.

"Yes, and I was surprised you were informed before I was. Derek asked me to marry him." She grinned. "I said yes, by the way. He tells me that you approved it."

Her father chuckled.

"Did you talk about a date?" her mother asked.

"We'd like to be married two weeks from today, except for one thing. That's when we have to return our library books."

Her father leaned back and roared, laughing. "From the looks of that bauble around your neck, your fiancé can probably afford the late penalty."

"What bauble?" asked her mother, and she put down her knitting needles. "Let me see."

Carrie sat beside her mother and let her inspect the necklace. "Oh, my goodness. I've never seen anything like that." Her eyes were wide, and her mouth agape. She gazed at Derek.

"Well, we know he didn't steal it," said Johnson jokingly.

"I'll confess now that I had Carrie's grandfather, Attorney Wolf, look you up in the criminal records of the county as a precaution. Of course, he didn't find anything. I also checked the criminal records back in Philadelphia. I wanted to know the man Carrie would spend the rest of her life with. Now that it's done, I feel foolish for checking. I should have trusted you. Welcome to the family, Derek."

Derek's knees nearly buckled at the thought of someone checking the criminal record. By a stroke of luck, he had never been charged with a crime, but he was still guilty. The guilt sometimes overwhelmed him.

His thoughts were quickly replaced when Carrie boldly approached him and threw her arms around him in front of her family.

Her mother smiled. "Sit down, everyone. I'll make some tea and bring some cookies. We'll talk about the wedding." She brought the snacks in.

"I know a new dress should be my last concern, Mama. It seems like a frivolous waste of money, but I'd like one."

"We can go shopping in Lamar. This will be the only wedding you ever have. Let's make it beautiful."

"Then I think we can be ready in two weeks. We'll talk to Pastor Waverly and reserve the church." She turned to Derek. "Do you think we can move into the house without any more furniture?"

"We don't need much. We could use chairs for the kitchen, a sofa, and a dresser. I don't want to buy anything else until we find out if we'll get any wedding gifts. Of course, we'll need pots and pans."

"I can give you some of my spares to get you started," her mother said.

There were so many details to work out. The next two weeks would be dizzy with activity.

Chapter 15: Dolly Rooney

The following day, Derek accompanied Mrs. Steuben to church. As he stepped from the carriage, he turned and put an arm around her shoulders. "Thank you, Mrs. Steuben. I'll have dinner with the Johnsons. I won't be riding home with you."

"It's getting serious with Carrie, is it?"

"She's accepted my proposal."

Mrs. Steuben grinned. "Congratulations, son. I'll get the details later."

He left her and took his seat with the Johnson family. The service was as humdrum as usual, but at least Derek could spend it beside Carrie. She sat primly with her hands in her lap but glanced up at him occasionally with an admiring smile. He took that as a sign she had as much trouble concentrating on the pastor's words as he did.

At the end of the service, Mr. Johnson was called aside by one of the other church members for a conversation. "Derek," Johnson said, "I'll be a few minutes. Would you mind bringing the carriage around?"

"I'd be happy to do that, sir." Derek strode to the front of the building, where the carriage was tied to the rail. As he untied the horses, someone brushed against his back. He turned to see Dolly Rooney. He whirled around, glaring at her face-to-face.

"Miss Rooney, what do you think you're doing? This is outrageous, and right here in front of the church. Someone will see you."

She gave him a catlike smile and whispered, "I know something about ye, Mr. March."

Derek paled and dropped the reins. "And what would that be?"

She slinked to the side of the carriage, leaned against it, and raised her brows.

"Now, if I told ye, I'd be in danger."

"What do you want from me?" he demanded. "You must want *something.*"

"I dinna want anythin.' Ye dinna deserve a peaceful life, and I'll see y' never get one."

His mind went into high gear. He had plenty of secrets; he didn't know which one she referred to. Could it be when he nipped that old lady's purse? Or the time he stole three bottles of scotch from the liquor store? Or, heaven forbid, that he killed the jeweler? Frustrated, he decided to counter her threats with a threat of his own.

"I don't know what you think you know, but I should hope you're not trying to threaten me. You don't know who you're dealing with."

"Ah, but I do. Your Miss Johnson had best be careful."

Derek's blood froze, and he raised his voice. "That was an open threat. Let me tell you this," he hissed, "you'll leave Miss Johnson and me alone, or you'll find yourself in more trouble than you thought you'd ever have."

"Ye don't frighten me. I know somethin'. Don't forget that." She reached up to fondle a button on his coat. He slapped her hand away. She laughed in derision and walked away. Derek turned to see his future mother-in-law on the church steps, watching their conversation.

Red-faced, Derek turned his back to Dolly and continued

loosening the horses as Matilda approached. Dolly slipped away and went somewhere. Derek didn't care where.

"What was that all about?" Matilda asked. Her voice and eyes were full of suspicion.

"That wicked girl has been bothering me since I moved to town, but that's the most brazen she's been. She's getting worse. I need to figure out what to do about her. Do you have any ideas?"

"The only way I know to combat evil is to pray. I'll do that."

Derek thought her prayers wouldn't hurt, but they wouldn't help either. He would have to take matters into his own hands. Dolly must know something, or she wouldn't be making threats. Obviously, she didn't know everything, or she would have been afraid to threaten him. He had already disposed of one person who blocked his plans and put another in an institution. One more wouldn't make that much difference, but he didn't want to taint his future for Carrie's sake. He would have to think long and hard about this problem.

Matilda climbed into the carriage, and Derek pulled it around to the front of the church. When the rest of the family got in, Carrie sensed his angst from the back seat.

"You look troubled, Derek. What's wrong?"

From the driver's position, Derek opened his mouth to answer, but her mother answered for him. "It's that nasty Dolly Rooney. She keeps bothering Derek. He's quite angry with her."

Carrie bristled. "Hmpf. I'll have a word with her myself. Then she'll leave you alone."

Derek caught his breath. That was the last thing he wanted her to do. That would give Dolly a chance to hurt her or tell her whatever secret about Derek she was holding. "You don't need to do that, Carrie. This is a problem a man should handle. I'll take care of her."

"As you wish. But if you need help, I'm ready."

Matilda leaned over toward her daughter, and Derek heard her whisper, "Let the man handle the problem, dear. It's not the woman's place. Besides, you don't want to look too possessive."

He strained to hear Carrie's response over the clip-clopping of the horses, but she said nothing.

After a good meal, Derek and Carrie went for a walk in the chilly air.

"I want to know about Dolly Rooney," Carrie said. "What does she want from you?"

"I don't know, but she's been stalking me since I moved to town. She's more forward than any woman I've ever known, batting her eyes and sashaying around. I don't like it."

"I wish I could help."

Derek had a partial solution. "There is something you can do. I don't think Dolly will bother me if you're around, and she won't bother you if I'm around, so you can stay beside me when we're in public."

Carrie smiled. "Then it's settled. I'll take that on as my assignment."

Derek relaxed a little. If Carrie stayed close to him, Dolly wouldn't have a chance to harm her or spill any secrets to her, at least while they were together. He would have to devise another plan to protect Carrie when they were apart.

Chapter 16: Preparations

Carrie and her mother took the carriage to Lamar the next day to look for a wedding gown in case one needed to be custom-made.

In Lamar, their first stop was the dressmaker's shop. Carrie stepped inside eagerly. This was a dream she had had since she was a girl, getting married in a beautiful gown to a handsome man. And here it was, coming true.

Matilda approached the dressmaker. "Hello. I'm Mrs. Joshua Johnson from Spencer's Mill, and this is my daughter, Carrie. She's getting married in two weeks. Can you help us with a gown?"

The petite lady smiled. "You've come to the right place."

Carrie was already taking in the dizzying selection of dress fabrics and styles. Her breath was taken at the possibilities. She wanted to touch the cool smoothness of the silks and satins, the rich velvets, and look at each style of lace.

"Miss Johnson, since your wedding is only a few days off, and you live so far away, I strongly suggest you find a dress already made."

Carrie's face fell, but her mother concurred. "I think she's right. If we can buy something today, that would save another trip back to Lamar to pick up the dress, and you'll need all the time you can get to make preparations. You'll be surprised at how quickly the time passes."

"You're probably right." Reluctantly, Carrie followed the dressmaker to a short rack of bridal gowns. She tried on three and found one that fit her perfectly. It was a satin gown with a ruffled overskirt, a plain bodice with a modest jewel neckline, and long sleeves. The sleeves were each accented with three satin-covered buttons near the wrist. She gazed at her reflection in the dressmaker's full-length mirror and nodded. She twirled around to see how the overskirt flowed.

"That's my design," the dressmaker said proudly. "You'll never see another gown like it. All my gowns are originals."

"I'd like this one, Mama. Can we buy it?"

"That's a good choice. Choose a veil to go with it."

The dressmaker helped her try on several veils. Once the choice was made, her mother paid the bill. "Thank you, ma'am. We'll come back and pick them up this afternoon."

Mother and daughter walked to the Old English Tea Room and lingered over a tasty lunch. Then they struck out on foot to visit the shops around the town square, looking at furniture prices. They went from the retail stores to an auction house.

"One day, you'll probably be able to afford new furniture," said her mother, "but as you're starting married life, you'll find that a good quality used sofa will save you money. That's money you can spend on something else."

They browsed the selection on hand, and Carrie found one she would have bought had she been prepared with cash.

"I'll come back after the wedding and buy this one."

Her mother smiled. "It will probably have already been sold, but there will be others. Don't worry. When you come, ask Grandpa to borrow his buckboard so you'll have a way to get it home."

"I have a lot to learn, don't I, Mama?"

"Yes, but you're a smart girl. You'll learn quickly."

They returned to pick up the wedding dress and veil. The

dressmaker slipped them into a long paper bag, and they carefully took it to the carriage. Carrie laid the bag with her finery in the back seat as gently as possible and spread a quilt over it for extra protection from the dust on the road.

On the way home, Matilda let the horses take their time, cherishing these hours with Carrie. This was the best opportunity to talk to her daughter about private things every bride needed to know about keeping a husband happy. Carrie blushed several times at what her mother told her but valued this precious exchange.

Chapter 17: Becoming One

Two weeks later, on Saturday afternoon, Carrie and Derek were at the church to get married instead of returning their library books. Trinity Chapel was packed with people dressed in their best. The picturesque little white church on a hill was perfect for a wedding. It stood beside a field where ancient oak trees shaded the grave markers. Many of the townspeople began life at Trinity and ended life there.

On this happy occasion, two popular people were getting married, and the small sanctuary buzzed with excitement. The grandparents, Christian and Susannah Wolf, sat on the first row, reserving the seats the bride's parents would occupy. Alvin and Cynthia sat with their grandparents while Carrie's adult brothers, Francis and Herbert, were on the pew behind. Aunts, uncles, cousins, and many church members also attended. It was a joyous celebration.

Carrie was in a side room of the church, stepping into her gown. Her heart beat wildly, and her hands shook. Lizbeth was there, dressed in a rose-colored bridesmaid's gown, to help Carrie stay calm.

The Johnsons entered and talked with their daughter before

giving her away.

"Dear, you look beautiful," her mother said. She reached up to smooth Carrie's hair. "My heart is bubbling over. And you look beautiful, too, Lizzy."

"Thank you, Matilda."

Papa shifted his weight from one foot to the other. "Carrie, I feel I should give you some space, but forgive me if I can't," he said. He hovered closely. "I want to make sure you're ready."

"Papa, Mama has been training me for years. I know my responsibilities as a wife."

"This is the start of a new life for you, honey, and you have a big task ahead," he said. "Mama has taught you how to clean a house and cook meals, but she can't teach you how to be a wife to Derek. Each man has his own needs. You'll have to lean on God to tell you how."

"I know, Papa."

"A man likes a clean, peaceful house when he comes home from work. He likes to have dinner on the table."

"I know that, Papa. I'll do my best."

"I told Derek that if he ever hurts you, he will answer to me."

Carrie chuckled. "Papa. If I thought he would hurt me, I wouldn't be here. He loves me. He'll never hurt me."

"Your mother and I will pray for you every day."

"I know. And I'll pray for you."

Papa was out of advice, so he occupied a chair by the wall while the women fussed over the bride, making her perfect for the groom.

Matilda's lower lip trembled as she helped Carrie button her lovely white satin dress. She squeezed back tears as she arranged her daughter's hair. Then Lizbeth stepped in to help Carrie adjust her veil.

Her father stood and gazed at her, bursting with pride.

"Papa, you'll escort me up the aisle and give me away, right?"

"Yes, that's what I'm here for. I think Derek is already at the altar waiting for you. You've chosen well. He'll make a fine addition to our family and be an outstanding father to my grandchildren." He smiled tenderly at his daughter.

Lizbeth handed Carrie a gift, a white Bible topped with a pink satin bow. The long ribbons trailed down in front of Carrie's dress. "Here. Take this and carry it up the aisle." She sniffed just a little. "I feel like I should say something important right now, but I'm speechless. God bless your marriage, dear Carrie." She hugged her as the organist began to play, signaling the time for the wedding to start.

Matilda tenderly gazed at her daughter through tears. "I'm going in to sit beside Grandma on the front pew." She kissed Carrie's cheek and left.

The proud father offered his elbow. Carrie slipped her arm in his, breathless, her heart pounding so hard her pulse swished in her ears. She had dreamed of this day since she was a girl, and the most wonderful man in the world waited for her. How could she be any more fortunate?

They stood at the back of the little sanctuary, arm in arm, while Lizbeth started her bridesmaid's walk up the aisle, smiling, one slow step after another. Out of the corner of her eye, Carrie spotted a flash of red hair on the back row. It was Dolly Rooney, staring straight ahead at Derek. She sucked in a breath. *No! She mustn't spoil the wedding."* She glanced at Derek, and the look that crossed his face told her he had also seen her.

"What's the matter, Carrie?" whispered her father.

"Look, it's that horrible Dolly Rooney. How could she have the nerve to show up here?"

He leaned in closer to her ear. "Don't worry about her. I'll see that she doesn't make a scene."

"Thank you, Papa."

The music swelled. The bride and her father proceeded up the aisle, one step at a time. Carrie put Dolly out of her mind. She was so eager to belong to Derek that she could have sworn her insides were vibrating. Her eyes were glued on him. He stood beside Pastor Waverly, returning her gaze. Joyful tears moistened her cheeks.

At the end of the aisle, her father pushed her veil aside far enough to kiss her wet face. He whispered in her ear, "God bless you both," and handed her over to Derek. The ceremony began.

The couple held hands and gazed at each other, smiling. They said their "I do's," and Derek slipped a gold band on her finger. Pastor Waverly pronounced them man and wife. It was the most wonderful moment Carrie had ever experienced. Derek lifted her veil and gave her a gentle kiss. The organ music began the recessional as she and her husband turned to face the guests. She was so full of emotion that her body trembled.

They walked to the back of the sanctuary, and Carrie noticed that Dolly was gone. *What a relief.* Friends followed them out, hugging and congratulating them. Carrie had so many relatives present that her heart was sorry for Derek, who had none. Then she realized that now, they were all his relatives, too. Aunts and uncles crowded around them, along with cousins. Friends from school and church were there.

Some of them brought gifts, which were piled into Derek's carriage. Most eye-catching was the bedside table someone had wrapped in a blanket and laid in the back seat. Carrie wondered who had been so generous as to give up their furniture. That was wonderful. Now, they had a place to put a kerosene lamp in the bedroom. She would have to find out later where that gift came from.

Mrs. Steuben approached Derek with reddened eyes. "Best wishes for a long marriage, Derek. You were the best tenant I ever had."

Derek hugged her. "We'll still see each other at church. And we'll invite you over for tea and cookies."

Lizbeth wanted to speak with Carrie after most guests had filtered out. "Enjoy your honeymoon, Mrs. March," she said, hugging her fondly. "I'll see you when you get back. We'll still be friends, won't we?"

"Of course, we will. Don't be silly. We'll see each other often."

"That's all I wanted to hear. Have a good time."

Lizbeth slipped out the door and was gone. Only Carrie's parents and grandparents remained. Grandma put a hand on Carrie's arm. "Carrie, each time one of my children married, I said a blessing over them. You're the first grandchild to marry, and I want to continue the tradition."

Carrie held Derek's hand and gazed at her grandmother expectantly.

Susannah put her hand over theirs.

"Derek and Carrie, the Lord bless thee, and keep thee: The Lord make his face shine upon thee, and be gracious unto thee: The Lord lift up his countenance upon thee, and give thee peace."

"Amen. Thank you, Grandma…Grandpa."

Derek shuffled nervously. *If they only knew….*

Joshua pumped his hand. "Welcome to the family, son. Proud to have you."

"Thank you, sir," he said. "I'm proud to be part of the Johnson clan. We'll be off now. We're going to Lamar tonight for a brief honeymoon. We'll be back tomorrow night."

Her mother leaned in for one last hug. "God bless you both."

Derek escorted his bride to the waiting carriage. "We have lots of gifts. We'll drop them off at the house, change our clothes, then be on our way."

The thought of changing clothes in the same room as Derek gave Carrie pause. She was quiet all the way to the house, but Derek was sensitive, not wanting to push her too fast. "You change your clothes while I bring in the gifts from the carriage."

With relief, she went into the bedroom of that beautiful house. *This is my home now,* she thought as she unbuttoned her gown. She dropped it to the floor and carefully hung it in the closet. She was ready to put on her dress when Derek returned and opened the door. She clutched the dress to her chest, her face turning red.

"This is hard for you, I know," Derek said. "Would you let me help you with the buttons? Go ahead and put the dress on."

As uncomfortable as she was, she managed to get the dress over her head. She stood quivering as Derek fastened the seven little buttons down her bodice.

"I hope you'll come to enjoy this," he said.

She whispered back, "I think I will."

"You need to pack your bag for the trip," he said. "I'll be ready as soon as you are."

She folded one more dress and put her nightgown in the bag.

"It was a shame to take off that beautiful wedding gown after wearing it for an hour," she said as she packed.

"Yes, but maybe our daughter will wear it at her wedding twenty years from now."

Carrie stared at him, open-mouthed. "Yes. We'll have a daughter, won't we?"

"Probably. Take good care of that dress."

Derek couldn't wait any longer. He pulled her close, held her tenderly, and kissed her passionately. She was startled but a willing participant. The kiss left her breathless.

"That's a little preview of things to come," Derek said. "Now, let's be on our way. The sooner we start, the sooner we'll get to Lamar."

She nodded, too stunned to reply.

Wearing more comfortable clothing, they began their honeymoon journey. The weather was cool and dry, perfect for a four-hour carriage ride. Carrie slid close to her husband, and he wrapped one arm around her as he drove.

"You were a beautiful bride, Carrie. The most beautiful I've ever seen."

She chuckled. "I don't suppose you've seen that many."

He shifted in his seat. "I still know you were the most beautiful."

"And you were the most handsome groom I've ever seen."

"We're going to have a perfect marriage," he said. "We'll fill our house with fine furnishings and have some babies."

"Smart, beautiful babies." She smiled at him and snuggled under his arm.

Later down the road, she began to think of the house, that amazing home where they would raise their family. "While we're in Lamar, can we look for fabric I can use to make curtains? We can't feel comfortable until we have some privacy. The only curtains we have now are those sheets over the bedroom windows. Everywhere else, we're exposed to public view."

"Tomorrow is Sunday, so the stores won't be open. We can't stay over until Monday because Mr. Blackburn expects me back at work." He kissed her cheek.

"Mama and I could shop together next week while you're at the wheelwright's."

"Let's talk about that later. Don't worry; we'll get the house in good shape soon. I want to relish our honeymoon right now."

They enjoyed the rest of the journey together, making small talk. When they reached Lamar, they checked into the hotel. Carrie stood beside him at the check-in desk, watching every pen stroke as he wrote "Mr. and Mrs. D. March" on the guest register. Her heart soared.

Once their bags were safely in their room, they shared a delicious honeymoon meal at the Old English Tea Room and celebrated with pumpkin pie for dessert.

"This is a good meal, Derek, but it's not exactly Martinelli's, is it?"

He grinned at her. "No. We'll have to go back there again someday. How do you like your pie?"

"The best. The only thing better would have been chocolate cake. I'm sorry they were out." She licked her fork.

"If you're finished, wife, it's time to go to our room."

Carrie's heart fluttered. "All right, husband."

They left the restaurant, returned to the hotel, and climbed the stairs to their room hand in hand.

Chapter 18: The Drive Home

In the morning, Carrie packed the picnic food they had brought for their trip home while Derek checked out of their room. They decided on a quick breakfast of sweet rolls with coffee and tea at the restaurant, then stepped into the carriage.

"I have an idea if you're up to it," Derek said. "We have all day. We could take the long way home. I've never been that way before. Maybe there's an outdoor table near Fort Amanda where we could have a picnic."

"How long a drive is it?"

Derek shrugged. "I'm not sure. Why?"

Carrie brightened. "We only have enough food for lunch, so I hope we'll be home by suppertime. But let's take a chance. It will be an adventure."

He grinned and helped her into the carriage. He slapped the reins, and off they went, heading south, intending to turn west at the first opportunity. They came to a picturesque, covered bridge over a wide, flowing stream. The wood roof supports stood like well-trained infantry lined up at attention all along both sides. The clattering of the horse's hooves echoed inside the wooden structure.

"Kiss me quick," said Derek. "No one can see us in here."

Carrie laughed with delight and planted a kiss on him before they reached the end of the bridge.

They passed field after field of ripening vegetables and cow pastures. They made small talk as hour after hour passed. *This is not very interesting for a honeymoon trip,* Carrie thought. *We've passed countless fields and farmhouses, but nothing especially scenic. It's all the same. There hasn't even been a stream where we could stop for the horse to get a drink.* She kept her thoughts to herself, not wanting to cloud Derek's day. She wondered if he had the same thoughts.

She turned her face toward the sky and checked the sun's position. It was past noon. Their stomachs were empty, and they hadn't found a shady place to pull over and eat. "How long can we keep going?" Carrie asked. "There must be a place to stop soon. I feel a little faint."

"It might have been a mistake to come this way," Derek admitted. "I'm getting tired, too, and my stomach is growling. Even worse, can you see the clouds forming in the sky? We may get some rain."

"Yes, and I didn't think to bring an umbrella. What will we do if it rains? We don't have a convertible hood like those Landau carriages."

Derek chuckled. "I guess we'll get wet. Does that matter? I wouldn't mind seeing my wife in a wet dress." He winked at her.

Her cheeks warmed in a blush, and she turned her head away so he wouldn't see the smile playing on her face. He saw it anyway, responded with a gentle laugh, and hugged her.

"Do we have any food with us?" he asked.

"If you behave yourself." Still smiling, she brushed back some hair that had blown in her face. "We have some jerky and apples. There's some bread and cheese. And I brought a canteen of water. I'll get that out." She opened her basket and gave him a bite to eat as they rode along. "Here, start with an apple. Maybe we'll find a spot to get out of the carriage and relax."

At the end of the road, they turned north, hoping the landscape would improve.

There still wasn't much scenery to enjoy as they continued along their route. It was all farmland. There were no beautiful woods, no streams to break up the drive, and no hills. All flat farmland. The corn had already been harvested, and the stalks were brown. The effect was almost depressing.

"That looks like a diner up ahead," Derek said. "It's too bad we're traveling on a Sunday. Otherwise, we could stop and get something to eat."

A moment later, Carrie grabbed his sleeve. "Look at that, Derek. The sign says the diner is open. They must not enforce the Blue Laws out here miles from any town."

He pulled into the gravel lot in front of the restaurant and tied the horse to the rail. Carrie pointed at the sign over the door. Prancing horses had been painted at either end, framing the words, 'The Red Stallion.' They entered and were greeted by the aroma of baked ham.

The diner could most kindly be described as rustic. The uneven wooden bar carried stains from food spills and grease accumulated over the years. A line of old barstools provided a place for patrons to belly up, and several tables covered with oilcloth filled the dining area.

A large woman with gray hair and sagging jowls greeted them.

"Hello, folks. Are you here looking for a meal?"

"Yes, ma'am. We're surprised you're open."

"I'm always open. Can't afford to take a day off. Sit wherever you like, and I'll bring you some menus."

"Thank you, ma'am. We'll sit over here." Derek pulled out a chair for Carrie by the window and then sat across the table from her.

Carrie touched the window with her finger and left a mark. She giggled. "I think someone needs to clean the windows."

The woman returned with menus. "My name's Bertha," she

said. "Can I bring you some coffee?"

"Coffee for me, please, and a cup of tea with sugar for my wife."

Bertha went to the kitchen for the hot drinks, then returned. "Are you ready to order?"

"Yes, I'll have the roast beef."

"I'm sorry, I'm out of roast beef."

Derek's smile faded. "Oh, too bad. I had my mouth all set for it. How about the catfish?"

"Out of that, too."

"What do you have?"

"Ham."

Derek shot a glance at Carrie, who lowered her head and stifled a grin.

"We'll have two ham dinners."

"Good choice," she said. It didn't take her more than a minute to return with two dinner plates filled with steaming meat, boiled potatoes, and carrots. She placed them on the table with a butter dish, salt, and pepper. "What are you doing out here in the middle of nowhere on a Sunday afternoon?"

Derek smiled and stabbed a piece of meat with his fork. "We're on our honeymoon, headed home."

He filled his mouth with ham and waved his fork at Bertha. "This is really good."

"Well, congratulations, you two. I just baked a big chocolate cake with butter icing, and I can't eat it all myself. How about we have a piece of cake to celebrate? That'll be my wedding gift to you."

"That sounds wonderful." Carrie relished the idea of having chocolate, her favorite. It was a rare treat.

Bertha disappeared into the kitchen, giving them time to eat their meal, then returned to the table with three plates of cake. She pulled a third chair from another table and sat with them. "I wish you many happy years together. I hope you'll be as happy as Frank and I was for thirty-two years."

"Thank you, ma'am."

"Thirty-two years probably seems like a long time to you young folks, but believe me, it flies by."

Carrie smiled sweetly at her with her mouth full of chocolate cake.

"I told you my name. What's yours?"

Derek was still chewing, so Carrie swallowed and answered. "My husband's name is Derek March, and my name is ... Mrs. Derek March." She grinned broadly. She had never said that before.

"March? That sounds familiar...Hmm. There was a young woman a few years back named March. She went missing. No one knows where she went. Was she related to you?"

Derek choked on something, coughing and gagging. Carrie jumped up and patted him firmly on the back while Bertha ran to get some water. "Was there a bone in that cake?" she asked, laughing.

Derek forced a smile and patted his chest. His eyes watered. "You would think so, wouldn't you? I'm glad that's over with."

"Did I say something wrong to make you choke?" Bertha asked.

"Oh, no, ma'am. For some reason, I tried to breathe cake. I'm over it now."

They finished their cake and conversation, thanked Bertha for her hospitality, and left.

Down the road, Carrie's curiosity overcame her. "Derek, when Bertha asked you about a woman named Julia—was she related somehow?"

Derek sucked in a breath and answered more sharply than he intended. "I wish people would stop asking me that. No, unless she was related to a distant cousin or something."

Carrie's eyebrows raised in surprise. "I'm sorry. I didn't mean to upset you."

Derek recovered and put on his even-tempered mask. "You didn't upset me. I'm just tired. It's been a long drive. Coming this way was probably a mistake, but we'll be home in an hour."

He raised one arm and cradled his wife. Carrie snuggled

closer to him, content to be on the way home...*their* home.

Chapter 19: Life Interrupted

The two of them were weary when they arrived home from their honeymoon, but Carrie was eager to look at the wedding gifts. She lit their only oil lamp and placed it on the bedside table.

Derek brought their bags in from the carriage, then sat on the edge of the bed with his wife to help her open the wrapped gifts.

"I apologize for snapping at you back on the road," he said quietly.

She had a large bundle in her arms, a gift from the Beaveys. "Think nothing of it," she said. "I know you were exhausted. So was I." She patted his knee. When his lips formed a smile, she kissed him.

Some gifts had been offered to them without wrappings, but some had been lovingly enclosed in newspaper and tied with string. She tore the newsprint back from the package in her arms, which turned out to be a handmade quilt. "That's beautiful. I'll have to thank Mrs. Beavey. And look here. Mrs. Steuben sent a crate with plates and bowls from her kitchen. Now we can eat from dishes like civilized people." They laughed at the prospect of eating dinner from a shared pot, relieved they wouldn't have to.

"Look at this, Derek," she said excitedly. The package she picked up next came from Grandma and Grandpa Wolf. It was long and flat. "Grandma had an Italian majolica platter with pierced rims that belonged to my great-grandmother. I wonder if this is it."

She ripped the newsprint away. It was the platter she had secretly admired all those years when it was displayed in the curio cabinet. Tears came to her eyes. "How did Grandma know I loved this platter so much? It's a family heirloom. I was sure it would eventually go to Lizzy."

"We still don't know who gave us the bedside table, do we?" asked Derek.

"No, there was no note on it. I'll have to ask around."

Smaller gifts, mostly handmade, came from friends and would be cherished.

In the following days, the Marches settled into their own home despite the sparse furnishings. Her parents donated some extra pots and pans from their kitchen and allowed her to move her old dresser to her new home, but the rest was up to the newlyweds.

Carrie transitioned into the life of a married woman smoothly, shopping for food, cooking, managing the house, and doing laundry. She had been well trained. She was quite content, except that they had only two kitchen chairs, which she purchased after a week of marriage. She couldn't invite guests in with no place for them to sit.

They also needed a sofa to relax in front of the fireplace during the evening. Sitting in a straight-backed chair was better than the edge of the bed, but a couch would be far more comfortable.

After three weeks of blissful married life, she convinced Derek that she needed to take the carriage to Lamar to buy a sofa. "Our parlor has been empty for three weeks," she said. "It would feel more like home if we had a comfortable place to sit and relax."

Derek agreed.

"I'd like to go tomorrow."

He took her on his knee and chuckled. "Only if you promise to come back. You're not going to leave me, are you?"

"Only if I find a man more handsome than you," she teased.

He laughed. "I saw myself in the mirror this morning, so I'm sure that won't happen. All right, you can go." Then he became serious. "It's a long way to Lamar, Carrie, and a little risky for a woman alone. So I want you to stop at your grandmother's house to ask for the loan of their buckboard. That's halfway to Lamar. Maybe you can get your grandmother or Lizbeth to go with you. Then tomorrow night, you stay at their house and come back the next morning."

"How will you get to work?"

"You can take me, and after work, I'll walk home. It's not that far."

"Thank you, my love."

"Just buy something pretty you'll want to keep for the rest of your life."

Carrie wrapped her arms around her husband and planted a long kiss on him. "I will."

The following day, she rose early and prepared breakfast for Derek. Then she dropped him off at the wheelwright's shop and headed east alone. The horse stepped along at a trot. The trees were beginning to change into their fall colors. She enjoyed the scenery, watching a stray leaf flutter down. Canadian geese headed south overhead.

She spoke to God along the way. "Father, thank you for my husband and our beautiful home. I couldn't be more blessed. Please be with him as he works, and be with me. Please guide me, help me find a suitable sofa at a fair price, and be conservative with Derek's money. Amen." She sang hymns with a joyful heart, except when another carriage approached. Then she hummed until they were out of earshot.

Once she arrived at her grandmother's house, she asked

Grandma Wolf if she and Lizbeth could go on her shopping trip with her.

"Oh, Carrie, I wish I had known about this earlier. Do you remember Lottie Mae Skinner? She's engaged to be married, and I promised to teach her how to knit today. She'll be coming by soon. Oh, I'm so sorry."

Carrie was disappointed but determined to go on. "Is Lizbeth here?"

"Lizbeth is at the school in Lamar, substitute teaching today."

Carrie's shoulders sagged. "Derek didn't want me to make this trip alone, but I'll continue anyway. I'll be fine. May I trade you my carriage for Grandpa's buckboard for two or three days? If I find a sofa, I'll need a way to get it home."

"Of course. I'll get the caretaker to hitch up the horses. Can you handle that team by yourself?"

"Oh, yes. And may I stay here tonight? Derek doesn't want me making a round trip all in one day."

"You know you're welcome here. If you get to Lamar in time, maybe you can stop at Grandpa's office and go to lunch with him."

Carrie brightened. "That's a good idea. I'd better be going. I'll see you this evening."

She switched to the wagon and headed out for the second leg of her trip with plenty of time to enjoy her thoughts. All went well until she reached her grandpa's law office.

Robbins, his clerk, met her in the reception room. "Miss Johnson, good to see you," he said.

"You haven't been told the good news. I'm Mrs. March now."

Robbins smiled, the first time she had ever seen him do that. "Then best wishes, Mrs. March. Best wishes for a long and happy marriage."

"Thank you, Robbins. Is Grandpa in?"

"I'm sorry, he's in court and isn't expected back for another two hours."

Carrie's heart sank. This was her first time in Lamar alone, and she would have enjoyed his company. "Please tell him I stopped by."

Carrie took the wagon to the town square. From there, she could make the rounds of the stores selling sofas.

She loved shopping in Lamar because it was such a busy place. There were other shoppers on the sidewalks taking care of their business. The open trolley rode by on rails down the middle of the street, its bell clanging. The passengers laughed and chatted among themselves through the open windows. Their good humor lifted Carrie's heart. She stepped into the street to cross the intersection, watching where she put her feet down lest she step into something dropped by horses.

First, she wanted to stop at the used furniture store where she had bought her chairs. If they had anything suitable, she could save money by buying there. But when she browsed their inventory of sofas, she was disappointed. She decided to move on.

She took her time at Sheffield's Furniture and found a beautiful sofa in a dark green color, but the price was stiff. She thought she should look for something else.

At the next stop, she found a lovely old Chesterfield with beautiful lines and leather upholstery. She ran her hand over the gently curved wood trim along the back, which was accented with brass tacks. It would fit perfectly in the parlor. The store owner told her it had been brought in by a man whose parents had passed away. She inspected every inch of it, looking for flaws, but besides being comfortably worn in, it was perfect. She even found an end table to hold a lamp. She negotiated with the shopkeeper, arrived at a price, and said she would bring her buckboard to the store to load up.

"Let's do the paperwork, and I'll get payment before you go for the buckboard." He got his pad of sales forms and his pen. What's the name?"

"March. Mrs. Derek March."

The shopkeeper raised his eyes slowly. "Did you say Derek March?"

"Yes."

He pursed his lips. "I don't know whether to tell you this or not – this is such a coincidence. The sheriff and his deputy were here yesterday, asking if we knew him. Of course, I said no."

Carrie's heart was pounding. Something wasn't right. "Are you sure they said Derek March?"

"Oh, yes. I remember it clearly. They said they were asking all the shopkeepers and bartenders."

"That doesn't make any sense to me. Why were they looking for him?"

The shopkeeper shrugged. "I don't think he's in any trouble. They just want to ask him some questions about a jewelry store robbery. The store owner was shot and died."

Carrie went pale. "Maybe Derek knows something about it, but he never mentioned any robbery to me."

"Oh, it happened six years ago, just down the street at the jewelry store. It was big news back then."

"It couldn't have been Derek, then, because he's only been in this area since June."

The storekeeper picked up his pen. "I'm sure it's nothing, then. Now, how about that payment?"

Carrie reached into her bag and came up with the money. The shopkeeper counted it and thanked her.

"I'll have my men put the sofa on the dock out back. They'll wait for you there. Thanks for your business."

She smiled at him weakly. Mission accomplished. She walked back to the wagon, weaving in and out of groups of people on the sidewalk. Some wandered along slowly to peer in the shop windows, while others stood on the sidewalk to chat with friends.

Along the way, she told herself she wasn't bothered by the rumor. Now, she and Derek could sit in front of the fireplace together. She imagined them snuggling there. Usually, that

155

thought would have made her smile, but she couldn't smile today. The more she thought about what the shopkeeper had told her, the more she trembled, and the blood drained from her face. She barely paid attention to what she was doing. *How could he have known anything about what happened in Lamar six years ago? He would have had to be here, but he said he came from Philadelphia. Could he have lied to me? Certainly not. It had to be a mistake.*

She tried to shake it off, knowing she must pick up the sofa and table she had just paid for. But then she needed to go to the law office to find Grandpa Wolf. He would know what to do.

She climbed onto the wagon seat, trembling and nearly hyperventilating. She sat for a moment, trying to calm herself down. *God, help me, help me,* was all she could think.

She steeled herself, slapped the reins, and guided the horses to the furniture store. Once the furniture was loaded, she drove straight to Christian's law office. He had returned from his court hearing.

"Grandpa, Grandpa," she cried, running into his lobby. He rushed from his office to see what was wrong.

"Carrie, what happened?" he asked. "Come in and sit down."

She sank into one of the client chairs, shaking. Christian took the chair next to her and put his hand on her arm. "Try to calm down, Carrie. It can't be all that bad. What's wrong?" He called his clerk. "Robbins, would you bring us a glass of water?"

Carrie spoke in a coarse whisper, not wanting anyone else to hear. "Grandpa, there's a rumor that the sheriff and his deputy are looking for Derek for questioning."

"Why? What would they want Derek for?"

Tears flowed down her cheeks. "They want to question him about a robbery and shooting at a jewelry store."

"Well, that's just silly," Christian said. "That robbery happened several years ago before Derek moved to this area. It must be a different Derek March."

"Wait, something else has been bothering me, too. On the way back from our honeymoon, we stopped at a diner. When we told the woman our name, she asked Derek if he was related to the man named March, whose wife disappeared a few years ago."

"I wouldn't worry, dear. March isn't a common name, but it's not rare, either. Poor Derek. He must have a distant cousin with a similar name."

"When I asked him about it privately, he snapped at me and said he was tired of people asking him that."

Christian sat back in his chair. "Hmm. Well, don't stress over it. I'll ask some questions around town and get this all cleared up. When I find out the details, I'll tell you what I learned, and we can have a good laugh over it. How's that?"

Carrie's shoulders relaxed. She dabbed at her tears with her handkerchief. "Thank you, Grandpa. I feel relieved, but it will take some time to recover from this shock. My knees are still shaking."

"Try not to worry. I'll take it from here. You go home to your husband."

"Well, he wants me to stay at your house tonight. I'm traveling alone, and he doesn't want me to make the round trip in one day."

"Then you can stay in my office until closing. I'll tie my horse to the back of the buckboard. I'll take the reins so you can relax."

She smiled and nodded. "That sounds good. I'll do a little window shopping until then."

"All right. I have just one errand I need to run before I lock up for the day. I'll see you about five o'clock."

The two of them started down the sidewalk on foot. When they reached Main Street, Christian went one direction and Carrie the other, to gaze into store windows.

Christian walked with a purposeful stride another two blocks to the newspaper office. Entering the front door, he asked to see the editor. The gentleman was at his desk and stood to greet Christian. "What can I do for you, sir?"

"I came to inquire about a news story that would have happened a few years ago. I hope you can remember it. There was a robbery and shooting at the jewelry store. Does that sound familiar?"

"Yes, it does. It's odd that you should ask about that today because the sheriff was in here a while ago asking for details on the same story. Wait, I'll pull the clippings I showed him."

He laid an article on his desk. Christian picked up the brittle, yellowed paper and began to read about Derek March, wanted for questioning in the robbery and murder of the jewelry store owner. There was no proof, but his name was turned in on an anonymous tip.

Christian laid the paper on the desk and stared into the distance for a moment, lost in thought. "Were there any more stories about this same case?" he asked.

"No, it went cold after that. As far as I know, the whole March family left town. But there was something about March's wife going missing. After I remembered that, I found those clippings, too. The sheriff organized a search, but Julia was never found."

He had another file folder and handed it to Christian. He scanned through the file and learned that Derek March was the son of Dr. Ivan and Bella March of Lamar. He had had a terrible run of luck. His wife, the former Miss Julia Sternbach of Florissant, had gone missing. When the article was written, it had been a week since anyone had seen her. Derek said she had gone to visit a sister in Columbus but never made it. He was reported to be distraught over her disappearance.

Christian's brow was wrinkled as he rubbed the back of his neck. "Where did the March family go?"

"I couldn't say."

"Could they have gone to Philadelphia?"

"I guess they could have gone anywhere."

"Could you keep those files handy for another two days? I have someone else I want to see them."

"Yes, I can do that."

Christian left the newspaper editor. Stepping onto the sidewalk, he went directly to the telegraph office, sending a wire to his friend, investigator Phineas Fletcher in Florissant: PLEASE COME AT ONCE STOP MATTER CONCERNING CARRIE JOHNSON STOP CHRISTIAN WOLF.

Back at his office at five o'clock, Christian tied his horse to the rear of the buckboard and waited for Carrie. When she arrived, he kept what he had learned to himself. He wanted to save Carrie from worrying until he had solid answers. The two of them climbed into the wagon and made light conversation back to the house.

At dinner, Carrie mentioned the affair to her grandmother and Lizbeth, but Christian minimized it. "Carrie, I don't think you need to say anything to Derek about this. It would only upset him. Wait until I make some inquiries and have something solid to tell you."

"That's probably good advice, Grandpa."

When Christian and Susannah were alone in their bedroom that night, Christian told her the whole story.

"Christian, this is horrible. Carrie's whole future is in jeopardy."

"I know, dear, but I don't want to do anything hasty. What if it is someone else by the same name, maybe a cousin? Derek would never trust us again if we accused him of something like that. And we can't tell Carrie. She wouldn't be able to act normal with Derek until we find the truth. That would jeopardize an otherwise happy marriage."

Susannah blew out the oil lamps and climbed into bed. "You're right. It needs to be kept a secret for now."

The following morning, Carrie drove the buckboard with her Chesterfield sofa and table the rest of the way to Spencer's Mill.

Derek was already at work when she arrived, so she had no choice but to leave them in the wagon until he came home. She could hardly wait. She decided to make a special dinner with candles on the table. She would fry some chicken, boil some potatoes and turnips, and serve carrots and peas. Derek would smell the delicious aromas before he came into the house. It would be a romantic evening.

Chapter 20: The Investigation Begins

The following day, Phineas Fletcher arrived at Christian's office after an hour's train ride from Florissant, where he and his wife owned a bed and breakfast. He was a self-styled investigator with a good reputation, having solved many cases in the past decade.

"Come on in, Phineas, and thank you for making the trip on such short notice. I need your expertise on a serious matter involving our family. It's Carrie."

Phineas was well acquainted with her. She was the niece of his son-in-law, Danny. Phineas had once solved a case involving Carrie's brother Herbert, an admirable young man.

"I came as soon as I could. The Johnson family is dear to my heart. I'm sorry to hear there's trouble. What happened?"

"Please have a seat, Phineas. I'm sure you know she recently married Derek March, a man we gladly welcomed into our family. He's respectful, treats her well, and goes to church every Sunday. We had nothing but good things to say about him."

"I can almost hear you saying 'but.'"

"Yes. But… we have become aware of rumors. Yesterday, a shopkeeper told Carrie that the sheriff and his deputy were looking to bring Derek March in for questioning about a

161

robbery and shooting. I learned it took place at the jewelry store in Lamar."

"Oh, I remember that case. That was a few years back. The place was wrecked, most of the jeweler's inventory was stolen, and the owner was shot. He later died, didn't he?"

"Yes, he did, without naming his murderer. As I pieced it together from newspaper reports, here's the whole story: First, the crime was committed at the jewelry store. The identity of the murderer was unknown. It was reported that Derek March's wife, Julia, had disappeared. Poof. Right off the planet. According to the news report, her husband was all upset and had no idea what had happened to her. She presumably went to Columbus to visit a sister but never arrived. She hasn't been found to this day. Third, someone sent an anonymous note that the sheriff needed to question Derek March about the robbery and shooting, but they couldn't find him when they went to pick him up. The whole March family had moved away from Lamar to points unknown."

"Hmm. Mighty suspicious, wouldn't you say?" Phineas asked. "Odd that he would move away if his loving wife, upon her return, wouldn't know where to find him. Either he knew where she was or was certain she wasn't coming back. That sounds sinister."

"Yes, but I want Carrie protected from knowing about the investigation until we have all the facts."

"Of course."

"Can I turn this over to you? You'll find out if the Derek March of the newspaper story is the same one who married Carrie? If he is, she may be in danger. Naturally, I hate to think that of him. He's such a gentleman and so good to her."

"I'll give this top priority. I'll also search for Julia March. If I find her alive, she can confirm whether Carrie's Derek and her Derek are the same man. Do you know anything about where the March family could have gone?"

"Derek says he's from Philadelphia. You might check there. I'll pay your usual rate."

"I can probably do this by telegram without going to Philadelphia, but I'll take my wife if I have to go. It would give her a little break from running the bed and breakfast."

"I was at the newspaper office yesterday. They're holding some clippings for you to look at."

"I appreciate that. I'll look them over, then visit the sheriff's office."

"Please don't tell them you know where Derek March is until we get more information."

"That's no problem, Christian. I don't know where Derek March is."

"Right. Well, please keep me informed. And hurry, Phineas. I fear for Carrie's life."

Phineas left Christian's office with a sick feeling. There might have been two men named Derek March, but he thought it unlikely. March wasn't that common a name. His first task would be to read those newspaper accounts. After he studied them and recorded his thoughts in his notebook, he walked to the sheriff's office. Fortunately, Sheriff Beeler was in.

"What can I do for you, sir?"

Phineas grinned. "You don't remember me. Nine or ten years ago, you deputized me for about three hours while we rescued Marcolus Banks from his kidnappers."

A flicker of recognition lit the sheriff's eyes. "Oh, yes. Phineas Fletcher. I do remember you. That was quite an operation." He chuckled. "We've both aged a little, haven't we?"

"I'm afraid we have. May I sit down?"

"Of course. What can I do for you?"

Phineas didn't want to reveal everything he learned from Christian, so he switched to investigator mode. "I've decided to write a book about a collection of unsolved crimes committed in Ohio. Do you remember a robbery at the jewelry store a few years ago?"

"Oh, yes. That one is still unsolved; you're right. Most

interesting case. The jeweler died from his injuries, unfortunately. We never caught the criminal."

"Do you remember any details that would make an interesting story?"

"Let me think. I remember that nearly every piece of jewelry in the store was taken. The cuckoo clocks were untouched. Say, I think I still have a list of the stolen jewelry we pieced together from purchase and sales records. Would that help you?"

"That would be excellent if you could lay your hands on it."

"I'm sure I can." The sheriff crossed the room to an old file cabinet, leafed through some file folders, and pulled one out of the drawer. "Here it is. It's quite an extensive list."

Phineas glanced at the record he was handed. "I'll be staying in Lamar tonight. Would you mind if I borrowed this list so I could copy it? I'll return it tomorrow."

"It's an old case I doubt will ever be solved, so I'm sure I won't need it tonight. Go ahead and take it."

"Do you remember anything else?"

"I remember there was an anonymous tip mailed in. Someone sent a letter suggesting that we question a fellow named Derek March. There was a doctor here in town named Ivan March, but he and his wife moved away at about that same time, so we couldn't question him. And we never found anyone named Derek. Although…someone who used to know him told my deputy they had seen him recently. Funny that you should take an interest right now. Do you know where he is?"

"No, I don't, but I intend to make some inquiries. Do you still have that letter?"

"Yes, it's right here in the file."

Phineas inspected it in detail. "It looks like a woman's handwriting. Surprisingly, it looks like a European hand wrote this letter. Do you see how the letters are formed vertically on the page, with no slant at all? Most right-handed Americans write with a forward slant. Left-handed Americans write with a backward slant."

"That's not conclusive, but it's something to keep in mind."

"Was there a return address on the envelope?"

"Sadly, no."

"What about a postmark?"

"Postmarked Lamar. That wasn't much help. There were thousands of women living in Lamar, even back then. And possibly hundreds of European immigrants." He handed Phineas the letter and envelope.

Phineas turned it over. "There's nothing remarkable about the envelope or paper. It looks like the woman used black ink, available anywhere. There isn't even anything distinctive about the way she forms her letters. No special swirls or flourishes at the end of words."

"I agree. I must have stared at that thing a dozen times, looking for clues."

"Yes. Well, thank you, Sheriff. I'll be going. If I learn anything more about the case, I'll pass on the information."

The two men shook hands, and Phineas left with the list of stolen jewelry. He checked into the Lamar Hotel and carefully copied the entire list into his notebook.

As he lay on his pillow that night, the details marched through his mind like the proverbial sheep that one counts to go to sleep. Only there wasn't much sleep for Phineas. He mentally reviewed the facts: Derek March was suspected of the robbery and murder by a woman, possibly European, who wrote an anonymous letter. If that were true, he had been in Lamar then, though he claimed to be from Philadelphia. And he had a wife that disappeared mysteriously at about that same time. Was it Carrie's husband who committed the crime? What happened to the jewelry? And who was the mysterious woman?

Day #2 of the Investigation

The next day, after returning the borrowed document, he went to the courthouse and searched for references to anyone named March. Nothing was in the criminal record, but he found a record of a Lamar property formerly owned by Dr. Ivan March.

It sold the same year as the robbery. He found the record of a marriage between Derek March of Lamar and Julia Sternbach of Florissant six months before the robbery. He also found the recent record of the marriage of Derek March and Carrie Johnson. There was no divorce record and no record of death for Julia. A divorce could have happened in another county, even another state. And maybe there were two men named Derek March, possibly cousins. He would like to believe that.

He thought to compare the signatures of Derek March on each marriage license. He tried to find similarities but was unsure if it was the same man. He penciled in his notebook: Inconclusive.

He had neglected to get a description of Carrie's husband. *My, my, Phineas. You're slipping,* he thought to himself. *That's a rookie mistake.*

He trudged back to Christian's office and got the details. Phineas jotted the information into his notebook: Derek was tall, twenty-seven years old, with dark hair, brown eyes, and a distinctive dimple. *Not many men have a dimple worth noting. That will help identify him.* Christian also remembered a small scar on the back of his left hand.

Next, Phineas collected his belongings from the hotel and checked out. He walked to the train station, purchased a ticket to Florissant, and left on the two o'clock run.

As the train rolled across the Ohio plain, he had plenty of time to plan his next steps. He would look for Julia March in Florissant. Maybe she had returned to her hometown. Perhaps she would have information on her husband. Phineas hoped her husband was a short, bald man. That would make his job easy. He chuckled at the unlikely thought.

At the train station in Florissant, he hired a Hansom cab to take him home. Reaching Fletcher House, he hesitated and stretched his legs before trying to step down from the cab. He was getting to the age where a kinked muscle could lead to a fall.

It was good to be back home with Adelaide. She greeted him with open arms when he walked into Fletcher House. Adelaide had stayed to check guests in and out and supervise the staff.

"Welcome home, dear. Tell me about this case."

"It's Carrie Johnson," he said, shaking his head slowly. "She married a young man Christian and Susannah admire, but now there are little hints of a problem. A serious problem."

"What's that?"

"He may have been married before. He never mentioned that to them or Carrie's parents. Or Carrie, for that matter. There's even a question about whether he is still married to her."

Adelaide's face was stricken. "Poor Carrie. If this information has substance, it could ruin her young life. She doesn't deserve that kind of problem."

"I intend to do some research in Florissant. The woman's maiden name is Sternbach. I'll check the courthouse and talk to Sheriff Milligan." He smiled and reflected on his long, happy relationship with the sheriff. "I don't know what I'll do when he retires."

He turned to his wife. "Do you want to come to the courthouse with me?"

She shook her head. "I know how long you usually spend there. I'd be bored. I'll stay here unless I can help with your research."

"You could search the death records while I look for evidence of a divorce or property owned by someone named Sternbach."

Her eyes lit up. "Well, if I can be useful, let's go. I'll get my bag."

The horse trotted along at a good pace, pulling the carriage. Phineas wanted to get there early enough to do a thorough search. They entered the clerk's office and asked for divorce and death records. Adelaide seated herself in the back of the room to look for a death certificate while Phineas searched for a divorce. The clerk browsed the land records and quickly found a residential property deeded to Dieter Sternbach.

"What's the address of that house?" Phineas asked.

"It's at 532 Baxter Street."

"What was the date of purchase?"

"Hmm. It was purchased in 1883. The ink on the date is smeared, so I can't be certain of the month or day."

"1883 is close enough. Thank you. So he has lived there for a while." That was five years before the robbery.

Adelaide carefully pored over the records but found no evidence of Julia March's death. Neither was there a record of divorce.

Phineas rose and closed the book he was researching. "Let's go to Baxter Street and see if Mr. and Mrs. Sternbach are home."

Approaching their destination, they arrived at a single-story, well-kept home with a fresh coat of whitewash. Their knock was answered by a lanky, tired-looking man. "Ja?"

Phineas offered one of his cards in his outstretched hand. "I'm Phineas Fletcher, an investigator looking into the marriage of Julia Sternbach to Derek March. May we come in?"

The expression on Mr. Sternbach's face twisted into a frown. His eyes bore into Phineas.

"What is your interest in my daughter?"

"I'm sorry to intrude this way. Our interest is in our young relative who just married a man named Derek March. We want to assure ourselves it isn't the same man who married your daughter."

Sternbach's hand flew to his chest. "Ach. Come in. We'll talk."

He showed Phineas and Adelaide to chairs in the parlor and called to his wife before taking a seat on the sofa. "Frieda, come, please. We have guests."

A tall woman in her fifties entered the room with a smile. Her braided hair was wound around the back of her head.

"Welcome, friends."

"Frieda, this is Mr. and Mrs. Fletcher. Mr. Fletcher is an investigator. They're interested in Julia."

Frieda tilted her head. "Why?"

Phineas said, "Mrs. Sternbach, we have a young relative, my son-in-law's niece, who was married recently. Her name now is Mrs. Derek March."

"What?" She clutched at her chest. "You'd better watch out for that girl. Derek March destroyed our daughter's life. He'll likely do the same thing to her."

Phineas turned both his palms toward her to calm her. "Wait, we don't know if it's the same Derek March. The one who married Carrie is tall, twenty-seven years old, with dark hair and brown eyes."

The Sternbachs exchanged a knowing glance. "That sounds like our son-in-law. How can he get married? He's still married to Julia."

Adelaide asked, "Where is Julia? May we speak to her?"

Tears came into Frieda's eyes. "She's not here. Derek admitted her to a sanitarium in Toledo. Legally, we can't get her out because it would take Derek's signature. He's her husband and the one who admitted her. They won't let us get her out because he said she was delusional and a danger to herself. They try to keep her sedated, but sometimes she outwits them." She laughed. "Our Julia is not as sedated as they think."

Mr. Sternbach said, "He's keeping her prisoner there." His voice was bitter. "We didn't know where he was. Where is he, anyway? If I get my hands on him…."

"If it's the same man, we believe he's probably living in the village of Spencer's Mill, a few miles west of Lamar."

"We visit Julia once a month when we can," Freida said. "You're probably wondering why he admitted her. The only thing she says is that she witnessed him commit a crime. When he realized she was there, he wanted to be certain she would never be a believable witness. You see, she had been hiding in the shadows and spying on him to find out why he had been acting so secretive."

"What was he doing that made her suspicious?" Phineas asked.

"Money was disappearing. Even though Derek had a good job, there was never enough to pay the rent. And he would go away one evening a week. She didn't know where he went. It turned out her worry was justified. He had run up high gambling debts and wanted to pay them off by stealing. But then he claimed she was imagining crazy things and might hurt herself. As long as he pays to keep her there, they're happy to keep her medicated and compliant. It's been six years of her life. He might as well have killed her." Frieda burst into sobs. "We wanted Julia to live a happy life. We wanted grandchildren. She's our only child."

Adelaide moved toward Frieda and put one arm around her shoulder. "Take heart, Mrs. Sternbach. My husband is a good investigator. He'll do everything he can to get her out."

Phineas' eyebrows raised. "So that story about her visiting a sister in Columbus was a lie…a diversion. Mrs. Sternbach, what is this crime that you mentioned?"

"Julia said he robbed a jewelry store in Lamar and shot the shopkeeper. The poor man died of his wounds."

Phineas nodded. "That fits in with what the sheriff told me in Lamar. That makes it a murder charge if he's caught. He'd likely be hung. This is getting worse."

Adelaide's hands began to shake. "Phineas, do you think there is still a chance this is someone other than Carrie's husband?"

Phineas tilted his head and shrugged. "The only way to find out is to get Mr. and Mrs. Sternbach in the same room as our Derek March and see what they say."

Mrs. Sternbach shook her head. "No, I'm sorry, we can't travel. The doctor told us that my husband has a poor heart and must stay close to home. You see how thin and pale he is. At times, he gets very weak."

Phineas paused. "I'm sorry to hear about your health

problems. So, then, our only other choice is to get Derek to the sanitarium or get Julia out. We could take her to Spencer's Mill to look at Derek there."

Mr. Sternbach laughed bitterly. "That will take some doing. Good luck."

"Please give me the name of the sanitarium. Adelaide and I will go see her and find out what it will take to get her out, one way or another. We'll keep you informed."

"It's the Maplewood Sanitarium. It's on the east side of Toledo."

Phineas nodded and jotted that name in his notebook. They rose to leave, and the Sternbachs showed them to the door.

"God bless you, Mr. Fletcher," said Frieda. "We'll pray for your success."

Chapter 21: Liberating Julia

Phineas and Adelaide returned to Fletcher House, discussing what they had learned. Adelaide's head was in a spin. "What's our next step, Phineas?"

"I need you to come with me, Adelaide; I really do. You'll soften my effect on the people at the sanitarium just by being a woman's presence. That will be important. They'll be less suspicious of a man and woman together. I don't know if we can get her out legally, or if we'll need to resort to kidnapping. We need to make certain the bed and breakfast is well-staffed during our absence."

"Oh, my." Adelaide's eyebrows raised, and her hand flew to her mouth. "I need a moment to let the word 'kidnapping' sink in." She chuckled nervously. "It's good that we have a long history of working on your cases together. Otherwise, I might object to being a part of that."

"So here's an idea. If anyone there asks who we are, we'll tell them we're Aunt Adelaide and Uncle Phineas from Detroit. That way, if we have to flee with her, they'll look north toward Michigan while we escape to the south."

Adelaide spoke softly and reached for both his hands. "This

is just like in the old days, Phineas, working on your cases before we were married. I'm both excited and scared to death, just like I was then."

Day #3 of the Investigation

It took all of the next day to pack for the trip and schedule the staff to run Fletcher House Bed and Breakfast in their absence. Adelaide fussed over the details of packing clothes and food for the four-hour journey to Toledo. Phineas oversaw scheduling staff members to work the extra days for them. The only way to contact them was in person at their homes. It turned out to be a long task.

Day #4 of the Investigation

On Sunday morning, they began their long drive after breakfast. The October air was crisp, and the warmth afforded by the fur collars on their winter coats was luxurious. Adelaide grabbed an extra quilt should they need to cover their legs for warmth.

"I love driving in the cool air when the sun is shining," Adelaide said, snuggling close to Phineas for warmth.

Later, as they continued their journey through the flat Ohio farmland, the sun became warm enough to unbutton their coats. They arrived at their destination, the Hotel Rossford in Toledo, late in the day. After a light supper, they took a short stroll beside the Maumee River, where they enjoyed the reflection of the gaslights on the rippling water.

They planned to go to Maplewood Sanitarium the next day and ask to see Julia March.

Day #5 of the Investigation

Despite the temperature on Monday morning, they enjoyed the drive to the sanitarium. The air was still chilled, but the sun was bright and warm, the sky a brilliant blue. Toledo was a modern, thriving city. They passed factories and a bustling business district with three-story buildings. As they drove, they prayed for Julia and success in getting her released.

Their route took them through the public park, which was mostly empty since the children were in school, but an elderly gentleman sat on a bench tossing corn to the pigeons. The pigeons trilled and cooed as they pecked at the man's offerings, their feathers changing from gray to purple in the sunlight. Adelaide and Phineas enjoyed watching as the birds strutted about with heads bobbing, dancing and chasing each other.

Adelaide watched a young mother out for a walk, pushing her fussy baby in a pram. As they passed her, the baby squealed and grabbed its toes. Adelaide waved at the mama and got a wave back.

After arriving at the sanitarium, they entered through double doors with large glass windows. A pleasant woman behind the reception desk greeted them.

"How can I help you?" she asked.

Adelaide flashed her best smile. "We came to visit our niece, Julia March."

The receptionist asked them to sign the guest register, then beckoned an orderly. "Will you please take these folks to see Julia March?"

The orderly turned. "This way, please," he said and escorted them down the hall to a door marked Room 23. They entered and found a young woman asleep in her bed.

"May we sit here and wait for her to wake up?" Phineas asked.

The orderly nodded and stepped outside into the hall. He pulled the door so it was mostly closed but left it open a crack. Phineas assumed he was standing guard in the corridor and would be listening to everything. He tapped Adelaide's arm to get her attention, then pointed at the door while holding his finger to his lips. She nodded.

The room was small and plain but clean. There was only an

iron bed, a two-drawer dresser, and two straight-backed chairs. Phineas mentally analyzed the room. *The washing facilities must be in a separate room. Julia has one window that faces the outside. That knowledge will come in handy, but there are iron bars over the window. I'll have to take a closer look.* He planned later to make a tour of the grounds so he would be able to recognize Room 23 from the outside in the dark.

He and Adelaide took chairs and sat patiently until the girl woke.

In a few minutes, she began to stir. She stretched her arms and opened her eyes, only to see strangers in her room looking at her. "Who are you?" she asked.

Phineas was not surprised at her slow speech. Medication would do that.

"We're Aunt Adelaide and Uncle Phineas, dear. Don't you remember us?" Phineas put his finger to his lips and pointed at the door, hoping she would get the clue that she should watch what she said.

She sat up and ran her fingers through her untidy hair. She nodded her understanding. "Oh…yes. Thank you for coming to see me." She held her hands with palms up and shrugged. Her raised eyebrows registered her confusion.

She couldn't know why two strangers were sitting beside her bed, claiming to be relatives. It was a dangerous situation, with the orderly listening at the door. What if she asked questions? Phineas dug for his notebook and pencil in his pocket and began writing her a note while Adelaide made small talk for a few minutes. When they were interrupted by a nurse with a breakfast tray, he hastily stuffed his writing materials back into his pocket. He peered into the hall while the nurse was in the room and spotted the orderly still in the corridor, just as he suspected. The nurse delivered the food and left.

"How are you feeling, dear?"

"Pretty good, Uncle Phineas." Julia's eyes were clearing. She made writing motions with her hand as she locked on to Phineas' eyes, then took a bite of her egg. "Mmm, the egg is

175

especially good today. I wish I could offer you some."

"That's all right, dear. We had breakfast before we came."

Phineas took his notebook and pencil from his pocket and put them on her tray.

"Have you seen my parents?" she asked. She grasped the pencil and wrote quickly.

"Yes, we visited them a couple of days ago. They send their love."

She handed the notebook back to him. "I miss them."

"I know you do. They plan to visit soon."

He read the page in the notebook. It said, "Can you get me out?"

As he wrote, "We're going to try," Adelaide asked Julia if she was being treated well.

"Oh, yes," she said. "They're very kind to me here. They let me have social time with other women from two to four o'clock every afternoon; then, I return to my room to rest. They have good cooks here. Dinner comes to my room at six o'clock. We have lights out at eight o'clock. I do enjoy the structure we have."

She rolled her eyes and shook her head silently. Her lips formed the word "Help."

Adelaide placed her hand gently on Julia's arm. "Have you seen Derek lately, dear?"

Julia's eyes widened, and her head jerked back as if she were stunned, but then she recovered. "I think he was here recently, but I didn't get to talk to him. So, I'm not sure it was him. My mind gets so foggy sometimes." She glanced toward the door. "He probably comes often. I'm just asleep when he comes." She made a sour face and shook her head. "I forget where you live," she said. "Do you still live in Toledo?"

"No, we moved to Detroit. But we'll come to see you again."

Phineas walked softly to the window and unlatched it while the women continued their conversation.

"I hope you do."

"Can we bring you a book or your Bible the next time?"

"That would be lovely, Auntie. So nice to see you again. I love you both."

"Goodbye, dear. We love you, too. Our prayers are with you." Adelaide patted her hand, and they walked into the hall. The orderly escorted them to the front door.

Once outside, Phineas exhaled heavily. "Whew, they keep tight security there, don't they?"

Adelaide laughed. "Those residents are their only source of income. They don't want them to escape...or get well. That's bad for profits."

"You're right. I'm impressed that she thought to give us her daily schedule. She's a smart girl. If we sneak her out of here, it will have to be after eight o'clock at night."

They toured the well-kept grounds on foot, taking time to admire the flowers in case someone was watching. Phineas paid particular attention to the iron bars on each window. They appeared to be recently installed, so there was little rust. They were each attached by four large screws.

Phineas and Adelaide made their way back to the carriage by walking along the side of the building. They had gone to the fifth window before they found the room where Julia rested on her bed. When they strolled by, she smiled and waved.

"Fifth window," Phineas said. "She'll probably be drugged. It might take two of us to get her out through that small opening."

"What are you going to do about the bars?"

"I'll bring a heavy screwdriver. It will take a minute or two, but I think I can get them off."

"I'll do everything I can to help. I'd better wear sturdy shoes."

They returned to their hotel. They spent time in sincere prayer, asking God to keep the orderlies busy while they tried to get Julia out of her prison. They asked for a successful escape.

It was a long day. They did some strolling through stores to keep themselves occupied. Phineas found a lumber supply store that stocked tools and bought a screwdriver with a heavy shaft.

"Phineas, I just realized it's going to be cold tonight, and Julia probably doesn't have warm clothes."

"We have a quilt with us."

"Yes, but it would be hard to hold a quilt around her all the way back to Florissant."

"We won't be going all the way to Florissant tonight. I don't want to travel that far in the dark. We're only going as far as the edge of town, and then we'll look for another hotel. We'll continue our trip in the morning. But you're right; she'll need a coat to stay warm."

They found a clothing store on the next block, where they bought a winter overcoat they estimated to be Julia's size. They had a hearty dinner at a local restaurant, then went to their hotel room to wait. There was no rest for them. Adelaide paced the floor while Phineas checked his matches and fuel for the kerosene lights on the carriage.

They rehearsed their plan during the hours of waiting. They hoped Julia wouldn't be too medicated to walk on her own. As soon as she was in the carriage, they would drive away, still in the dark, until they reached a road where Phineas could safely light the headlamps.

"This is dangerous," Adelaide said, shivering. "I hope nothing goes wrong. If it goes badly, we could be arrested and thrown in jail."

"I know. Keep praying, dear."

At eight o'clock, they left their hotel. Adelaide neatly folded Julia's coat and the extra quilt and stowed them under the rear seat. Phineas lit the headlights, and they drove a half-hour to a spot within two blocks of the sanitarium. When they stopped, their nerves were strung tight. Adelaide's hands trembled as Phineas swung down from the carriage and extinguished the headlamps. They drove the rest of the way in the dark until they parked along the stone wall outside the sanitarium. The horse shook its head and quietly snorted. Phineas gave his nose a reassuring pat.

"It's time to rescue Julia," he said. "Come, dear. It will be all right." Over the years, he had become practiced at exhibiting more confidence than he had. Secretly, he felt a little sick in his stomach.

The two of them crept from tree to tree in the darkness, not a dignified thing for people to do at their age. When they reached a large buckeye tree across the gravel walk from the fifth window, the only way to cross the walkway was in the open. This was the beginning of the dangerous part of the operation. Adelaide grasped Phineas' hand for reassurance. He smiled in the pale moonlight, patted her back, and turned away. "Let's go," he whispered.

They each took a deep breath and hurried across the gravel walkway, stones crunching under their feet. They prayed no one would hear them. Then they hugged the wall of the sanitarium near the window. Phineas peeked around, and there was Julia, sound asleep. He reached into his pocket for the screwdriver, but it wasn't there. "God help me," he whispered in panic. "I've lost the screwdriver. I had it when we left the carriage."

"You wait here," Adelaide said. "I'll look for it."

"Please hurry, dear. I'm completely exposed standing here if anyone looks in this direction."

She stepped as lightly as she could over the gravel and retraced their steps, going from tree to tree. Moonlight glinted on the screwdriver blade near an oak. "Thank you, Jesus, that it dropped in a spot bare of grass," she whispered. She retrieved the tool and carried it to her husband.

Phineas started with the two bottom screws and laboriously turned them until they dropped. The noise was minimal, but to his ears, it might as well have been a brass band. He cringed at each turn of the screwdriver.

Next, he started on the top screws. "Adelaide, when I take this screw out, the bars will swing loose. You'll have to hold the frame so it doesn't scrape against the building until I get the fourth screw out."

She took her position. "Will it be heavy?"

"Oh, yes. Please be ready and do your best."

The third screw came out, and the bars tried to swing, but Adelaide pushed back with all her strength. She puffed as she worked.

"Got it?" Phineas asked.

"Yes, but hurry."

The fourth screw came out, and Phineas grabbed the iron to help Adelaide with the weight.

"Set it down easy right over here," he said. So far, so good, but his nerves were about to snap. He glanced in both directions to ensure they hadn't been spotted, then lifted the window gingerly and climbed through.

"Julia," he whispered, jiggling the girl's arm.

"Hmmph?" she said.

"Shh. Be quiet. It's Phineas and Adelaide, here to get you out."

She shook her head. "I'm awake," she whispered. "When they brought me my pill before bedtime, I pretended to swallow it, then stuck it under my pillow."

"Come quickly."

"I need to get my clothes."

Phineas hadn't thought about that. "No, there's no time for that. We'll get you new ones."

There was a tap on the door, and they both froze.

"Miss Julia?"

She pretended to be groggy. "Hmpph?"

Phineas crouched on the floor behind the bed with no time to spare before the orderly opened the door. "Are you all right?"

"Yes, thank you. I must have been dreaming."

He backed out and closed the door. They waited until his footsteps were further down the hall before they made their next move. Phineas stood and rubbed his sore knees.

"That was close," he said. "Now, come on before he gets back."

Julia was barefoot and wearing only a nightgown. "I can't go out like this."

"Yes, you can. We'll get you everything you need. Now, please, Julia, hurry."

Adelaide waited outside to help her through the window, but the window frame was sharp on Julia's bare legs.

"This hurts!" she said in a stage whisper but continued to try to get through anyway.

Phineas darted back to her bed to get her pillow and placed it between her and the window ledge. "Try that."

She stepped over, lost her balance, and rolled to the cold ground. She gasped.

Phineas worked his way through the window and closed it behind him as she struggled to her feet. "Now run!" he whispered.

They took off for the trees on the other side of the sidewalk, but the gravel cut into Julia's feet. She gasped again.

"Uncle Phineas," she said, "I think my feet are bleeding." She shivered hard in the cold.

This was another issue he hadn't thought through. "I'll have to carry you, but that will slow us down. Adelaide, take this pillow and go to the carriage quickly, but go carefully."

Phineas lifted Julia and tried to walk with her. He couldn't see the ground ahead and prayed desperately for divine guidance. "Lord, be my eyes," he prayed. "Julia, I can't see through you. Put your head down on my shoulder." His heart was pounding from the stress of the situation, and he was panting from the exertion of carrying Julia's weight.

The act of laying her head on his shoulder did a surprising job of redistributing her weight, and he was able to go more quickly. He had almost reached the carriage when orderlies with lanterns ran out of the sanitarium. "Stop...Stop," they shouted and raced toward Phineas as fast as they could.

"We've been found out," he said, and began to walk faster.

Julia hung on as if her very life depended on it, because it did. Fortunately, Adelaide was already sitting in the rear of the carriage. He slid Julia into the back with her and ran for the driver's seat. "Cover her up with that quilt back there," he said, slapping the reins. The two orderlies continued their pursuit. One of them leaped toward them and had a grip on the carriage.

"Hyaah!" Phineas shouted, and the horse took off. They went clattering down the street with Julia shivering in the back. The orderly held on and ran as fast as he could, but he couldn't keep up with the horse. His grip was loosened, and he finally fell behind. White-faced, Adelaide watched him recede into the distance as the horse kept pace. They all hung on tightly as the carriage bounced over bricks and cobblestones.

When it was safe to slow down, Adelaide tried to get the quilt unfolded around Julia, who was still crouched on the floor, trembling from fear and the cold night air. Her thin nightgown was doing nothing to keep her warm. Goosebumps covered her slender, shivering body.

"Tuck this quilt around you tightly," said Adelaide, "or you'll catch your death." She grabbed the overcoat they brought for Julia and threw it over the quilt.

They wound their way through side streets, making themselves difficult to find until Phineas thought stopping and lighting the kerosene headlamps would be safe.

He was still breathing hard, and Adelaide was trembling and pale. Julia continued to shiver violently on the hard floor.

"They'll notify the local sheriff that there's been an escape," Phineas said. "The police will be looking for us. Julia, you'd best stay on the floor with your pillow and quilt in case we're stopped. I'll head south out of Toledo, but I can't go too fast, or we'll draw attention."

Adelaide said, "Why don't you get up for a minute and put that coat on properly? Get your arms through the sleeves. Then draw the cover around you again."

Julia's shivering shook the carriage as she lowered the quilt, then slid into the coat. Her eyes were large, and her chin trembled. She crouched down again, and Adelaide tucked the quilt around her. After a moment, Julia said, "Oh, that's better. Thank you. Now, only my feet are cold."

"Stay covered, including your head, dear."

"Yes, ma'am."

The carriage bumped along through the south side of town. "How are you doing?" asked Adelaide.

"A little uncomfortable here on this hard floor, but it's a small price for freedom. Where are we going?"

"What did you say, dear? Your voice is muffled under that quilt."

Julia uncovered her head. "I said, where are we going?"

"We're going to find a hotel for tonight; then tomorrow, we'll go to Florissant. You can see your Ma and Pa tomorrow."

Julia laughed. "I hope I'm wearing clothes when I see them."

"We'll get you some clothes and shoes to wear. Then we have a lot to talk about."

They found a small, shabby hotel on the south side of Toledo. Some of the paint had peeled away from the trim, and there was evidence of a roof leak in the lobby, but the rooms were clean. Phineas rented two rooms while Adelaide managed to slip Julia in, barefooted and wearing her coat.

Day #6 of the Investigation

In the morning, they all gathered in Julia's room to plan the day. Phineas and Adelaide checked out of their room but left Julia in hers while they went out to find a general store nearby. There, they bought cheese and apples for breakfast and asked the storekeeper if a clothing store was nearby.

Minutes later, they returned to the hotel with a new dress, shoes, and stockings for Julia. They were startled to spot a uniformed sheriff and deputy entering the hotel. They stared at each other, terrified. Phineas' hand went to his chest, and he gasped for air. Adelaide became weak in the knees as her courage left her.

"Phineas, what do you suppose they want? Should we go in or wait here?"

Phineas hesitated. "We would look suspicious just sitting here. Let's go in and face whatever happens."

Reluctantly, they climbed out of the carriage with their packages. Hand in hand, they walked into the hotel lobby. The sheriff and his deputy were at the front desk, asking the clerk about an escapee from a sanitarium. Fortunately, their backs were to the Fletchers, and the two tall officers blocked the clerk's view. Phineas ducked into the hall, where he could overhear their conversation.

"Yes, someone suspicious did check in last night," said the clerk. "There was an older couple with a younger woman. The thing that caught my attention was that the girl was barefoot. Why wouldn't she wear shoes on a cold night like that? But I'm just the clerk here. I mind my own business. It's bad policy to irritate the guests by asking too much."

"Yes, yes," said the Sheriff. "But we need to ask those questions. It was a kidnapping, and that girl could be in danger. What room are they staying in?"

The clerk answered, "I'm sorry, sir, they've already checked out."

"We'd like to see their registration."

There was a pause. "Let me copy that address," said the sheriff. "I'll telegraph the Detroit authorities to pick them up when they get home." He scribbled in his notebook and then continued his questioning. "Did they say anything else about where they were going?"

"Yes, sir. They asked for directions to the general store."

"Thank you," the deputy said and strode out the door with his colleague, hoping to catch up with the barefoot girl and her kidnappers.

Phineas turned to Adelaide, surprised at what had just happened. He whispered, "God is with us, dear. That clerk forgot we rented two rooms and didn't alert the sheriff."

With relief, Phineas and Adelaide opened Julia's door, but no one was inside.

"Where could she have gone in her nightgown?" Phineas' nerves were still raw, and now he was near panic. "Do you think someone snatched her?"

"You mean someone other than us?" Adelaide realized what had happened. "Phineas, where do women go in a hotel in their night clothes? She must have gone to the washroom down the hall."

A moment later, the door opened. Julia entered, wearing her coat over her nightgown. She had a freshly washed face and recognized Phineas' distress. She hesitated. "I'm sorry I frightened you. I needed to wash up and have a look in the mirror. This is one of the few times in six years I haven't been medicated when I woke up. What a wonderful feeling."

"It's all right, dear. An old man forgets that young women need to take care of themselves when they travel. Here are your clothes. Adelaide and I will wait in the hall while you dress. We have breakfast for you in the carriage."

"We should check her out of her room," Adelaide said.

"No, under the circumstances, we can't," Phineas said. "I don't want to alert them that the barefoot woman is leaving. The clerk may send for the sheriff again. They will figure out later that she's gone when the housekeeper sees the empty room."

"We can't cheat the innkeeper," Adelaide insisted, cringing at the memory of someone cheating her at her bed and breakfast. "Leave the money on the dresser, Phineas."

He relented and left payment, even though he thought the innkeeper would never get it. The housekeepers would find it and assume it was a generous tip left for them. But if it would help appease Adelaide's conscience...

When Julia was ready, Phineas went first, going far enough down the hall to spy on the front desk clerk without being detected. As soon as the fellow stepped into the back office,

Phineas waved his hand, motioning Adelaide and Julia to come quickly.

It didn't take long until all three of them were in the carriage, properly dressed, and heading south to Florissant. It was another sunny day. Few clouds were in the sky, and the leaves showed off their fall colors.

Adelaide opened the bag of apples and cheese and passed it around.

"Do you know how long it's been since I breathed fresh air?" Julia asked. "What a joy! I'm having the time of my life." As they traveled to Florissant, the conversation was light and pleasant, except for the danger hanging over their heads.

Phineas was still on the alert. "Adelaide, would you check behind us every few minutes and see if horses or a carriage are approaching fast?"

"Yes, dear." Adelaide took that assignment seriously and looked back often to check for dust being raised on the horizon. Fortunately, there wasn't any.

Phineas turned to Julia. "I just remembered a question I wanted to ask. Did you write a letter to Sheriff Beeler in Lamar suggesting that he question Derek about the murder of the jeweler?"

"Heavens, no. Did someone do that?"

"Yes. The sheriff still has the letter in his file. I read it myself."

"I can think of only one person who could have done it. You see, I was nervous about following Derek after dark. I had recently met a new friend in Lamar, and we quickly became close like sisters. I doubt if Derek ever met her. We would meet to go shopping together when Derek was at work. I confided in her about my suspicions and asked her to go with me to find out what he was doing. It was a dangerous business, and I felt safer not being alone. She was there and saw the whole thing, but Derek didn't see her."

"What was her name?"

"Dolly Rooney."

186

Chapter 22: Carrie's Determination

C hristian Wolf's office door opened, and a young man called out, "Telegram!"

Robbins met him in the lobby and took the envelope. He read the message and quickly delivered it to Christian's private office, where the attorney was with a client.

"Mr. Wolf, there's a telegram from Phineas Fletcher. You'll want to see this right away."

"Excuse me for a moment," Christian said to his client, and read the message: JULIA MARCH WITH US STOP NEED HER TO IDENTIFY DEREK STOP HAVE YOU ANY SUGGESTIONS STOP PHINEAS.

Christian's back straightened, and his eyes focused in the distance for a moment. Then, he remembered he still had someone in his office.

"Sorry for the interruption," he said. "Let's continue." But his heart wasn't in it. After the client left, he concentrated on how to get Derek in the same room as Julia and still keep her safe. He could have her travel to Lamar by train. He would devise an excuse to get Derek to his office, where Julia would be waiting. He could supervise their meeting and observe their reactions.

He would have to give it some thought. He may be able to

think of a better plan.

At home, he told Susannah the details. "Julia March, who is also married to a man named Derek March—she's at Fletcher House with Phineas and Adelaide. I'm trying to work out the best way to have her see our Derek and see if she recognizes him.

"What if you told Derek there was a woman named Julia March at Phineas' house?"

"No, that wouldn't do. We need him to be unaware that we're delving into his past. If he's innocent, after all, I wouldn't want him to mistrust us for the rest of our lives. I have a better idea. We need to get Julia to Spencer's Mill. I could drive her past the wheelwright's shop while Derek is at work and see if she recognizes him."

"That sounds like a wiser plan."

"I'll telegraph Phineas when I go to work tomorrow."

Day #8 of the Investigation

The following day, after Christian left for work, Susannah couldn't get her mind off this new development. Her heart ached for Carrie. The girl was worried and utterly unaware of anything being done. She thought her granddaughter's mind would be relieved if she were informed that Phineas was on the case. It wouldn't hurt to tell her.

She asked the caretaker to hitch up the carriage and then drove to Spencer's Mill to see Carrie. She found her baking an apple pie in the kitchen.

"Grandma," Carrie said. "This is a lovely surprise. Sit here, and I'll make some tea." She grabbed a rag and cleaned scraps of pie crust and flour from the tabletop. Then, she filled a saucepan with water. "We don't have a teakettle yet," she said. "But I can use this old saucepan of Mama's."

"Those things will come in time, dear."

Carrie grabbed the teacups and saucers, gifts from Mrs.

Steuben, from the cabinet.

"I thought you'd like to know what's going on," Susannah said. "Maybe I shouldn't tell you this, but I know you've been worried about Derek. I came here to assure you that your questions will be resolved soon, and you can return to normal life." She beamed at her granddaughter. Mission accomplished.

Carrie turned her attention back to her pie and slid it into the oven. Wiping her hands on a towel, she said, "That's good. The whole thing has been eating at me day and night. Keeping it from Derek has taken so much emotional energy that I'm worn out from the effort. Can you give me any details?" She reached for the sugar bowl.

Susannah reconsidered the wisdom of giving her any details, but she had gone this far. It probably wouldn't hurt to tell her just a little bit more.

"I can tell you only this much. Grandpa called on Mr. Fletcher to see if he could dig into these mysterious allegations and find the truth."

Carrie smiled with relief. "If anyone can get to the bottom of it, that would be Mr. Fletcher."

It came out of Susannah's mouth before she could think: "Yes, well, Grandpa got a telegram from Mr. Fletcher yesterday saying that Julia March was with him. He wants to get her close enough to Derek to see if they know one another."

Susannah didn't expect the reaction she got.

Carrie wheeled around. "What? So there is a Julia March, and she's a real live person? I need to meet her myself, Grandma. I'm going to Florissant. I still have your buckboard; I'll drive it back to your house. Then I'll take Derek's carriage to the train station if Lizzy isn't using it." She whipped her apron off and prepared to leave. "I'll take the pie out of the oven and leave it on the table for Derek."

Susannah was taken aback, fearful that she had created a whirlwind. "Carrie, don't be hasty. There's no need for you to go to Florissant. Mr. Fletcher will bring Julia to Spencer's Mill in a few days and drive her past the wheelwright's shop. There's no need for you to go. Why do you even want to? You need to stop this nonsense."

"No, Grandma. I'm going. This is too serious for me to sit at home and wait. What would you do if someone told you Grandpa was also married to another woman?"

Susannah had to pause for a moment. The girl had a point. She remembered overreacting once when a false rumor went around that Christian was seeing a young lady before their marriage.

"But what about Derek? What will he say when he comes home and his wife is gone?"

"I'll leave him a note. I'll say I'll be back in a couple of days. I'll say there was an emergency with my Uncle Phineas in Florissant, and I was needed there."

Susannah paled and leaned forward. "He's not your Uncle Phineas. That would be a lie. You don't want to lie to your husband."

"He's close enough to be an uncle. He solved a case involving my brother one time. I don't think you understand how this has been haunting me. I've hardly been able to think about anything else. I have to know if Derek is truthful or if he has a past he's not telling me about. He's a wonderful husband, and I love him dearly, but I need to know if there is some threat to our marriage." She took off her apron and threw it on the chair. "I'm going to Florissant."

"Oh, Carrie." Susannah sighed, shaking her head. Carrie was a good girl, but she had always been headstrong. "Now I'm sorry I told you anything. Can we at least have a cup of tea first?"

"Yes. I'll pour it. Then I'll write a note for Derek."

As Susannah stirred a spoonful of sugar into her tea and took a sip, Carrie hastily scribbled a note to leave on the table: MY DEAR HUSBAND, EMERGENCY IN FLORISSANT. WENT TO HELP MY UNCLE PHINEAS. BE BACK IN TWO OR THREE DAYS. SORRY ABOUT THE SHORT NOTICE. I LOVE YOU.

Carrie threw some clothes into a bag and grabbed her coat. "Let's go, Grandma."

Susannah's head was in a whirl. "Carrie, this is not proper behavior for a wife. I beg of you to change your mind."

"I'm going, Grandma."

"At least tell your mother what you're doing."

"I'll tell her when I get back."

"This is not what I expected when I left home this morning," Susannah said. "This has gone all wrong. I hope your grandpa doesn't get upset about this."

Even the idea that her beloved grandfather might be upset didn't deter her. "I do, too. Let's go."

An hour and a half later, when they reached Susannah's home, Carrie was determined to keep going. She left the buckboard and took Derek's carriage, which was still there from before her shopping trip, and continued to Lamar, arriving in time to catch the afternoon train to Florissant.

Hungry and exhausted, she boarded the train and found a seat where she could be alone. She waited until the train chugged away from the station, then found her way to the dining car to get something to eat. Hot food in her stomach strengthened her, and she returned to the coach in a better frame of mind.

It was mid-afternoon when her train pulled into Florissant. Carrie hailed a cab and told the driver to take her to Fletcher House Bed & Breakfast. She entered the lobby, lugging her bag.

Adelaide was at the front desk. "Carrie! What are you doing here?"

"I need a room, please, if you have one. And I need to talk to Mr. Fletcher."

"Room 3 is vacant. Here's the key. Take your bag up, then come back downstairs. Phineas has gone out to run an errand, but he'll be back soon."

Once Carrie was back downstairs, Adelaide invited her into their private apartment to wait. Carrie sunk into a parlor chair, sighing heavily.

"It's been a whirlwind trip. This morning, Grandma told me

that Julia March is here."

"Yes, but I'd like you to wait for the details until Phineas is back. Oh, here he is now."

The door opened, and Phineas walked in. At the sight of Carrie, he took a step back. "Carrie. What in the world?"

"I need to know what's going on, Mr. Fletcher. Grandma said Julia March is here. You must have found her when you checked those rumors about Derek."

Phineas took a seat beside her. "I'm sorry your grandmother told you before we were ready with the whole story. But now that you know that much, I suppose you deserve to hear the whole story. It's your life." He hesitated as he noted the necklace around her neck.

"What a beautiful necklace!" He squinted to inspect it more closely, then stood back with his hand on his chin.

Carrie smiled. "Thank you. Derek gave it to me the day he proposed at Martinelli's." She fingered the stones on the chain.

"All right, let me tell you what's going on."

Carrie cocked her head and waited.

"Adelaide and I did some research at the courthouse and found out there had been a marriage between Derek March and Julia Sternbach in 1888..." He ran through all the details so she would have a complete picture. "...We still don't know if it's your Derek or a distant cousin with the same name, so it's not worth worrying about yet."

"Where was Julia all that time? Surely she wasn't in Lamar."

"No, the sanitarium was in Toledo,"

"Toledo!" Carrie said. Her eyes widened, and her hand went to her chest. "That's where Derek went to help his sick aunt. He was gone for almost a week."

"Yes, well, Adelaide and I went to Toledo and found the young woman. She had been confined to the sanitarium for six years."

This story had Carrie's full attention. "Six years? That's horrible."

"Bottom line, we got her out. She's here in Florissant."

"So they discharged her anyway without her husband's permission?"

Phineas chuckled. "No. Adelaide and I snuck her out a window. Some people would call it kidnapping, I suppose. I prefer to think that we liberated her."

Carrie sat with her mouth agape. "What does she say about Derek?"

"She says he committed her, saying she was delusional. She witnessed him burglarize a jewelry store and shoot the clerk. I suppose he didn't want anyone to believe her if she took the witness stand. The sad thing is, a wife can't be compelled to testify against her husband, but maybe he thought she was so angry she would have volunteered."

Carrie's eyes bulged, and her chin dropped. She stared at Phineas in horror. "Then that couldn't be my Derek. He would never do such a thing."

"I agree. Your Ma and Pa say Derek is a fine man. By the way, I'll mention this on Julia's behalf: I read the newspaper clippings. That robbery and shooting did take place, so Julia is not delusional. The criminal was never caught. The sheriff has a letter someone sent anonymously advising him to investigate Derek March. I suspected Julia had sent that letter, but she said she hadn't. She thinks a friend of hers sent it. Anyway, shortly after the crime was committed, Derek's parents sold their property and moved out of Lamar. Possibly just a coincidence."

Carrie stared at the floor and sighed heavily. "Where is Julia now? Can I meet her? I want to question her about her husband to satisfy myself that her Derek and mine are different men. My heart will be more at peace when I'm certain."

"She's staying with her parents. We'll invite her here tomorrow, and you can meet her then. She's quite a sweet girl. She's smart and personable, a lot like you. You'll like her."

Chapter 23: The Note

After a long, hard day, Derek left the wheelwright's shop, looking forward to a good meal with Carrie. He found that physical labor was exhilarating. Every day when he went home, he was weary with a good kind of tiredness, and he anticipated seeing his beautiful wife. She always made him smile. He would thank God for such a wife if he thought God was listening… if he thought God had anything to do with it.

He put his horse away, then walked into the house, wondering what Carrie had cooked for supper. But there was no welcoming aroma of beef or ham. There was only an empty kitchen, with an unbaked pie and a folded note in the middle of the table.

In alarm, he picked up the paper. He had to read it twice to believe what he read. MY DEAR HUSBAND, EMERGENCY IN FLORISSANT. WENT TO HELP MY UNCLE PHINEAS. BE BACK IN TWO OR THREE DAYS. SORRY ABOUT THE SHORT NOTICE. I LOVE YOU.

What? He thought he had met all her aunts and uncles at the wedding. There was no Phineas among them. What could this be about? He pulled a chair away from the table and sat in a daze. *What could have caused her to rush off like that? Her parents must have come to tell her of an emergency. She must have*

194

gone off in her grandpa's buckboard because it's not here anymore. What was such a dire event that she couldn't even stop by the wheelwright's shop and tell me about it before she left?

At that moment, there was a tap on the door. *This is not the time for visitors.*

When he answered the knock, there was Dolly Rooney, her lips in a sensual smile and her eyes closing and opening lazily.

"What the devil are you doing here?"

"I know your lovely wife ain't here. She drove away earlier, and I was passin' by."

"Keep passing. I have no time for you. Ever."

She tried to step inside, but Derek grabbed her by the wrist and twisted it so hard she was forced to turn around.

"Ow! You're hurting me."

"Don't you ever come back here!"

"Don't forget...I know things."

Still gripping her arm, he demanded, "Alright, missy, tell me what you think you know."

She broke into derisive laughter as if she were confident of her control over him. "I'll keep ye guessin', but I will tell ye this much...what I know is worth diamonds and gold."

He paled, shoved her backward, and slammed the door. *That laugh...I've heard it before. Why would she mention diamonds and gold?*

Forgetting his hunger and his dirty, sweaty clothing, he dashed to the barn to hitch his horse to the carriage. He swore when he realized his horse and carriage were at the Wolfs' home, taken there so Carrie could borrow their buckboard. He had to get there somehow.

He thought her parents would probably loan him their rig, so he walked to the Johnson home, full of angst. Was this just a ruse? Was Carrie's actual intent to leave him? He didn't think so. Their lives had been blissful since the wedding. But maybe she found out something he didn't want her to know. No, that was impossible. Would he never get those horrible memories out of his mind? Would he have to put up with this torment forever? Would he never again know peace?

He arrived at her parents' home and pounded on the door like a wild man. His mother-in-law answered. "Derek, is something wrong?"

"Where is my wife?" he demanded.

Matilda took a step back. "I thought she was home. Come in, and I'll get you a cup of tea."

Derek shook his head. "Thanks, but I need to find Carrie. Look at this note she left me."

Matilda took the scrap of paper and read the short message. Her eyes grew large, and her hand went to her mouth. "Oh, my. I don't know anything about this. It's Carrie's handwriting, but—"

"I believe you," Derek said as he snatched the note back from her hands. "I have to go find her. She took our carriage to her grandmother's house. Can you loan me your horse and carriage?"

Joshua entered the room and learned the details of the crisis. "I'm sure everything will be fine, Derek. Try to calm down while I hitch the horse to the carriage for you."

In short order, Derek climbed into the Johnsons' carriage and headed toward the Wolf home to see if Carrie's grandmother knew where she was. He drove like a man possessed, unable to quiet his mind. Even the beautiful colors of the turning leaves didn't hold his attention. Red and gold leaves fluttered down, filling the air. Migrating geese squawked in the blue sky overhead, but he was oblivious. He only concentrated on the road.

He rehearsed in his mind how he would act when he found her. Should he act as if nothing had changed and be the gracious, loving husband, or would she already know things she shouldn't? In that case, what could he do to protect himself? He had already put Julia in the sanitarium. Was there another sanitarium somewhere else for Carrie? Or should he find a remote place to move and take her with him, cutting her off from communicating with other people?

Oh, God! He let out a long, anguished scream, startling the horse. He was aware that his thoughts were deteriorating, sliding away from the idyllic reality he wanted to create. He recognized he was teetering on the edge of something dark and frightening, like balancing on the very edge of hell.

His heart pounded hard; the veins in his neck throbbed. He was in a sweat despite the cool weather.

The horse's hooves thudded against the ground. They didn't stop until he went up the long driveway at the Wolf house and pulled on the reins to stop in front of the wide veranda.

He climbed from the carriage and stood by the panting horse, breathing hard, shaking his head, trying to rid himself of the darkness surrounding him. He needed to put on the face of the patient, understanding husband until he found out how much damaging information the family had.

He relaxed his tense muscles, put a smile on his face, and knocked.

After a long moment, the housekeeper opened the door.

"Mr. March," she said with her best welcome smile despite his disheveled condition. "Please come in. I'll tell Mrs. Wolf you're here."

"Thank you, Hannah."

He stood in the foyer, waiting, shifting his weight from one foot to another, until Susannah came to greet him. She wondered at his sweaty clothing full of sawdust. What could have brought him in such a state?

"Derek, what a surprise. You look...unusual. Do you need something to drink?"

"That would be nice, thank you. I left in a hurry."

Susannah told the housekeeper to bring two cups of tea.

They went into the parlor to talk.

"I'm sorry about my appearance. I'll take the leather chair so my dirty clothes don't soil your Chesterfield," he said.

"What brings you here, Derek?"

"I'm looking for my wife. There was only a note on the kitchen table when I got home. She must have left suddenly. I remembered that she had your buckboard, so I hoped she would still be here. Can you tell me where she is?"

Susannah swallowed hard. She crossed her hands over her knees and lowered her head for just a second, trying to choose her words carefully.

"She said she's gone to visit Phineas and Adelaide Fletcher in Florissant. She shouldn't be more than two or three days."

"What was the nature of the emergency?"

"I've told you as much as I can, son."

Derek fought for control of his emotions. *She's hiding something.* He gripped the arms of the chair until his knuckles were white. When he spoke, his voice came across more sharply than he intended. "You're the only one who could have told her about an emergency. You don't know what the emergency was, yet you came to get her and took her away without my knowledge?"

Susannah stiffened her spine. "That's not what happened. I visited Carrie and mentioned that Phineas and Adelaide had a visitor. Carrie became upset and said she was leaving. I urged her to stay, but she was determined. So she came back here in the buckboard and took your carriage."

"But why? Who was the visitor, and why was Carrie so upset that she would leave that way?"

"I don't have any answers for you, Derek. I'm sorry. You can get this all sorted out when she gets home."

"I won't sit around while my wife has left me. I'm going after her."

Susannah paled. Derek stared at her trembling hands and lifted his eyes to her face. *She's afraid. Something is going on.*

He said, "I need the address of this Uncle Phineas, if he is an uncle. It's funny she never mentioned him before, even when we were talking about people to invite to the wedding."

Susannah ignored his last remark. "I don't know the street number, but it's easy to find. As soon as you get into Florissant on the main road, it's just a few blocks farther on the right, and it has a big sign out front that says Fletcher House Bed & Breakfast. You can't miss it. But, Derek, it's a six-hour ride to

Florissant in the carriage, and it's getting dark. Traveling is not so safe at night. Why don't you have dinner with us, stay in one of our extra bedrooms, then be on your way tomorrow? Who knows, you might even meet her on the road as she returns."

Derek surrendered to the hopelessness of his situation. As much as he wanted to strike out immediately, driving in the dark without sleep would be crazy. He agreed to stay.

It wasn't long until Christian returned home from work. "Good to see you, Derek. This is a surprise. What brings you here? Is Carrie with you?"

Susannah intervened. "Carrie left this morning to go see Phineas and Adelaide. She left a note for Derek, which he found when he got home. He's beside himself with worry. He wants to go get her."

Christian's brow knit in confusion. "What? Why did she do that?"

"I think it's my fault. I visited her this morning. During our conversation, I mentioned that Phineas and Adelaide had a visitor. To my surprise, she became upset and insisted on going to see them. I was shocked at that reaction. Despite my objection to her plan, she returned our buckboard. Then she hitched up Derek's carriage and took off."

Christian sat in the nearest chair. His legs were crossed, and his right foot bobbed up and down. "What was going through her head? She's normally a sensible girl."

"Who was this visitor?" Derek asked.

"It's someone we don't know."

Derek's frustration emboldened him. "You're hiding something." His voice became demanding. "Does my wife have a past I don't know about?"

Christian's brow knit, and he rose to his full height. He spoke in his best commanding voice. "If she does, we don't know about it, either. You two will have to work this out when you see her. We can't help you."

The mood had taken an ugly turn, but Susannah tried to rescue the conversation. "Derek will be having supper with us and staying the night. In the morning, he'll leave to go to Fletcher House."

"I see. Well, I'm going upstairs to change out of my work clothes. I'll be down when supper is ready."

"I believe Hannah will be putting it on the table soon."

Christian left the room. Derek lowered his head and put his hands over his face. "Mrs. Wolf, I'm sorry I said what I did." But it was too late to take it back. He could only try to smooth it over as the evening went on.

She regarded him with her lips pressed together tightly. "I hope so. It wasn't a good idea to speak to Mr. Wolf that way."

"I'll leave now if you like."

She shook her head. "It's too dangerous to try that trip at night when you're so distraught."

"I appreciate your putting me up," he said. "I'll leave early in the morning. Are you sure you don't have the address?"

Susannah sighed and went to the old writing desk. She pulled out a notebook of addresses. "I'm sorry, I never wrote it down because we didn't need it. But you'll find it the way I told you."

"Thank you, Mrs. Wolf. I'm very grateful."

Supper that evening was strained. Derek didn't try to force a conversation but devoured his meal quickly and went upstairs to the guest room. He left before sunrise while Susannah and Christian were still in bed.

Day #9 of the Investigation

In the cold darkness before dawn, Derek drove the Johnsons' horse and carriage down the road at a hard pace, bumping over uneven ruts, dirt clods, and tree roots. The horse's hooves pounded the dirt, and the carriage wheels clattered. He was sure demons were chasing him. His well-laid plans of a life with Carrie were threatened. His past dogged him, and he couldn't escape. He needed more information. He needed to know if Carrie had learned his secrets. There was still a chance she didn't know anything, that she had gone to see her Uncle Phineas to deal with some unrelated emergency. He swore. If only she hadn't run off the way she did. This situation forced him to realize something frightening: he had only a shaky hold on his sanity.

He needed someone to blame. First, he blamed God, the God he believed had abandoned him when he needed Him most. His parents were also to blame for forcing him into a religion that deserted him when it mattered. Then he blamed Carrie for running off suddenly without even talking to him about it. That was no way for a wife to behave, and here, they had only been married for a month. He didn't know what he would do about it when he found her, but it certainly required some action. He couldn't allow her to take that kind of liberty whenever she felt like it. He would show her who was in charge.

He thought about how they cuddled and teased each other just yesterday morning before he left for work. As he continued to travel, his view of their marriage turned black, and it was Carrie's fault. It was all her fault. What decent wife behaves the way she did? At that thought, he pounded his fist on the seat of the carriage.

When the horse needed rest, he reluctantly found a creek and stopped. He gave the horse an apple and let him drink from the stream.

But the demons wouldn't stop. He lay in a pile of crisp leaves and closed his eyes, thinking of Carrie. He thought about her sweet smile, the gentle way she cared for him, and her warmth as she slept beside him. He thought about their day at the library and their Italian dinner when she sipped the wine. Then his emotions flipped again to anger. He realized how corrupted his soul was, how unstable his mind. Who was he, really? Was he the loving husband or the corrupt criminal who committed murder and consigned his wife to a sanitarium? He didn't know. He didn't know if he could be both. But he did know he was out of control, switching back and forth between two personalities.

After a brief rest, he shook his head to clear his thoughts, climbed back into the carriage, and continued. He tried desperately to keep his mind blank, but it was impossible.

Chapter 24: The Meeting

Four rooms at the Fletcher House were occupied that night. The guests all came downstairs in the morning for breakfast. Adelaide hustled around the kitchen cooking, and Phineas was busy serving as Carrie entered the dining room.

"Good morning, Carrie. How did you sleep?" asked Phineas.

She smiled. "Not well, despite the very comfortable bed in my room."

"Pick a table and pull up a chair. I'll bring your breakfast to you."

Carrie chose an unoccupied table and seated herself. Phineas brought her a plate filled with an omelet, sausage, and a sweet roll.

"Thank you. That looks delicious."

"You've never had one of Adelaide's breakfasts, have you? They're exquisite. I hope you enjoy this." He poured her a cup of tea, set the pot on the table, and sat with her. He lowered his voice. "We didn't get a chance to talk much yesterday since we were so busy. It takes a lot to run a bed and breakfast. But Julia will be here early in the afternoon to discuss her options. Her first problem is that she's in danger of being arrested and put back in the sanitarium. Adelaide and I could also be arrested for kidnapping."

Carrie's eyes widened in shock. "I didn't realize you were at so much risk."

"I hope it will all work out. The first thing Julia needs is an attorney. I want your grandpa to handle her case, but he's fifteen miles away."

"I feel sorry for her, to have married someone she loved, only to have him turn on her. Are they still married?"

"It's anyone's guess. There was no record of a divorce at the courthouse in Lamar and no record here. But her husband could have gotten a divorce anywhere else. Of course, then he would have no authority over whether she was kept in the sanitarium. My guess is that there was no divorce."

Carrie lifted her teacup and took a sip. Her eyes flooded in sympathy for Julia's plight. She stared at her plate and wagged her head slowly.

"Why don't you borrow one of Adelaide's books and spend some time reading this morning? Or you could take a walk. Julia will be here in a few hours."

"That sounds good, Mr. Fletcher. I'll stretch my legs and walk awhile."

His heart tightened in his chest for her. He feared the future unfolding in her life since the expensive necklace around her neck matched one on the list of items stolen from the jewelry store. His mind raced to find a way to make her comfortable talking to him. She would need someone to lean on when her world crashed.

"By the way," he said, "Julia calls me Uncle Phineas. Why don't you do the same? You've known me long enough."

She laughed and hugged him. "All right, Uncle Phineas. I'll help Aunt Adelaide wash the dishes; then I'll go out for a walk."

The cool air was stimulating. Carrie pulled her coat closer around her and walked as fast as she could. When the wind blew, the air filled with leaves fluttering to the ground to be crunched underfoot. She wished the breeze could blow the confusion from her mind. She got a whiff of smoke rising from the chimneys of neighboring homes. It smelled like autumn, her favorite season, but she was too stressed to enjoy it.

Her thoughts turned to Derek. *I shouldn't have rushed off the way I did. I hope he wasn't upset. He's such an exceptional husband. This investigation is probably a foolish waste of time. I should have had more faith in him. I can't wait to get home and feel his arms around me. Surely, the rumors are false. Surely, he is not the man who shot a shopkeeper. Surely, he didn't have another wife when he married me. Of course not.*

She walked past quaint little houses and shops. She wandered into the milliner's and tried on a wide-brimmed hat decorated with ribbons and silk flowers. She checked the mirror, and sure enough, it was very attractive on her. *I wonder if Derek would mind if I bought a hat? I should probably wait until we have all the furniture we need.* She thanked the shopkeeper and left the hat on the counter.

She stepped into a candy shop next door where trays of fudge lined shelves in a display case. Her mouth watered, and she longed to buy some. She thought about taking some home to Derek, but again, she wanted to wait to purchase frivolities until after the house was furnished. She left the candy shop empty-handed and retraced her steps to Fletcher House.

Derek was still on the road, pushing the horse as hard as he dared. His anger mounted with every passing minute. *Carrie should never have left the house the way she did. What was she thinking? Her responsibility is to me. I'm the head of the house. I sold everything I had to buy that house for her, even deeding it to her before we were married, and this is the way she repays me. I'll get her straightened out when I find her.*

His eyes flooded with tears, and he sobbed as he flew down the road.

I hope I can find the Fletchers' place when I get there. Mrs. Wolf should have given me better directions. I'll bet she had the address all along and just wanted to make it harder for me to find my wife.

The demons in Derek's head were having a heyday.

Early in the afternoon, a carriage pulled up to Fletcher House with Julia March and her parents, Dieter and Frieda Sternbach. They trooped into the lobby and rang the bell at the front desk. Adelaide emerged from the owners' quarters to meet them.

"It's good to see you all again. Phineas will be here in just a moment."

Phineas came around the corner with a smile on his face. "Why don't we go into our private quarters to talk? If you don't mind, I'd like to include Carrie March, who is resting upstairs after a long walk this morning. Her husband is also Derek March, but she needs to be assured we're not talking about her husband."

Julia gasped. "I hope her husband wouldn't do to her what Derek did to me."

Mr. Sternbach said in his heavy German accent, "I'm sure it is a different man."

Adelaide directed them to the apartment while Phineas went to bring Carrie downstairs. After introducing her to the Sternbachs, Phineas said, "We'll discuss the two husbands in a moment, but first, let's figure out how to keep you safe, Julia. We need to consider the options and try to find the best one."

"Do you have to know where a man is before you can divorce him?" asked Mr. Sternbach. "Julia thinks he was in Toledo some weeks ago, but we don't know where he lives."

"You would need an attorney to answer that question," said Phineas. "I can recommend an excellent attorney, but his office is in Lamar. There may be other good attorneys in Florissant who would be more convenient for you."

Carrie interrupted. "The attorney he's talking about is my grandfather, and he's the best. He'd be worth the trip. It's only an hour by train."

Julia turned to Carrie. "Uncle Phineas says you're married to a man named Derek March. That's quite a coincidence. At least, I hope it's a coincidence. Tell me what he looks like."

"He's a tall, good-looking man with dark hair and gorgeous brown eyes."

Julia smiled. "That could describe a lot of men. How old is he?"

"Twenty-seven. He has a scar on his left hand."

"Hm. My husband would be twenty-seven now, but many men would still fit that description. The last I saw him, he had no scars."

"Julia, would you be willing to come to Spencer's Mill with me?" Carrie asked. "We could drive past the wheelwright's shop where my husband works. He usually works outside. You could get a look at him and tell me if it's the same man."

"I would be willing to do that, but let me get my own situation resolved first. I'm still in danger of being arrested and returned to the sanitarium. I don't know if I'll need to go to court, or if I should still be watching over my shoulder to make sure some sheriff isn't coming after me. I have too many things on my mind. Once everything is settled, then I'll look at your Derek."

"Thank you. I'm sympathetic to your plight, of course, but the sooner we can do it, the better. This uncertainty eats at me night and day."

"Let's talk about the sheriff," Phineas said. "He's a friend of mine, but I don't know if I can get the information I want without alerting him to your presence—"

The bell on the front desk dinged. Then it rang again, ding-ding-ding-ding, frantically, like someone had an emergency.

"I'll see who it is," Adelaide said, jumping from her seat. "You continue."

Adelaide walked to the front desk. "May I help you?"

"My wife is here, and I want to see her. My name is Derek March."

Adelaide's face drained. The wild look on March's face

alarmed her. He was flushed with anger, and the man was filthy and unshaven. "One moment, please. I'll get my husband."

"No, not your husband. I want my wife. Where is she?" Derek spoke in a threatening tone.

Adelaide spoke firmly. "One moment." She turned away and went to get Phineas.

She trembled as she stepped into their private quarters. In a stage whisper, she said, "Phineas, a man at the front desk is looking for his wife. He says his name is Derek March. His aggressive pose, the look on his face...I'm afraid of what he might do."

Julia's face paled, and she grabbed her father's arm. Carrie flinched, but her concern was for Julia.

"All right. I'll talk to him. Go to the kitchen and arm yourself with whatever you can find in case we need to subdue him. Hopefully, we won't have to."

Adelaide slipped into the kitchen to find something that might serve as a weapon. She thought a knife would be too dangerous; then she spotted the iron skillets. Perfect. She took one of the smallest ones and concealed it in the folds of her skirt. Phineas was at the front desk, so she crossed the lobby and stood quietly a few feet behind March.

"Are you Uncle Phineas? I want my wife, and I want her now."

"What is your wife's name?"

"Don't act stupid. You know it's Carrie, and I know she's here."

Waiting in Phineas and Adelaide's apartment, Carrie recognized Derek's voice. She had never before known him to be that upset. "It's my husband," she said, alarmed. "He must be angry that I left him with only a note of explanation. I shouldn't have done that. I'll apologize." Her lips trembled as she started for the door, but Julia pulled her back.

"That's my husband's voice, too. You don't want to be around him when he's that crazy. Stay here, and let Uncle

Phineas get him calmed down."

As she coped with the realization that her worst fears were confirmed, Carrie broke down sobbing while Julia tried to comfort her. "I guess we know the truth now, Carrie. I'm so sorry you ever got involved with that...that...I can't think of a word bad enough to describe him."

Phineas used the most appeasing voice he could summon. "Why don't you have a seat? It will take me a few minutes to get her."

"There's no reason why it should." He shouted, "Carrie! Carrie!" He was not in the mood to wait.

When he reached across the front desk to grab Phineas by the shirt, Adelaide jumped into quick action. She swung her iron skillet and caught him on the back of the head. If she hadn't choked on her swing at the last second, she might have killed him.

She stared in horror as he sank to the floor.

Chapter 25: The Escape

When Derek opened his eyes, he was in more trouble than he thought he would ever be. Leaning over him were Phineas, Adelaide, the Sternbachs, his wife Julia, and his other wife Carrie. He groaned.

"It's all over, Derek," Phineas said.

Sternbach lunged at Derek, but Phineas restrained him. Sternbach's face was red and the veins of his neck throbbed. "Mr. Sternbach, you don't want to do anything crazy outside the law. And think of your heart. We need the sheriff. Would you mind going to get him?"

Sternbach spat out his reply. "I've never hated anyone as much as I hate this man." His jaw jutted out, and his fists flexed rapidly until he reluctantly backed away. "I'll be back with the sheriff." He strode toward the door to go on his errand.

"*Warten,* Deiter. Wait," called Mrs. Sternbach. "Let me go with you. Your heart!"

"Hurry up." They both left, leaving Julia to wait for them there.

"Let me help you to your feet," said Phineas, grabbing Derek by the arm. "Adelaide, would you mind getting a cold cloth for Derek's head? We'll go into the parlor to get this all straightened out."

Carrie stared into her husband's eyes. There was an angry blackness there she had never seen before. It was as if he were someone she never met. He stared through her, wild-eyed, as her own eyes flooded with tears. The mask he had carefully constructed for himself had shattered, and his dark soul was bared.

As Phineas pulled Derek to his feet and walked him toward the Fletchers' private quarters, Derek twisted in one violent motion and escaped Phineas' grasp. He darted toward the door and fled down the walk toward his carriage, which sat in front of Fletcher House where Carrie had left it. Phineas tried to chase him but wasn't as agile as the younger man. Quickly, Derek jumped into his rig and fled down the street, rounding the corner to elude anyone who wanted to follow. As he drove away, Phineas stared at the red spokes and red crown painted on his carriage.

The group in the lobby of Fletcher House stood in stunned amazement. "That was my husband," Julia said. "I hope I never see him again."

Carrie froze in place, covering her mouth with her palm. She was too shocked to cry. "I think I married a man who never existed, not really," said Carrie. "It's like one man with two personalities. I love him so much, but that man stared right past me like I was a stranger to him." Her face was white, and her knees went weak. "I feel faint."

Adelaide rushed to her. "Here's a chair, Carrie. I'll get you a glass of water."

Julia seethed with anger. "He sank to a new low, didn't he, committing bigamy along with his other crimes? Mr. Fletcher, what can we do to get out of danger from the sanitarium?"

Phineas sank into the nearest chair. "We need to see Christian Wolf."

Shortly, Dieter and his wife returned with Sheriff Milligan. "What's going on here, Phineas?" asked the sheriff. "Mr.

Sternbach is so beside himself I couldn't get the story straight. He was blurting it out so fast that half of what he told me was in German."

"Let's sit at a table in the dining room, and we'll tell you the whole story. But you should know the criminal has escaped."

Milligan shrugged. "I can't chase someone until I know who he is and what I'm chasing him for."

The group pushed two small tables together and seated themselves. "I'll start at the beginning," Phineas said.

It took several minutes to tell the story. It came out in bits and pieces. By this time, Carrie was hyperventilating. Adelaide helped her stretch out on the sofa and rubbed her arms to slow her breathing.

"Aunt Adelaide," she whispered, "I need to get him back. I want my Derek back. He's really a wonderful man."

Adelaide stroked her hair. "You're still in shock, baby. We'll talk about it after you rest."

Milligan finally leaned back in his chair. "Let me see if I understand this correctly. Derek March has committed robbery, murder, false imprisonment, and bigamy. Once we catch him, he'll be going away for a long time, or possibly hanged for murder, sorry to say. That leaves the two wives with legal problems only an attorney can sort out. And it leaves you with emotional problems that only God Almighty can resolve. Bless you all." He wagged his head. "As sheriff, I'd like to remain emotionally uninvolved, but I've never seen anything this shocking. My prayers are with you."

Phineas glanced at Dieter. "The Sternbachs have problems to deal with, too, and one of them is a struggle with forgiveness."

Dieter snorted. "That'll be no struggle for me. I never intend to forgive him."

Freida put her hand on his knee and patted softly.

The sheriff rose. "I'll see if I can find him. You say he took off to the north, then turned left at the corner?"

Phineas nodded. "Yes, but I'm sure that as a man

experienced at hiding himself, he was trying to lay down a false trail. He could be anywhere by now."

"I won't find him by standing here. I'll get going. Wish me luck."

"Wait, let's work out a plan, Milligan," said Phineas. "We'll take territories. You tell me where you're going to look, and I'll look in another area of town."

"That sounds smart." The two strategized, Milligan choosing the southeast quadrant of town to start with and Phineas agreeing to search the northeast. They would meet back together at Fletcher House at five o'clock.

"One piece of information that may be helpful," said Phineas. "March's carriage has red spokes with yellow accents and a red crown painted on the back."

"That's good to know. Grab your revolver and some rope to restrain him, Phineas. You're my deputy today."

Phineas ducked into the bedroom for his weapon. He was thankful he had plenty of experience with this. As the two men left, Phineas said a silent prayer, asking God to help them find Derek and bring him back successfully.

Chapter 26: The Crime Spree

Derek continued to drive like a madman, lashing the reins and bouncing over the uneven brick roads. The horse's hooves struck the ground so hard that some of the paving bricks chipped. He turned north again, nearly tipping the carriage. He reasoned that his pursuers would be less likely to find him if he went in a zigzag pattern.

Despite his panic, he realized he hadn't eaten a meal since dinner last night. He couldn't keep up this pace unless he could find some nourishment. It was certain he couldn't stop at a restaurant and risk getting caught. Hope rose when he came to a pumpkin field, but that was no good. Even if he had time and a knife to cut one open and scoop out the meat, raw pumpkin wasn't on his list of appetizing foods.

He kept pushing forward. Up ahead, he spotted an apple orchard. The red apples were inviting and would be quick to gather. He pulled the horse to a stop, jumped to the ground, and ran to the first tree. He managed to snag five ripe apples quickly, then leaped back into the carriage and continued on at a furious pace. He would stop and have an apple as soon as he thought he was safe. He'd give one to the horse, too.

I wish I had a town map. I think it's time I turned. I'd feel a lot better if I didn't have to guess.

He tugged the reins, and the horse veered to the right. He came to an area of stores where folks were out on the sidewalks, so he slowed his pace. He didn't want to appear suspicious like he was fleeing someone. He thought people stared at him as he passed, making him uncomfortable, so he turned left again. He nearly fainted when he realized he was passing the sheriff's office.

In another three blocks, he turned right into a residential area where other carriages were parked in the street. He felt safer there, blending in, but was compelled to continue. Staying in one spot was a luxury he couldn't afford.

I was one second from capture back there, he thought. *If I'm caught and found guilty, it'll be the hangman's noose for sure. There's no way I'm going to allow that to happen. I should never have tried to settle in Spencer's Mill. I wish I had never met Carrie. What a stupid plan that was. When I get to my next location, I'll settle where no one has ever heard of Derek March.*

He pressed on. Soon, the residences he passed took on a more rustic look, and the surrounding properties became larger. On the right was an old log cabin where a thin, brown-haired woman hung laundry on a line. His mind raced. He might be able to hide his rig behind her house and get some rest there before he continued his journey. She would give him some hot food; he would see to that.

His mind formed a quick plan. He would pull up in front of the cabin and subdue her with his revolver while he still had the element of surprise. He would force her inside and make her give him some food. Then he would leave her tied to a chair while he pulled his rig around back. If her husband came home, he would restrain him, too. It all sounded plausible to his weary mind.

He stopped his horse in front of her house, hopped out, and put on his friendliest smile. He was sorry his appearance was so unkempt.

"I'm lost, ma'am. Can you give me directions to Delphos?"

She paused in her laundry chores and turned to the west, shading her eyes from the sun. She lifted a slender arm and pointed in the distance. "You'll need to go that way, but I'm not sure how far…."

Derek pulled his revolver. "Stay calm, ma'am. I don't intend to harm you, but I will if you don't cooperate. I need some hot food and a place to rest."

She flinched and dropped a wet shirt at her feet. "You take that gun and get out of here, you dirty rapscallion," she shouted.

"You're right; I am a dirty rapscallion, but I'm not leaving until I get food and a little rest. Now move." He waved the revolver toward the house to get her to start walking.

She laughed derisively. "I'll give you food if you force me, but you'll not get any rest here."

"I'll decide if I get rest here. I'm the one with the gun." He muttered under his breath, "I can't believe she was fool enough to defy me."

With a smirk, she turned and trudged to the house with the revolver pointed at her back.

Inside the door, Derek's plan unraveled. Five children in the primary grades and younger were doing their lessons or playing with toys. When they spotted the stranger and his revolver, every child set up a howl, some in terror, the older ones in anger. The racket they set up rattled Derek, whose nerves were already raw.

He shouted at them. "Shut up, every one of you. Lady, make those kids shut up."

She crossed her arms and stared at him defiantly. The children continued their screaming. The oldest one, a boy wearing heavy brogans, ran at Derek and kicked him in the leg as hard as he could. "You leave my Ma alone!"

Derek's shin exploded in pain, and he swore. Now he had that pain to deal with, as well as the splitting headache from being assaulted with an iron skillet. He was tempted to fire his weapon at someone... anyone... maybe that ornery brat, but he still had enough sense to know when to retreat. He rushed outside, slammed the door behind him, and jumped into his carriage. His hands shook violently. As he took off, he glanced back at the cabin. The woman and all five children stared at him through the windows. The woman still wore that smirk.

What do I do now? Derek was so exhausted, hungry, and in pain that he couldn't think straight. He longed to sit in a quiet place with Carrie and fold her into his arms. But no, she had disrespected him.

Five minutes later, with his mind in turmoil, he came upon a farmhouse needing paint. Beside it stood a barn that was cared for more lovingly than the house. His eyes scanned the property for horses or wagons. He didn't see any.

Thinking that no one was home, he pulled his rig to the rear of the barn, then crept through an open window to find a place to rest. Once inside, he stepped over tools and paraphernalia typical of any farm. Bales of hay, hammers, saws, axes, hoes, and countless other tools hung on the walls or lay scattered on the floor. Sunlight streamed in, spotlighting a plow.

He dashed to the ladder going to the hayloft and scrambled up. Barn smells of hay and animal stalls were strangely comforting to him. Settling in, he pulled an apple from his pocket and had enough time to take the first two bites before the barn door opened.

Derek realized the farmer would be able to detect the crunching of the apple, so he laid it down carefully and drew his revolver as quietly as he could. Then he waited, trying to control his breathing.

The farmer below him was visible through the gaps in the floor of the loft, so Derek tried to shrink into the shadows where he wouldn't be spotted so easily. He waited with muscles tensed as the farmer moved silently toward the door, picked up the shotgun leaning on the doorpost, and aimed it at the loft.

"You come down from there right now." This farmer was

serious. "You have five seconds."

Derek held his breath, not moving.

"Five … four … three… two…"

Derek lunged to the edge of the hayloft, fired at him with his revolver, and missed. The farmer got off a blast of his shotgun and then ran back out.

He's probably waiting for me just on the other side of that door, Derek thought. *He'll probably jump me coming down the ladder when both my hands are occupied. I'll have to swing down without it, then run for that back window.*

He left his apples in the hay, shoved his revolver into his pocket as far down as possible, and lowered himself until he was hanging from the loft with his hands. He dropped quietly but twisted his ankle. It was all he could do to stifle a moan. He limped to the back window, climbed out the way he had come in, and mounted his carriage. One painful right shin and a twisted left ankle were curses placed on him by the Almighty, he was sure.

He slapped the reins, yelled, "Hyaah," and took off through the weeds at a gallop, trying to reach the road. The rear wheel dipped into a hole and jerked the carriage. Derek nearly fell out, but the carriage righted, and the horse kept going. The farmer ran around the back of the barn and shot at him. The blast echoed off the barn and a nearby house as the pellets sped dangerously close to Derek's ear. He thought the world was ending. Fortunately for him, the farmer had a faulty aim. Derek kept going as fast as the horse would take him. His heart pounded wildly.

What kind of life is this? All I wanted was to settle down and live a quiet life. God is supposed to be a God of love. Hah! That's a big lie!

He raised his fist and shook it at the heavens.

His wind-whipped hair lashed his face and interfered with his vision as he rushed down the road. He was obliged to continually push it aside with one hand.

Two men converged on the sheriff's office at about the same

time. One of them was the husband of the woman Derek had threatened with his gun, and the other was the farmer whose barn he had invaded. Neither had seen the perpetrator's face, but they compared notes when they discovered the sheriff was not in his office and realized they were both there to make a complaint.

"He held my wife at gunpoint," said the angry husband. "He had all my kids scared witless. At least my oldest boy had some guts. He kicked the intruder with his brogans."

"I bet it's the same guy. He tried to hole up in my hayloft. I blasted at him with my shotgun. I'm sorry to say I missed him twice. Do you know what he looks like?"

"My wife said he was a tall guy with a wild look in his eyes. She thought he was young, in his late twenties, maybe."

"I only saw his back as he escaped in his carriage. He had dark hair. Could be the same guy, but I can't be sure."

"I wonder where the sheriff is. We ought to leave him a note telling him the basic facts. If it's the same man, he's on a rampage. He might not quit. Lord knows how many people he could hurt."

The two men stopped a woman passing by and asked if she had any notepaper and a pencil in her purse. She did. "Why do you need it?" she asked.

Talking over one another, they described the actions of the man who had shot at the farmer and tried to force the other man's wife to give him food. Her eyes widened.

"Excuse me, gentlemen. Keep the pencil and paper. I need to go meet some other ladies."

The farmer chuckled as she hurried off. "She sure is in a hurry to spread the gossip, ain't she?"

"That's all right, friend. Folks need to be warned about this fellow. He's a danger to everyone in town."

Just then, Phineas rode up, hoping that Milligan had happened to stop by for some reason. He wanted to connect with the sheriff early, but instead, he ran into the two men writing the message. He started a conversation, then listened

219

patiently as the men told him what had happened.

"My wife didn't recognize him. She thought he was probably a stranger in town," said one man.

"I know who he is," Phineas said. "His name is Derek March, and he's dangerous. If you see him again, please take the information to the Fletcher House Bed and Breakfast on Main Street. The sheriff and I plan to meet there at five o'clock to coordinate our efforts. We're determined to catch that man. He's ruined a lot of people's lives."

The two men promised to be on the lookout. They gave their folded paper to Phineas to deliver to the sheriff.

Derek was in more of a panic than ever. His tidy, well-planned life was destroyed, and everything he had was gone: Carrie, his job, his beautiful house, and his box of jewelry. Even his bank account would probably be turned over to one of his wives. It was as if God Himself had plotted against him and tried to squash him like a bug. The more he thought of it, the angrier he became. He thought of cursing God, but when he opened his mouth, his tongue stuck. God even got in the way of his cursing. His rage toward the Almighty increased.

He traveled aimlessly, this way and that, trying to avoid capture. As he went, he wondered if God would show him favor if he asked for forgiveness. His Sunday School teachers said He would. He considered that idea while he continued down the road and was on the brink of surrendering, but finally decided that he had sinned too much. God would never forgive a man like him. He would have to make it through on his own.

He slowed down to give the horse a rest. He had pushed the poor beast too far but needed to survive as a free man. He finally devised a plan to rob the bank for enough money to give him a fresh start in Toledo. Then he would head up there. But which way was the bank? He was afraid he was traveling in circles, so he headed back toward the east, reckoning by the position of the sun. Whatever he was going to do, he would have to do it quickly before his weary steed collapsed.

He thought of selling the carriage and continuing on horseback. If he found a livery stable, he would see if anyone there would buy the carriage and trade him a fresh mount. But the most important thing would be finding that bank.

He wished he had a bandana to hide his face, but what difference did it make? No one in Florissant would recognize him except the Fletchers, the Sternbachs…and Carrie. The chance of one of them being at the bank when he held it up was very low. Before anyone caught him, he would be out of town, so the bandana wasn't necessary.

Soon, he came to the business section of Florissant and found the bank without much trouble. He stopped his panting horse in front. "Take a short rest, buddy," he said. "I'll be back in a minute." Taking a deep breath, he boldly entered the bank lobby with his revolver drawn. He was hungry, weak, trembling, and desperate.

He shouted at the few people in the bank: "Everyone, put your hands up. This is a robbery."

Startled customers whirled around to look at him and thrust their hands in the air. The bank manager sat at his desk, ashen-faced.

"I said get your hands up," he yelled at the manager, who complied. Derek collected the money from the teller's window and stuffed it into his pockets. He glanced at the customers' watches and jewelry but resisted the temptation to steal them. Time was of the essence. He turned sharply, intending to bolt out the door, but his sore ankle and shin forced him to stop. He limped painfully to his carriage, then clattered away. The whole robbery had taken less than one minute.

As Derek barreled north at full speed, he thought he spotted a bridge in the distance. *If there's a bridge, then a river flows through the town. That bridge will be my only route of escape.*

He swiveled his head to see if anyone was behind, chasing him. There was a carriage some distance back, matching his speed. His tension increased. It could have been the sheriff or

Phineas Fletcher in the carriage, but he wasn't sure, so he twisted in his seat to stare back at the driver. If only he could get a closer look without risking capture. Not looking where he was going, he nearly ran into a field, clipped a fence, and jerked the reins to correct his course.

Then, there was that familiar mocking laugh in his head. It was the old, familiar demon, jubilant that Derek was inching closer and closer to insanity. He must hold on, if only long enough to escape. Then, he could try to find his way back to normalcy just as he did after his trip to Toledo. He must hold on. Maybe he could go back and get Carrie. He could take her to another state where no one had ever met them, but no, she probably wouldn't go with him now. Maybe if he restrained her...

A litany of his sins ran through his head as he urged the horse on. If only he could stop it. If only his mind could blot out the memory of the jeweler lying in blood. If only he could change the day he forced Julia into that sanitarium. Maybe he should have killed her, as well. He was embarrassed about the easy skill with which he romanced Carrie into being his wife when he was still married to Julia. He thought about today's events: charging into Fletcher House and screaming at Mrs. Fletcher, the faces of the Sternbachs and both his wives staring at him together. He remembered knowing instantly that his life was shattered, and a demon was laughing...laughing...laughing. What about the laundry woman with all those kids, the farmer with the shotgun, and the bank robbery?

He opened his mouth, and a string of profanities sullied the air. Who had taken over his body? He used to be such a gentleman, respected by his peers and adored by the young ladies. What happened? He didn't deserve this. How could he escape his circumstances? He needed it all to stop. Just stop.

As Derek continued his furious race toward the bridge, wheels chattering noisily over the brick road, the mocking demon in his head took on a voice. "You could jump off the bridge. Why not end your misery? Jump."

At first, the idea shocked him. What a ridiculous notion. But then…why not? He wanted it all to stop, didn't he?

"Jump, Derek." The demon was no longer mocking, but entreating. "This is your chance to escape."

Derek's hold on his will to live slipped a notch. The thought of ending this miserable life took on some appeal. But no, that was crazy.

"Jump, Derek. Go ahead." A quiet, soothing voice.

He neared the bridge, still undecided.

The voice urged him gently, enticingly. "Jump, Derek. Your misery will end."

He checked behind him. The carriage behind him had made a turn. It wouldn't hurt to stop at the river. He needed a minute to calm down and consider his options. Besides, his horse needed a rest. Maybe he could clear his mind if he spent a minute looking down at the water. Flowing water had a soothing effect on him.

He drove onto the bridge and pulled his carriage next to the rail. Slowly, he stepped onto the pavement. He was still in pain from that drop he took in the barn and the kick to his shins. His head throbbed from the blow of the iron skillet.

He stepped to the rail and peered over the side. It was so peaceful. He was mesmerized by the dark ripples below, lapping at the caissons anchoring the bridge. The place was so calm…so quiet…the water so wonderfully dark. He lingered longer than he intended.

"Jump, Derek." The voice was soothing and kind.

He thought, *This is the kind of peace I need. I'll take a few more minutes here. If someone comes upon me unexpectedly, I can always escape by jumping into the water.*

Derek chuckled, amused. The railing was chest-high, so jumping wouldn't be an easy feat.

"Go on, Derek; things will be so much better."

Maybe. No one would miss me. I'm sure Carrie won't take me back.

223

"She doesn't deserve you anyway, Derek." The voice was so soothing.

That's right. Why would I want her back? She mistreated me. How could she do that after all I've done for her? I gave her the best of everything I had.

He stood on the bridge for another five minutes, gazing into the water and thinking over the new idea that he didn't want Carrie. He didn't want any woman. He could do better on his own. The water seemed to invite him to come.

Why did I deed that house in her name? What a stupid idea. Now I have nothing.

"Yes, now you're homeless. You can't go back to your job. You have nothing to live for. Why not end it?"

Derek wasn't sure if the voice was the demon's or his own. Everything swirled together in his mind.

"It would be so easy. Just stand on the carriage seat, step up on the rail, and it's one more short step."

Derek's shoulders relaxed as he gave in to the voice. He moved in slow motion as if someone else had taken over his body.

Is this me? Am I really considering this?

The voice again, entreating. "The water will wrap itself around you like a lover."

Derek smiled. As if dreaming, he climbed back into his carriage and stepped onto the seat. From there, it was one easy step to the concrete rail of the bridge. Lazily, as if in a daze, he realized his shin and ankle no longer hurt, and his headache was gone. He took the step and balanced himself on the rail. He felt so light.

"Jump, Derek." So inviting.

With a smile, he crossed his arms, stepped off the rail, and dropped toward the black water.

.

Chapter 27: Out of Time

As soon as Derek's feet left the rail in blissful serenity, it was as if someone slapped him in the face, and he snapped back to reality. That laughing—that evil, hilarious laughing—echoed inside his skull, and he knew he had made the worst mistake of his life.

Thoughts raced through his head faster than he had ever thought possible: scenes of his wasted life over the past twenty-seven years.

"Help me, help me," he shouted at no god in particular.

He gulped air, hoping that once he dropped into the river, he could swim to the surface. His arms and legs whirled madly to try to keep himself upright. He wanted more than anything for that laughing to stop.

Down, down, he dropped in sheer panic. Then, an intense pain as he hit a concrete caisson.

His time was up.

Chapter 28: The Water Recovery

At five o'clock, Phineas still wasn't back at Fletcher House. He returned late, closer to five-thirty. Sheriff Milligan was already there, empty-handed. The Sternbachs and Julia were also there with Adelaide and Carrie, eager to hear any news.

Phineas walked in slowly, dreading to pass on the information he had. The entire group turned toward him expectantly. Something was wrong; it was evident in his heavy steps and the pallor on his face.

Phineas opened his mouth to speak, closed it, hesitated, and opened his mouth again. "I found him," he said.

The sheriff's eyebrows knitted together, and his forehead creased. "Where is he, Phineas?"

"We'll have to pull him out of the water. I found his horse and empty carriage on the Commerce Street Bridge. I pulled up behind it and, on a hunch, leaned over the side of the bridge. His body is in the water, held against one of the caissons by the current."

Julia and Carrie both gasped. Carrie's hand went to her mouth, and she began sobbing anew. "I loved him so much! He was the perfect husband and friend."

Adelaide encircled her with her arms. "The man you loved was only a fantasy, dear heart. He was an actor in a play of his own invention."

Carrie would not be consoled. Adelaide continued to comfort her, stroking her hair and speaking softly.

Julia stood to the side, stunned but without emotion. "He was a good husband until he got into trouble gambling and thought he could pay off his debts with stolen money. I'm sure he never intended to shoot the store owner, but once the man died, Derek's soul went black. I've never seen such a change in a man. And then he stuck me in that horrible place." The more she talked, the more upset she became. She pounded her fist on a table. "I'm not sorry he's dead. Now, no one can keep me in that sanitarium."

"We'd better hurry if we're to get him before dark, before his body dislodges and gets carried downstream," said Milligan. "I'll contact my friend Joe, who has a rowboat. Can you come along to help, Phineas?"

"Yes, of course."

Sternbach stood. "I'll come, too."

"No, Deiter," his wife said in a pleading voice. "Your heart."

"I'll be fine. This is something I have to do."

Julia's hand went to her forehead. "Papa, he's not worth your life."

"I'm going."

It was dusk by the time they reached the river. Darkness rolled slowly from the eastern sky toward the west as four grim men filed to the dock and launched the rowboat. The night was still, except for the quiet lapping of the waves against the wooden hull and the gentle splash of the oars dipping into the water. The river smelled faintly of fish and crawdads in the chill night air. Phineas carried a lantern while Joe rowed steadily until they reached the body.

Milligan spoke in subdued tones. "Joe, take the lantern and see if you can hold onto that pylon to keep the boat from drifting. It won't be easy. Phineas, I'll grab Derek by the belt if you can get his shoulders and pull him in."

"I don't think I can get a grip on him that way. Give me that rope, and I'll try to get it around his chest to drag him over the side." Phineas made a loop with the rope and pulled it over Derek's head as far as his neck. He tried to work it down over his shoulders, but the force of the water current wouldn't allow it. "We can't pull him up by the neck. We might rip his head off."

"I doubt that, but let's try something else. When I pull on his belt, you see if you can grab his shirt. I'm ready to pull now, but he'll be heavy," he said. "Sternbach, you counterbalance our weight as we lean over."

Sternbach took his position and tilted his body over the opposite side of the rowboat.

Phineas and Milligan both leaned over to get the body, but the rowboat rocked dangerously, and they took on some water. Joe struggled to keep the boat in position. Despite their best efforts, aided by grunting and swearing, they could not pull Derek into the boat.

Milligan waved his hands. "Stop, fellas. This is too dangerous, and it's not working. We'll have to tow him behind the boat and row for shore. Then we'll drag him out of the shallows."

Phineas and Joe agreed. Sternbach clenched his jaw tightly and nodded.

"Since we couldn't get the rope around his chest, let's tie him by the ankles and pull him back that way." They pulled his body into position and got the rope securely around his ankles, making one loop through his belt for extra safety.

"It's a good thing the women aren't here to see this," Phineas said.

Rowing back was more difficult against the current and the drag created by the waterlogged corpse. Phineas held tight to the rope, praying he didn't let Derek slip off. As the body trailed behind them in the twilight, Phineas thought he spotted a few dollar bills float out of his pants pocket and get swept downstream. *That's odd. Did I see that right?*

Despite the cold temperature, Joe and the sheriff were covered with sweat when the boat reached the dock. The stars glittered in the black sky. The lantern had gone out, so only the light of the harvest moon allowed them to complete their task.

Joe tied the boat to the cleats on the dock, and the four men stepped into the cold water up to their knees.

"Let's get him on shore first," Milligan said. "You two take his shoulders under his arms. I'll carry his legs. Sternbach, you'd best sit this one out. Let's get him onto the floor of my carriage."

Joe shuddered. "He's looking at me."

"Close his eyes."

They lowered the body onto the grassy shore to allow Joe to pass his hand over Derek's eyes. He closed the lids. "He has a nasty gash on his head."

"Probably from where he hit the concrete pylon. Come on, let's get him loaded up."

Without warning, Sternbach's rage overflowed. He roared with a loud, agonized howl and kicked the corpse in the ribs as hard as he could. Water bubbled out of Derek's mouth. While the other three men looked on in shock, Sternbach collapsed to his knees in the weeds and sobbed.

The other three men stood frozen in place, their eyes bulging and jaws agape. Then Milligan moved toward Sternbach, knelt beside him, and put his arm around his shoulder. "We don't need to mention this to anyone, friend. The women will never know. Go ahead and get in the carriage. The rest of us will load the body."

Sternbach nodded. He rose, stumbled toward the carriage with tears still pouring down his cheeks, and climbed in.

It was a mighty struggle. Phineas and Joe managed to get Derek's head and torso on the back floor of the carriage, then the three of them shoved his legs and feet the rest of the way. He was folded up in the tight space like an Amish pretzel.

"We should cover him up," Joe said.

"I don't have a blanket with me," said Milligan. "It seems cruel, but he won't feel the cold. Thanks for your help and the loan of your rowboat, Joe. We couldn't have done it without you."

"You're welcome. I hope we never have to do that again." The two men shook hands, the sheriff clapped him on the shoulder, and Joe headed home.

Phineas and Milligan climbed onto the front seat of the carriage with a subdued Sternbach and drove to the undertaker's house.

A rotund man named Cooper answered the door in his nightgown, a little cross. "What do you have this late at night?" he asked. "I'm about to go to bed."

"We have a drowning victim," said Milligan. "His name is Derek March. We just pulled him out of the river."

"Take him to my workshop and put him on the table," Cooper said. "I'll get dressed and be right out."

Milligan, Phineas, and Sternbach carried the body to the workshop behind the house, and Cooper soon came along with his lantern. He made a low whistle. "He got beat up pretty bad, didn't he?"

"I'd say he did," Milligan said. "Make a nice box for him. He had a wife who loved him."

"And another one who didn't," muttered Sternbach under his breath.

Milligan shot a warning glance at him, hoping to keep him quiet. Then he continued, "He died either of that gash on his head, or maybe he drowned. He fell off the Commerce Street Bridge, and like I said, we just fished him out of the water."

"Fell? How could somebody fall off that bridge with the sides at chest level?"

"I don't know. I didn't want to say he jumped off. I wouldn't want to have to prove suicide in court. It would be easier on everyone if he just fell."

"Then that's what will go on the death record. What a

shame," he said. "What a waste of a life. Good-looking fellow, wasn't he?"

"That could have been part of his downfall."

Milligan, Phineas, and Sternbach returned to Fletcher House. Sternbach said no more but collected his wife and daughter and left.

Adelaide had prepared a late dinner. "Won't you join us and have something to eat, Sheriff?" she asked. "You must be starved." She took in the appearance of the two men. They were wet from the chest down, shivering, and grim. Her heart went out to them. "Did you get him out of the river?"

"Yes. We're both physically and emotionally spent. I don't know about Milligan, but that was the worst job I ever had to do." Phineas headed for their private apartment. "I need to change my wet clothes. Come on, Milligan. I'll loan you a pair of dry trousers and a shirt."

There wasn't much conversation at the table. The only sound was the clinking of silverware on porcelain. Finally, Phineas turned to Carrie. "I'll telegraph your Grandpa in the morning and tell him what happened. Do you have any idea what your plans are for tomorrow?"

"Can I see Derek?"

"That would be a bad idea. He doesn't look much like himself. He took on a lot of water, and his head has an open gash." He shoveled a spoonful of potatoes into his mouth.

Carrie reconsidered, her eyes squeezing back tears. "Then maybe I shouldn't see him."

Milligan nodded. "I think it would be easier for you to remember him as the handsome man he was."

"Do you want a train ticket back to Lamar, or do you want to take the carriage?" Phineas asked.

"Let Julia have the carriage. I'll go by rail, but I dread going back. There's nothing to go to. Maybe my parents will take me in again."

After the meal, they all went to their beds. Carrie cried

herself to sleep upstairs in Room 3, burying her face in the pillow to muffle the sound. Everything in her wanted to scream, but she didn't want to disturb the other guests. Eventually, she gave in to exhaustion.

Epilogue

The following morning, Carrie slept late. She had never known such despair and didn't want to leave the bed. Emotions swirled around her like a tornado, pulling her mind and heart in so many ways that she couldn't keep up. The horror of her situation rolled over her in waves. *How can I face the gossip that will surely flow in the aftermath of this fiasco? What will people say when they find out I was living with a man who was married to someone else? Who will ever want me after this? What will the rest of my life look like?*

She could see only empty blackness in front of her.

This was not the way she had planned her life. Up to this point, she had done everything right, behaving properly, obeying her parents, and making what she believed were wise choices. She had dedicated her life to being a follower of Jesus. And look at how it had turned out. She longed to stay in bed, pull the quilts over her head, and stay there for a month, drowning in tears.

At ten o'clock, she finally rose and dressed herself.

Downstairs, Phineas greeted her. "I arranged for you to travel tomorrow, but I don't think you should be alone on the train. I sent a telegram to your mother, asking her to come to Florissant to accompany you on the ride home. And I'll ask your grandpa to meet the two of you when you get into the station in Lamar."

In Carrie's numbed state, she nodded her assent.

Her mother arrived in Florissant the next morning with tickets for the return trip to Lamar. When she learned the whole story and realized they had all been duped, she dropped into a chair. Her face was flushed, and she nearly fainted. "I can't believe he's gone. I just talked to him the day before yesterday. He came to look for Carrie."

Phineas took her hand and patted her arm.

Once recovered from the initial shock, she stood to wrap her arms around her daughter. She whispered, "I am so embarrassed at how we misread our son-in-law. Carrie, can you ever forgive me for not being able to see this coming?"

"Mama, I didn't see it coming either. I feel like a fool. We were so happy together. If only I had stayed home…."

Adelaide interrupted. "Then you would have been living a lie, dear. It had to come out at some time."

Later, Carrie said a wistful goodbye to Adelaide and thanked her for everything. She and her mother climbed into the carriage with Phineas to go to the train station. They waited in the carriage until the conductor called, "All aboard!"

She hugged Phineas before climbing out of the carriage. "Goodbye, Uncle Phineas," she said. "I owe you a lot. I don't know how I can ever repay you."

"Don't be silly, dear. You take care of yourself. Let me know if there's anything else I can do for you. Have your Grandpa send a telegram." Carrie nodded and walked numbly to the train platform with her mother. They climbed the steps to their coach, found seats, and settled in. The train's whistle was as mournful as Carrie's heart as the engine began its chug…chug…chug. Soon, they were speeding toward Lamar across the Ohio farmland. She stared out the window, seeing nothing.

Her thoughts took on a life of their own. *If I had stayed home instead of running to Florissant, maybe Derek would still be alive. We would still be living our happy life. It was a wonderful four weeks.*

Then she remembered she would have been living a lie. Adelaide was right; it all would have been exposed eventually. Better sooner than later. Better now than after they brought children into the world.

It took about an hour to reach Lamar. Carrie collected her valise and stepped onto the platform with her mother.

"Look, Mama, Grandpa is waiting for us." Carrie ran into his arms. He had received only basic details from Phineas but couldn't imagine the rest. It was too bizarre.

"Come back to my office, both of you," he said. "I've canceled my appointments for this afternoon. I need to know every detail. I only got from Phineas' telegram that Julia was found, Derek is dead, and you were on your way home. I can't imagine…."

Christian picked up Carrie's luggage, and the three returned to his office. Carrie tried to start at the beginning, but the story came out disjointed and interrupted by bursts of crying. She had to keep backing up to fill in the details. Christian could only stare at her in shock as the story unfolded. He asked for explanations for parts he didn't understand.

Finally, he spoke. "I think I have a clear understanding of what happened. Derek committed a crime that Julia witnessed, and he admitted her to a sanitarium to keep her quiet. But he wanted a wife to live with, so he came here and had his eye on you, even though he was still married."

Carrie nodded, tears running down her face. "That's the short of it."

Christian handed her a handkerchief. "I'm exhausted just thinking about all of that. So where is his body?"

"The undertaker in Florissant has him. I don't know who is responsible for burial plans. I suppose it would be Julia since she is his wife. I'm nothing more than a mistress." She burst into sobs at the humiliation that brought her.

"Stop that kind of thinking, Carrie," said Christian. "We must decide how to handle this so your reputation isn't blemished. You did nothing wrong with the information he allowed you to have. He fooled us, too, as well as your Ma and Pa and most other people."

"What do you mean, 'handle this?'"

"No one in Spencer's Mill needs to be told about Julia. All we need to report is that your husband died by drowning in the river. If folks ask you how it happened, you don't know; you weren't there. You're a widow, and while that is very sad, it's honorable."

"How can I keep people from asking me about all the details?"

"You'll be in mourning for a while. There's no need to be out among people during that time if you want to stay home. That will give you time to decide how much you want to tell people and what you want to do next. Do you want to go to college? Do you want to live in Lamar and get a job? Do you want to live with Grandma and me and work in my law office? You have a lot of options open."

"What do I do about our house? Right now, I don't want to go back there to live. It's a beautiful house, but it would remind me too much of Derek. We were so happy together...." A sudden thought struck her. "Besides, it's not even mine."

Christian stopped her. "You'll be surprised to know that when Derek bought the house, he titled it in both your names, even though you weren't married yet. That's unheard of. But if he hadn't, that house would now belong to Julia. I think God might have prompted him to do that."

"Julia deserves it for the six years he had her locked up in the sanitarium."

"Don't be hasty and make decisions based on emotion. I sympathize with your feelings for her, but keep a cool head. The court will probably award her his bank account, which is substantial, as well as his horse and carriage. But that means you're penniless. We'll pray about what to do about the house. If you decide to move back home with your parents, you could sell the house, but I recommend you find renters and give yourself a regular income."

"When can I go home?"

Christian turned the office over to the care of his clerk for the afternoon. Carrie's grandmother and father must be informed of Derek's death and the surrounding events. They both took it hard, especially her father. The news that Derek had drowned spread quickly throughout the community. Mrs. Steuben was distraught, and Mr. Blackburn was caught without a valuable employee. His business suffered when he couldn't fill orders. The only person who smiled over the tragic news was Dolly Rooney, who suspected there was more to the story than a simple drowning. She figured he got what was coming to him.

Carrie was not the same inexperienced girl she had been a few weeks ago, before her marriage. She had matured. Now she had known life as a wife, and a horribly betrayed one at that.

After the initial shock wore off, she could think more clearly. One day, in the kitchen, she asked her mother, "Why didn't God stop me from marrying Derek? He could see Derek's heart and knew he wasn't the man he pretended to be."

Matilda thought. "Sit down at the table with me, and let's talk about this." She put down her dishtowel. The two pulled out chairs and sat facing each other.

Matilda grasped her daughter's hand across the table. "I, too, have wondered why God didn't give you a warning to stop you from marrying Derek. I've wondered why Papa or I didn't see what was coming. I only know His ways are higher than ours, and He allows things we don't understand."

"I wish I could understand it."

"This ordeal will undoubtedly make you a strong woman if you rely on Him. God already knows the future events in your life and what strength you will need to get through them. Maybe this experience was allowed to build your strength."

"Right now, that doesn't help."

"I know. But at some point in your life, you'll fall back on lessons learned from this ordeal. You'll have insight and wisdom that few people have."

Carrie's eyes flooded with tears. "I'm sorry, Ma…That doesn't help me right now. I'm overwhelmed with grief."

Matilda rested her elbows on the table and put her hands to her head. "I wish I could help you. I feel so frustrated."

Carrie wiped her wet face with both hands. "The only thing I'm thankful for right now is God's presence. He's closer to me than before. It's like His arms are around me, protecting me. I've never known such peace, even though sometimes I think the grief will kill me."

Matilda nodded. She had had a similar experience when her father died. "Some people won't believe you when you say that, but I know it's true. That's the 'peace that passes understanding' the Bible talks about."

Carrie stared at the floor. "But I did everything right. Isn't God supposed to reward us when we live right?"

"I don't have all the answers, but I know we're not promised the outcome we want just for behaving ourselves. He will reward you in time, in His way. He still has a plan, and He will carry it out."

Carrie continued. "And then I think about Derek. What a tragedy. If he had only dealt with the sin in his life when he was gambling and turned it over to God, he would probably still be alive. Maybe he would be a better person, living happily with Julia."

Her mother nodded.

A year later, Carrie had survived the tragedy, and her life was much different. Her house in Spencer's Mill had been rented to a young doctor, his wife, and their little boy, who loved playing in the backyard. She had moved to her grandparents' home, occupying a bedroom across the hall from Lizbeth, and was employed as Christian's new assistant clerk. Since Robbins had announced his intention to move away to care for his aging mother, he was tasked with training Carrie to take his place. She was delighted to learn about her grandfather's work. She was even more thrilled that an old schoolmate of hers was graduating from law school and was being taken into her grandfather's office as a junior partner.

A peek into the future would have revealed that Carrie and the new law partner, Grayson Davidson, were planning to marry and live in a lovely home in Lamar. When Carrie told Grayson the whole story of her marriage to Derek, he wanted to marry her anyway. The couple would eventually raise a family and take their place as loved and respected pillars in the community.

Did she keep the necklace? Yes, for its beauty and value, but she tucked it away where no one would see it. She never wore it again or told anyone where it had come from. When her daughter reached her eighteenth birthday, she passed it on to her as a birthday gift. The symbol that represented tragedy to Carrie became, to her daughter, a symbol of her mother's love.

A NOTE FROM THE AUTHOR

Thank you for reading "A Man With A Mask."

To show my appreciation, I'd like to offer free downloads from my website.

◆ Downloadable Phineas Fletcher short story for easy evening reading
◆ Downloadable resources for your book club
Also:
◆ Articles of interest
◆ Updates on upcoming books

Visit my website:

www. CherieHarbridgeWilliams.com

Please enter your email address so we'll know where to send your free downloads.

OTHER BOOKS BY THIS AUTHOR

Teacups and Lies

In Spencer's Mill in 1886, Susannah Reese loses her husband suddenly and still has three children at home. She must deal with overwhelming obstacles, including sabotage by one of her sons. Leaning on her faith, she relies on her attorney/advisor and falls in love. She and her family work through loss and betrayal to confrontation and repentance.

The Rippling Effect

This sequel to "Teacups and Lies" is the story of the consequences of John Reese's betrayal as he pulls his life back together. His wife and children experience the loss of his income, uncertain future, and treachery. But ultimately, they find their way to the security of total dependence on God.

The Phineas Fletcher Mysteries

Phineas Fletcher debuted in "Teacups and Lies" and became an essential force in "The Rippling Effect." In "The Phineas Fletcher Mysteries," he stars in his own series of fun short stories. He is involved in a string of investigations in unusual circumstances, ending in a heart-rending story about his family.

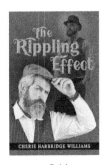

Made in United States
North Haven, CT
21 December 2023